Callum and Marsaili

"I have struggled
in vain to conquer
my desire for ye."

Series by Julie Johnstone

Scottish Medieval Romance Books:

Highlanders Through Time Series
Sinful Scot, Book 1
Sexy Scot, Book 2
Seductive Scot, Book 3
Scandalous Scot, Book 4

Highlander Vows: Entangled Hearts Series
When a Laird Loves a Lady, Book 1
Wicked Highland Wishes, Book 2
Christmas in the Scot's Arms, Book 3
When a Highlander Loses His Heart, Book 4
How a Scot Surrenders to a Lady, Book 5
When a Warrior Woos a Lass, Book 6
When a Scot Gives His Heart, Book 7
When a Highlander Weds a Hellion, Book 8
How to Heal a Highland Heart, Book 9
The Heart of a Highlander, Book 10

Renegade Scots Series
Outlaw King, Book 1
Highland Defender, Book 2
Highland Avenger, Book 3

Regency Romance Books:

A Whisper of Scandal Series
Bargaining with a Rake, Book 1
Conspiring with a Rogue, Book 2
Dancing with a Devil, Book 3

After Forever, Book 4
The Dangerous Duke of Dinnisfree, Book 5

A Once Upon A Rogue Series
My Fair Duchess, Book 1
My Seductive Innocent, Book 2
My Enchanting Hoyden, Book 3
My Daring Duchess, Book 4

Lords of Deception Series
What a Rogue Wants, Book 1

Danby Regency Christmas Novellas
The Redemption of a Dissolute Earl, Book 1
Season For Surrender, Book 2
It's in the Duke's Kiss, Book 3

Regency Anthologies
A Summons from the Duke of Danby (Regency Christmas Summons, Book 2)
Thwarting the Duke (When the Duke Comes to Town, Book 2)

Regency Romance Box Sets
A Very Regency Christmas
Three Wicked Rogues

Paranormal Books:

The Siren Saga
Echoes in the Silence, Book 1

When a Scot Gives His Heart

Highlander Vows: Entangled Hearts, Book Six

by
Julie Johnstone

Dedication

This book is for the Wenches! Many of you have been there with me from the first book that was ever published. I appreciate greatly the support and eagerness you always give me and my books!

Author's Note

Dear Readers,

I have taken great pains to make sure the words I used in writing this story were as historically accurate as possible. However, given that I am writing to a modern audience, there are some instances when I chose to use a word that was not in existence in the fourteenth century, as they simply did not have a word at that time to correctly convey the meaning of the sentence.

If you're interested in when my books go on sale, or want to be one of the first to know about my new releases, please follow me on BookBub! You'll get quick book notifications every time there's a new pre-order, book on sale, or new release with an easy click of your mouse to follow me. You can follow me on BookBub here:
www.bookbub.com/authors/julie-johnstone

All the best,
Julie

Prologue

1358
Scotland

Marsaili Campbell stood upon the ramparts of Innis Chonnell Castle as her father's warriors filled the courtyard below. The battle-hardened Highlanders spilled out from the sanctuary, past the iron-spiked, tower-manned gates and down the stone path to the loch that surrounded the Campbell stronghold. Rain poured from the sky, turning the hill into a stream of raw, red, slippery earth that could easily cause a man to lose his footing and tumble down the rocky cliffs to his death. The throng was a terrifying sight to behold, which was what her father, the Campbell laird, had wanted.

As if he sensed she was thinking of him, her father raised his arms, his black cape billowing in the wind in front of her. Before he said a word, a deafening cheer rose from the masses. Whether it was out of adoration or fear, she could not say for certain, but she suspected it was the latter. She would never dare utter such a suspicion aloud, however. A shiver ran through her just thinking of the penance cell in the dungeon where she'd spent many a night for speaking her mind. At eighteen summers, she fully understood to keep her thoughts to herself by now.

"The Gathering is upon us!" her father shouted to his

men.

"Steward sworn!" came the thundering reply from the warriors, as well as her mother, brothers, Colin and Findlay, and sister, Helena, who were by her father's side. Marsaili stood alone at the back of the rampart. It used to vex her being set apart from her family, but now she secretly considered it a badge of pride. She was different from them. She had honor—or she hoped she did, anyway.

Her father motioned for silence, and a hush immediately rippled through the crowd, leaving it so quiet that a squawk from a bird flying above made Marsaili twitch in surprise.

"Today marks a bold step toward taking the throne from King David," her father began. He paused as another cheer rent the air.

Marsaili forced a smile in case one of her siblings, her mother, or God forbid, her father turned around and saw her face. She could ill afford to appear anything but enthusiastic about all the Scottish lairds, lords, and their chosen representatives arriving at the Campbell hold today. Some of them had come most willingly. Others, she knew from eavesdropping at her father's solar, had been enticed with promises of greater wealth and land, and still others had been threatened with reprisal from her father if they did not attend the Gathering and pledge their support to Robert Stewart, who was known simply as the Steward due to his title, High Steward of Scotland. He was the nephew of King David II, King of the Scots, and he wanted his uncle's throne.

"We will nae tolerate a king who does nae care what his people think, feel, or want!"

Swords clanked against shields with a vibrating hum that filled Marsaili's ears. She wanted to spit her disgust, but she swallowed it instead. Her father was a wordsmith at best, a perverse liar at worst. She had heard from his very mouth the real reason he had pledged his support to the Steward. It was because King David was a strong king whose views on how to rule Scotland differed from those of the wealthy lords and lairds, and he neither needed nor wanted greedy men like her father telling him what to do. And it was because the king believed the common people of Scotland were as important as the wealthy, if not more so. The commoners gave the king their full support; therefore, he was rewarding them with land and coin that he was taking from men like her father, men who thought to rule the king himself.

"For the next two fortnights," Father went on, "I will gather support for the Steward and ensure the pledges that have already been made are still strong! We must show our strength to all friend and foe!" Cheers and shouts of agreement rose from the crowd. "We go forth with the hope that the Steward will take the throne, but we must ready ourselves for every possible outcome. Every man who steps foot on my land these next two fortnights, from the squire of a Highlander to the powerful English Earl of Ulster, must ken my power. They must nae forget that I am an ally they need. Must nae forget to fear ever crossing me. *Ne obliviscaris!*"

"*Ne obliviscaris!*" roared the warriors and Marsaili's family alike.

The Campbell clan motto, *Forget not*, reverberated in her ears. She had the untimely urge to laugh, which sometimes happened when she was disgusted. *Forget not*, her father had chanted. Forget not his greatness, he'd told them. Forget not his power, he'd said. What she could not forget was his cruelty, his harshness, his greed.

"Go forth to yer posts," he continued. "Our guests will soon be arriving."

He turned from the men below to face his wife and her siblings, and Marsaili supposed her, as well, though he never looked at her unless she angered him. He never spoke directly to her unless to reprimand, either. She pressed back against the stone wall, wishing she could fly away like a bird. Her father raised a questioning eyebrow, and her family immediately burst out in praise of his speech.

When they fell silent, her mother said, "I was nae aware that ye had extended an invitation to King Edward's son."

"That is because ye are but a woman and nae made aware of all I do. Do ye forget yer place, Wife?" he challenged, his tone sharp.

"Nay, Husband," Mother said. She was wise enough to know when to grovel.

Her father nodded, a satisfied look sweeping his face. "Inviting the Earl of Ulster 'tis a recent development. I've heard whispers that King David might relent to King Edward's demands to name Edward's son, the earl's elder brother, John of Gaunt, as David's successor if David fails to produce an heir. John is happily married, but Ulster... I happen to ken that Ulster's wife is near dying and that he is searching for a leman and, eventually, a new wife. I see opportunity there."

His calculating gaze raked over Marsaili, much to her dismay, and her nerve endings flared to life. She knew that look. He was plotting something, and she feared it involved her.

"David is weak," Father snarled, "to even consider relenting to the English king's demands, but I will take advantage of his weakness."

"Well, King David must consider it, nay?" Mother

asked.

"Aye," Father answered. "He kens well the Scottish lords and lairds will nae pay the debt he owes King Edward. The ransom for David's release from that blasted English prison should nae be our responsibility. 'Tis David's own fault he was captured and imprisoned."

"Aye," agreed her mother.

Her father's lips twisted into a gruesome smile. "Were I on the throne, I'd find a way to fulfill my debts that did nae require bowing to the wishes of King Edward."

Mother quirked her mouth. "Will ye tell me of yer cunning plot involving Ulster?"

He smiled. He did so love to be indulged. "I must cultivate alliances with all who could possibly be named king while still maintaining my outer show of fealty to David."

"If we truly want a position of favor, perhaps ye should make a match between Ulster and Helena," Mother offered.

Marsaili tensed. Her mother was wily, too much so, and knew how to state her opinions in a way that usually did not anger Father by the mere fact that she had been so bold as to give an opinion. But presently, her father's eyes narrowed and his nostrils flared. She had not been quite manipulative enough this time. Marsaili wanted to laugh, then felt a flush of guilt at wishing ill on her mother, in spite of the poor way she treated Marsaili.

Oblivious to their father's ire, Marsaili's sister nodded. "I'd like that, Father." Helena's eyes gleamed; she was just as hungry for power and wealth as Father. Marsaili had to grind her teeth to keep from speaking.

He chuckled, indulging her sister, whom he favored greatly. "I'm sure ye would, lass, but I have other plans for ye."

Helena pouted, and Marsaili's mother frowned. "Might

I inquire what they are?"

Marsaili's father scowled at his wife. "Silence yer questioning tongue, woman. I'll tell ye my intentions when the time for ye to ken them is at hand. Besides, I just told ye the earl is currently married."

"Aye," her mother said, clearly disappointed that he wasn't sharing more.

"However, my cunning wife," Father continued, "use yer soft, female mind to recall that his wife is verra ill, and it is said she will nae live much longer."

"Excellent!" her mother replied, which made Marsaili's stomach turn. "Except," she went on, "we've nae a daughter to put forth for Ulster if ye have plans for Helena."

"There's Marsaili," her father said. Now Marsaili's stomach dropped in shock at her father's words. She had been correct about his look earlier. All eyes swiveled toward her. "Is she nae a lass and our daughter?"

A disgusted look came to her mother's face. "Aye," she bit out, "but—"

"But what?" her father snapped, his color rising with his temper.

Marsaili pressed herself harder against the stone wall, disliking being the object of this conversation or her father's notice.

"She could nae catch the earl's attention," Helena snipped, looking down her nose at Marsaili. The bite of shame from her sister's cruel words heated Marsaili's cheeks.

"Aye, and she's a daft lass," Colin, her eldest brother, said.

Her other brother, Findlay, agreed. "The earl would nae wish to marry a half-wit."

Marsaili clenched her jaw, bombarded with anger and

humiliation at the same time. Her father's cold gaze settled firmly on her. "Leave us," he said. His hard words brooked no argument, not that Marsaili cared to argue. It would do no good.

She turned to make her way toward the stairs when her father said, "Nae ye, Marsaili." Marsaili cringed as she faced her father once more. He looked over at their family.

"Us?" Her mother gasped. "Why do ye wish us to leave?"

Marsaili backed up a step when her father raised his arm as if to strike her mother. "Do ye question me again, woman?" She shook her head as she cast her gaze down. "Away with ye now," he commanded and motioned to all but Marsaili. "Helena, select a gown—yer best—for Marsaili to wear tonight to meet the earl."

Helena opened her mouth as if to protest, but when Mother shook her head, Helena pressed her lips together and nodded.

"Findlay, ye will greet the Earl of Ulster with me and then invite him on a hunt, which Marsaili will attend."

"Ye are plotting, Father," Colin said, his admiration clear in his tone.

"Always," her father answered with a boastful smile. "And ye have a part in this, too, Colin. Ye will make certain ye dunnae win the hunt. The earl needs to be in front of ye, so that it will appear ye are taking aim at the wild boar when ye accidentally shoot the earl. His arm is most preferable, I think. And then Marsaili will be the one to tend his wound. She can rip her dress to do so. A nice touch, aye?" he added with a nefarious laugh.

The way her father so easily plotted to purposely hurt another made Marsaili's stomach roil once more. Her nostrils flared as she tried to subtly suck in more air to calm herself.

Colin nodded and departed quickly behind Findlay, Helena, and Mother. Marsaili's father caught her gaze but said nothing for a long moment. Finally, he said, "Ye have proven ye are a survivor, Marsaili. Cunning, too."

"I'm nae cunning," she replied, wishing immediately she had not spoken.

Her father gave her a condescending smile. "Ye are. I ken ye think yerself unlike the rest of us, but ye are verra much like us. Ye have used cunning to contrive a way to mostly escape yer siblings' and yer mother's notice. Ye have convinced them ye are a simpleton, but I ken ye are nae."

Dread trickled down Marsaili's spine.

"Ye are a clever lass." He paused and cocked his head, as if considering what else to say. "Ye are plain, though," he finally said, his eyes narrowing. "Dunnae forget that. Dunnae think to tempt a man to yer bed with yer appearance. Ye will only have a man by my good graces, my negotiations on yer behalf, and my say so."

That statement almost made her laugh. Her father had no good graces, just plots to make himself wealthier and more powerful.

"Do ye ken me?" he demanded.

She nodded dutifully, her mind turning, as it often did, to where she would go if she ever managed to flee her home. The problem was that she had nowhere to go, no one to call on for aid, no one who cared for her. When she was younger, she had daydreamed of meeting a man and falling in love. He would take her away in her silly fantasies, but she knew better now. No man ever saw her; they all looked through her. Of course they did. Her father had been right that she strove to appear the simpleton to escape as much notice as possible from her family. She rarely received new gowns, and she rarely washed the ones of quality that she did have. Her hair was usually knotted, her face dirty, and she had perfected a blank stare, as if she did not have a thought in her head. It had served her well with her brothers, sister, and mother. They were still cruel to her, but her ruse had blunted the sharp, sometimes physical, edge of their cruelty.

"Ye will marry the Earl of Ulster," her father pronounced.

Her breath caught in her throat. Surely, her father did not intend to kill the earl's wife!

She kept her voice calm and cautious. "Ye said the earl was married."

"When she dies, ye foolish lass," her father snarled.

"But I dunnae ken the earl, and he dunnae ken me. Ye said yerself, I'm plain." She knew she was no great beauty, but she also knew her father liked to make her feel ugly. Honestly, she was unsure if a man would think her pleasant to look at if she took care with her appearance.

"Ye will find a way to enthrall the earl in spite of that. And ye will do so strongly enough that he will wish to have ye as his mistress. Ye will let him join with ye then, until ye are with child, and when his wife dies, ye will compel the man to marry ye."

Heat singed her cheeks, her neck, her chest. "Ye would make me a whore?"

"Aye," he replied, matter-of-fact. "I would make my own mother a whore to get what I want."

All her silly dreams of girlhood flooded her mind once more—her lost hopes, her fantasies. In that moment, her anger exploded and fear fled. "Nay," she said, tilting up her chin. "I'll nae do it."

Her father brought his hand up in a flash and gripped

her chin in an iron hold. He jerked her face so close to his
that she could see the cracks in his yellowed front teeth. "Ye
will do as I bid, or I will have the healer, Maria, killed slowly
and painfully. I ken ye have formed a friendship with her."

Marsaili sucked in a sharp breath. Maria was her only
friend. She was the one person who had shown kindness to
Marsaili. She did not want to do as her father ordered, but
she was certain that he'd kill Maria as he'd threatened.
However, if Marsaili agreed, she'd be relinquishing all hope
of happiness—unless the earl actually proved to be a kind
man, one she might even fall in love with, which was
doubtful. Regardless, the idea of luring him, of tricking him,
disgusted her. She could not refuse, though. Maria's life was
more important to Marsaili than her own happiness.

"I will try," was all she said.

Her father released her immediately. "Excellent choice.
Now off with ye to make yerself presentable before our
guests arrive."

"Callum Grant, halt, damn ye! I demand ye halt!" Edina
Gordon screamed at Callum's back as he strode outside,
toward his horse and away from the stable, where he had
just discovered his intended wife naked in the stable hand's
arms.

For a moment, he considered simply mounting his
destrier, continuing on his journey to the Gathering at the
Campbell hold—he'd been ordered to attend for his father,
the Grant laird—and dealing with breaking his vow to wed
Edina after the Gathering. The idea of letting her fret over
what he might reveal, what he might say until he returned
to speak with her appealed to him, but he recognized the

dishonorable thought and came to a stop.

He was angry, but only because he'd almost allowed himself to be wed to a woman he had never cared for and who had been claimed in body by another man. She would have brought betrayal to their marriage that would have been difficult at best.

Edina hurried toward him, tugging the laces of her bodice together. She stopped in front of him, cheeks flushed from her tumble in the hay with the stable hand. "It's nae what ye think."

For some reason, that amused him. "Is it nae?" He raised his eyebrows. "I've nae joined with a woman myself, given I've been promised to wed ye since I was ten summers, but I'm fairly certain what I just saw ye and the stable hand doing in the hay was a joining."

Her gray eyes narrowed as her mouth puckered. "Dunnae stand there and lie to me, Callum Grant. Ye are a laird's son, and a fine-looking one at that. Ye kinnae tell me ye have been true to me. I've seen the lasses flirting with ye."

"Aye," he agreed, "they flirted. But my father made a vow to yer da that I'd wed ye when ye were eighteen summers, and as much as I did nae wish to take ye to wife, our clans had an alliance, and I intended to honor it."

She gasped. "Ye still have to honor it! I may be with child!"

"Then marry the stable hand," Callum said calmly. "Ye two seem to like each other verra much." How any man could have been enticed into Edina Gordon's arms perplexed Callum. She was lovely enough, but it was surface deep.

"I kinnae marry a lowly stable hand!" she bellowed.

"A man's station in life dunnae determine his quality," Callum said through clenched teeth. He hated that so many people, including his own parents, thought that it did.

Edina clenched her hands into fists. She had a spiteful-ness about her and a jealous tendency to be cruel to anyone she thought might be prettier than she was. He'd asked his father more than once over the years to break their promise to wed, but his father had refused every time, reminding Callum that their alliance with the Gordon clan only existed because of the impending marriage. Callum gave a quick thanks to God that Edina's mother had insisted she reach eighteen summers before they wed. If not for that request, he would already be well and shackled to a woman without honor.

"I'll tell ye, as I have before, that my father's warriors are the reason yer family is still in possession of Urquhart Castle." Edina gave him a haughty smile. "If it were nae for them, the MacDonald clan would have taken the castle from yer father shortly after it was granted to him by King David. We both ken the MacDonald laird has a much greater force than yer father does. So ye kinnae renounce our upcoming union," Edina said smugly. "Ye will marry me, and ye will keep what ye saw a secret. And if I should have a bairn, ye will raise it as yer own."

Callum felt as if his blood were boiling. He had known for a long time that Edina was a spoiled lass, but he had misjudged the depth of her lack of character. It was true that the Lord of the Isles did have many more men at his disposal than Callum's father had. It was also true that Callum's clan had desperately needed an ally to help them defend Urquhart against sieges by the MacDonald clan because their laird had wanted to advance his holdings farther north.

"Ye dunnae ken me Edina, and ye did nae ever. I am nae a man to be told what to do. I'll nae shame ye by telling all that ye gave yerself to another man, but I'll nae marry ye. Ye may consider our promise to be wed broken."

"Ye kinnae do that! Yer clan needs the alliance!"

He nodded. "Aye, we do, but we dunnae need it so greatly that we will sacrifice honor. We will find another alliance."

She glared at him. "Yer father will nae allow it, and I'll nae consider yer vow to wed me broken until yer father has agreed."

"My father kinnae force me to wed ye and neither can yer threats." Callum turned and strode toward his horse with Edina bellowing his name.

He kept going until he was mounted and riding away from her. He felt liberated, though also burdened by what was to come next. He suspected his father, and most assuredly his mother, would try to compel him to mend the rift. But he'd not bind himself to a woman like Edina for life. That would not be good for the clan, nor for any children they might have. For too long, Callum had obeyed his father's commands, despite his doubts, but no more. He'd not wed Edina, but he would do all he could to ensure his clan made another alliance.

The best way to do that would be to travel with haste to the Gathering and speak to the other lairds who'd been called there by the Campbell laird. Callum hoped that some of them had doubts about pledging loyalty to the Steward, too. His father disagreed with Callum's concerns, but his father would not always be laird. It would be Callum's duty someday, and he intended to be informed thoroughly about the politics of his land and choose his loyalty based on the honor of a man, not how the man could increase the Grant clan's wealth.

Marsaili sat on a plaid in the grass with her mother and sister, as she had been ordered to by her father. The lords and lairds who'd been invited to the Gathering, including the Earl of Ulster, had ridden off into the woods some time ago for a Bow and Stable hunt. Her father had chosen to hunt a wild boar as opposed to the usual prey of a deer, and the animal had taken off with a squeal. The men, all assembled on horseback with their bows ready to shoot, had set off after it. The winner would receive a purse of coin and his choice of lass to dance with at the feast tonight. Her brother Colin was the best shot she had ever seen, and under normal circumstances, he would be the winner. Except today, of course, he'd been instructed to let the Earl of Ulster pull ahead for the win so he could shoot him from behind.

Marsaili picked unhappily at a blade of grass. She listened with little interest to her mother and sister, who were speaking extensively on the eligible men present, making a list of their attributes, which apparently included their clan's wealth, their clan's strength, and finally, the man himself. Not of his honor, of course—her petty mother and sister were judging each man by his appearance.

Marsaili listened half-heartedly, but most of her thoughts were occupied with the horrible predicament in which she found herself.

She'd met the Earl of Ulster when he had arrived. He'd only managed to draw his gawking gaze from her cleavage, which Helena had ensured was almost spilling out of Marsaili's gown, when her mother had inquired after his wife. His answer had been disturbing and telling of his character. Marsaili had quickly concluded that he had little merit when he had complained that his wife was "still stubbornly clinging to life" despite his best physician assuring him that the woman would succumb to her sickness within a few months. He'd noted, with a scowl, that it had been six tiresome months.

It disgusted her to think upon his callous words and uncaring attitude. She did not want to do as her father had demanded. She did not want to gain the earl's attention, become his mistress, and then wed him, either. But she had little choice if she wanted to protect Maria.

"They approach!" Helena cried out and scrambled to her feet. The sound of the hunting dogs barking filled the air. "Mother! Callum Grant is leading the hunters!" she gushed.

Marsaili looked up from the grass. She did not know who Callum Grant was. She'd only been present yesterday when the Earl of Ulster had arrived, and then her father had commanded her to her room until today's hunt. She lifted her hand to shield her eyes as she stared at the rider who was coming hard and fast at the boar, the hunting dogs on his heels. The Highlander had his bow raised, and Marsaili could see, even from a distance, that he had quite powerful arms.

"Where is Colin?" Mother moaned. "Callum Grant is nae meant to win!"

"There!" Helena exclaimed, pointing. "He is ten paces behind Callum."

Marsaili rose to her feet, getting embroiled in the excitement of the hunt despite her worry. Colin had never lost a hunt, and she wanted to be in a position to see him finally bested. He'd been especially cruel to her all her life. He was the one who often locked her in the penance cell and said she had done things she had not. Sin or not, she would enjoy watching his defeat. He was as prideful as they came, and this public loss, which also would disturb their father's carefully laid plans, would sting his pride.

"Do ye see the earl?" her mother demanded.

"There," Marsaili said pointing, "he's coming up beside Colin." The thundering of the horses' hooves reverberated in the air, and the ground trembled beneath her feet. Marsaili held her breath in anticipation as Callum Grant closed in on the boar, backing it against a wall of rock. He cocked his head slightly, and she knew he was lining up his shot. Behind him, her brother and the earl raced onward, the earl pulling ahead of Colin. The minute he did, Colin raised his arm, and Marsaili cringed, knowing her brother intended to shoot the earl and not the boar.

The barking dogs grew frenzied, Callum released his arrow, and at the same moment, Colin released his. The boar fell and an exalted shout came from Callum, but then a bellow rang out as the Earl of Ulster yanked his destrier to a halt. He reached for his arm and awkwardly dismounted his horse.

"Make haste," Marsaili's mother said calmly. "Ye ken what ye're to do."

She started toward the earl as her father and the men gathered around him, but her feet would not carry her quickly. It felt as if she were wearing stone shoes. When her father glanced her way, his gaze narrowed dangerously, and she forced herself to increase her pace. Soon, she was running.

As she drew near the earl, so did Callum Grant. His gaze locked with hers, and her breath caught. She felt as captive as a hawk in an iron cage. Eyes the color of a rich honeyed mead assessed her frankly, and then his heavy eyebrows drew up as if he were shocked by something. By what, she didn't know. The urge to smooth her gown and put order to her hair gripped her, but she fought it. When the earl groaned loudly, she remembered all too clearly the task at hand. She turned her attention to the earl, even as Callum moved to stand beside her. His arm brushed hers briefly, sending a tremor of odd recognition through her, as if her body were familiar with his.

"I can tend to the earl if someone can withdraw the arrow from his arm," she said, inhaling in a desperate bid for calmness.

The Earl of Ulster swung toward her, face mottled red and fist raised in anger. Her instinct was to scuttle backward, but Callum stepped slightly in front of her. She blinked in shock at his boldness and at the fact that he would place himself in harm's way to protect her, a woman he did not know. No one had ever done such a thing for her in her life.

The earl raked his flinty gaze over Callum before settling it on her once more. "There'd be no need to withdraw an arrow if that fool—" he glared at Colin "—had aimed with more care."

"I am terribly sorry," Colin replied, but his stiff tone alerted Marsaili immediately that her brother's quick temper had been lit. Her father must have realized it, as well. He placed a hand on Colin's shoulder, and she saw him squeeze it until his knuckles turned white. Colin's jaw began to twitch, but he gave an almost imperceptible nod of understanding. "I can remove the arrow," he said, exactly as their father had planned.

"If you believe I'd let you near me, you're mad!" the earl bellowed and then grabbed Marsaili by the arm. "You will do it. I'll take a woman's touch."

To dress an arm was one thing but to remove an arrow?

"I kinnae, my lord. I—"

"Ye dare defy me?" He shot her a menacing glare.

Callum moved forward so quickly, she didn't even realize what he was doing until she heard a snap, and then in a flash, he yanked the arrow out of the earl's arm. "There," he said, throwing the two halves of the arrow on the ground. "'Tis done."

Marsaili was too astounded and too grateful to speak for a moment. The earl appeared enraged, as his face twisted into a grimace, but he bit out through clenched teeth, "Thank you." And when he looked down at the steady stream of blood coming from his arm, he paled.

Marsaili's instinct to help anyone in need took over. She took up the hem of her dress and ripped off a long strip of material without a thought. She didn't realize until she was wrapping it around the earl's arm with great care that she had unwittingly done her father's bidding. She ground her teeth, though she would not have changed aiding the man. "There now, my lord. That should hold ye, but I compel ye to make yer way immediately to the medicine woman."

"An excellent idea," he replied, his gaze sliding from her face to her chest. "You will show me the way, of course."

"Aye, she would be happy to," her father answered for her.

She bit hard on her lip but nodded. She was trapped, exactly as her father had intended. The earl gave an impatient wave for them to depart. As she turned, her gaze caught Callum's once more. The look of understanding he gave her filled her with an unexpected sense of hope, but she quickly shelved it, knowing how foolish hope was.

The beautiful Marsaili Campbell stayed in Callum's thoughts all day, even as he spoke with many of the other men at the Gathering. Many men talked highly of his father, which did bode well for making a new alliance, but with each person he spoke with, Callum's hopes to find a like-minded man, one who was doubting the wisdom of pledging his clan to the Steward, ebbed away. He tasked himself with delving deeper into the character of the king and his nephew so when the time came that he led the Grant clan, he'd be well-informed enough to make an unprejudiced decision.

When he entered the great hall for supper, the first person he saw—truly, the *only* person he saw—was Marsaili. She looked fragile, tense, and stunning as she sat on the dais between her father and the Earl of Ulster. Gazing upon her tightened Callum's chest and stirred his desire in a way it had never been stirred. He had no notion what was making her so unhappy, but perhaps it was the married earl's attention. The man was gawking at her. Not that Callum could blame him.

Marsaili Campbell had outer beauty, to be sure. Her mahogany hair shined and tumbled over her shoulders in inviting curls. And her eyes... Never had he seen eyes of such a pure, clear blue. God's blood, he would likely dream of her eyes tonight. They reminded him of the waters of the loch around his home. Yet, it was not the color he would dream of as much as the emotions they had conveyed. One minute her gaze had appeared guarded, then forlorn, and for one extraordinary breath, he'd sworn he'd seen hope there.

Not only did she have unforgettable eyes but the lass was all lush curves and softness. She had a body that God had created to be loved by a man. But for all the outer beauty she possessed, he sensed her inner beauty down deep to his very bones, and it drew him to her. It was the sort of beauty that would not fade with age but grow ever brighter, ever warmer, and would guide a man in his darkest hour and heat him on the coldest nights. He had to find out if what he had sensed was indeed true.

He strode toward her, anticipation filling him at claiming the victor dance with her. When he reached the dais, he inclined his head to her father, skimmed his gaze dismissively over the earl—whom he did not care for at all, even after just one meeting—and settled his focus on her. He allowed himself a long breath to soak in her beauty. He bowed to show her the respect she deserved. "I've come to claim my first dance rights."

Her eyes widened with surprise, with delight, and then shadowed with worry. He was uncertain what had caused the last, but each emotion proved what he had suspected: she was a complex lass, a knot to be untangled, and he itched to do so.

Her father scowled, as if he wanted to deny the request, but Marsaili rose, almost hastily, and descended the dais without so much as glancing at her father. Callum set his fingertips to the delicate slope of her back, and it felt right to guide her. He could not explain it. He did not want to explain it. He simply wanted to discover what these feelings were and where they might lead.

The floor was littered with couples dancing and did not lend the space for any sort of private conversation. Yet, when their palms met to begin the dance, it was as if he'd been struck by a powerful gust, and he could not resist one question. "Does any man have yer heart, Marsaili Campbell?"

Those expressive eyes showed her shock at his question,

but then a lovely shy smile touched her lips. "Nay," she replied in a low voice. "Why do ye ask?"

He slid his arm around her back to twirl her in the motions of the dance. For one spin, their bodies were pressed together, hardness to softness, man to woman. He finished the circle, and before releasing her into the next motion, he whispered in her ear, "I needed to be certain there was nae a man I needed to kill."

Her shy smile became a grin, and she released a throaty chuckle. "And why would ye be killing a man if he had my heart?" she whispered.

"Because," he said, wishing more than anything that they were alone, "I'll nae tolerate a man trying to claim what I ken is mine."

"By whose authority is my heart yers?" she asked, her look serious but her tone teasing.

"By God's." He snagged her hand in his and pressed her palm against his heart. "I recognized it here the moment I first saw ye."

"Marsaili!" her father's voice barked to Callum's right. "The dance has ended. Bid Callum good night."

She broke contact immediately and curtsied.

An almost desperate feeling came over Callum. "My lady," he called to her back, fearing that he might never see her again.

She turned quickly, looking over her shoulder once at her father, who was still striding through the crowd.

"What say ye, my lady, to what I told ye?"

She bit down on her lip, and for a moment, he thought he had overstepped, but then she said, "I say it is as I told ye. The stream to the east of the castle is verra picturesque in the early-morning light. If ye wish to find a spot to be alone, it is most recommended. I often go there myself." With that, she curtsied again and scurried after her father, who led her to the earl.

Callum watched her as she danced once with the man, who looked entirely too engrossed with her for Callum's taste. But Marsaili appeared miserable, which assured him that she did not care for the earl's attention. When her father fetched her from the earl, she seemed eager to leave, and Callum wondered if her father often made her dance with men who leered at her. It set his teeth on edge with anger, but as she was leaving the great hall, she smiled at him, and his anger dissipated. When he could no longer see her departing figure, he made his way to his bedchamber to dream of her, what tomorrow would bring, and all the days after that.

Marsaili awoke at dawn, giddy with the prospect that Callum might venture to the stream to see her. She sat up in her bed, waiting for the sun to fully rise so she could make her way there without it seeming peculiar. As she sat there, she thought on his words from last night and of how a man she had only just met could fill her heart with such hope. She'd spent her life cast in the shadows. When she was younger it had hurt her greatly, but she had learned that the shadows were the safest place to dwell. She did not want to live the rest of her life cowering in shadows, though, unable to find happiness.

She had been a fool. She had not escaped her father's notice; he had been biding his time until he was ready to use her as he wished. All her life he had made her feel ugly and unwanted, and she knew in her gut it had been purposeful. Mayhap, he had wanted her to be so grateful to leave home someday that she would do whatever he bid without argument. She would have to do as he insisted when it came to the earl so she could protect Maria, but she wished to know the tender touch of a man she desired, of a man who looked at her the way Callum had last night. If she must be chained to the earl for life, she would steal a taste of what true passion would have been like.

Anticipation swelled and with it, unexpected hope. She did not try to quash it as she usually did. Instead, she allowed it to take hold and spread like a vine within her chest. What if she and Callum fell in love? What if he wanted to wed her and she could take Maria with her, offer a position, and be free of this place and her father? She pressed her fingertips to the smile she felt on her lips, and she chuckled at herself. It felt good to laugh and to hope. However foolish it was, however unlikely, today she would pretend that her future was not yet plotted. She was the weaver of her fate for this day, even if it was the only time she ever was. With that in mind, she arose, dressed, and made her way into the great hall, where she rushed through breaking her fast and then departed for the stream.

When she entered the courtyard, her silly, foolish fantasy immediately came crashing down around her.

"Ah, Marsaili," the earl boomed. "I'm glad to see you before I have to take my leave."

Elation burst within her. "I did nae ken ye had to quit our company so soon," she said, hoping her voice did not reveal her happiness at the news. Perhaps she had failed to sway the earl to her as her father had wished. She sent a quick prayer up that this was so.

"One of my men arrived late in the night with an urgent message from my physician that my wife is finally dying." She sucked in her breath at his callousness. His gaze widened fractionally, and he said, "You cannot imagine what it has been like for me, Marsaili, married since my youth to a woman who has always been ill. She's never had vigor nor beauty as you do."

"My lord, please," she said, disgusted that he could talk so about his wife.

"I see my compliments make you blush," he said, running a hand down her cheek. "I very much like your modesty, Marsaili."

"I blush," she said, through clenched teeth, "because I am disheartened to hear ye speak of yer wife in such a cold manner."

A dark scowl swept his face. "Don't be, my dear. If you knew her, you would understand. She revels in being a burden, but soon I will be done with her. You are the exact sort of woman I always wished to have for a wife."

"I'm certain I am nae," she replied, desperate to change his mind.

"See," he said, smiling, "this is what I told your father this morning when I formally asked to make you my mistress and wed you once my wife is dead. You are modest about your own attributes."

"My lord, I fear ye are mistaken about me. I have spent a great deal of time in the penance cell for my stubbornness."

"Yes," the earl said, a twisted smile coming to his lips. "Your father told me. I rather like the idea of punishing you if you cross me."

The earl's eagerness at the prospect of punishing her made her cringe. Her father had to know the sort of man the earl was but simply did not care.

"With my wife," the earl continued, "I had to fear reprisal from her father, but from your father, I have no such fear. We will suit perfectly, Marsaili. If my wife should not breathe her last breath within a sennight, I will settle the nuisance in the country and send for you. I'm finished waiting patiently for her to die." With that, he pulled her to him and covered her mouth with his in a wet, sloppy kiss. He broke it as abruptly as he had started it, mounted his horse, and waved for his men to depart. She was left trembling with rage and disgust in the empty courtyard.

Her thoughts tripped over themselves, and in time, her mind settled on one: seeing Callum. She rushed to the stream, disappointed to find that Callum was not there, yet she clung to the hope that he would appear. As the sun shone down on her, she removed her slippers and sat in front of the water, listening to the wind rustle the trees and the trickling of the stream. After a long while, her certainty that Callum would come began to fade, and that's when a twig snapped behind her. She turned as he kneeled, his warm gaze assessing her. "I was starting to think ye would nae come," she admitted.

"A legion of warriors could nae have kept me away, though yer sister did delay me," he replied as he sat next to her.

His thigh pressed against hers, but she did not move. She reveled in the strength his powerful legs displayed. Her belly tightened, and her breath quickened. *This* was desire. She knew it instinctually. She welcomed it, even if it was sinful. This could well be her only chance to ever experience it.

Still, she frowned. "My sister? What did she want with ye?"

Callum looked suddenly uncomfortable, and Marsaili's cheeks flamed. She knew Helena well. She was a born seductress, and men succumbed willingly to her desires. She was beautiful whereas Marsaili was plain.

"I see," Marsaili said slowly, jealousy burning within her. "If my sister wishes yer attention, I'm surprised ye're here."

"Ye should nae be," he said. His gaze glittered as he studied her. "Yer sister has a skin-deep beauty. It will fade. It dunnae reach her soul." He gently rubbed his thumb against her right temple. "In yer eyes, I see goodness, kindness, and courage. I see beauty that will nae fade and reaches all the way into ye to envelop ye." He brought her untried senses to life, and the very air around them suddenly was buzzing, as if a storm were approaching. Yet it was not a storm; it was possibility and hope.

"I want to kiss ye," he said, his voice rough with emotion.

"I want ye to, as well," she whispered. His hands cupped her face, and a delicious shudder heated her body. As he brought his lips to hers, the thudding of her heart drowned out the wind and the stream. The touch of his mouth to hers was velvety and warm. He deepened the kiss, and she responded with every ounce of desire that he had brought to life within her.

His ragged groan filled her ears as his lips became more insistent, more searching. She parted her mouth, wanting to taste more of him, to become one with him. Their tongues met and circled as he possessed her with demanding mastery. When they finally pulled apart, her breaths came in short gasps, and it pleased her to hear he was affected the same way.

Without a word, he held his hand out to her, and she slipped her palm into his, interlacing their fingers. "Ye will be mine," he said simply.

Her heart clenched with joy. "I believe I shall," she

replied, willing it to be so.

The Gathering was to span two fortnights, planned this way by her father so there would not only be time to talk politics and pledges but for the men to go on lengthy, overnight hunts. When Callum was at her home and not away on an excursion, they met at the stream at first, and then they began to meet in a secret spot that Marsaili had discovered long ago where a cliff overlooked the loch, surrounded by thick brush. Purple heather encircled the grass on that spot and took her breath away every time she went there. It was the perfect place for her and Callum to become acquainted without fear of her father discovering what was occurring.

Each time a messenger arrived at the castle, she feared it would be a summons from the earl, but so far, no word had come. She considered it as a blessing from God, who she decided had finally remembered her and was giving her time with Callum. Time to know each other, time to forge a possible future before it was too late.

Every moment they shared strengthened the invisible bond between them, and it was this ever-growing bond that stirred guilt in her that she had not confessed to him her father's plans regarding the earl, plans that may well affect Callum's clan if her father decided to declare the Grants an enemy, which would most assuredly occur if she and Callum were to run off together. Of course, he had not asked her to wed him, but she hoped he would.

Then one night, while Callum was away on a four-day hunt, a letter arrived from the earl. His wife had still failed to succumb. Those were his exact words. He still intended to settle her in the country, but he had been called to his father, King Edward. He expected a delay of a fortnight, perhaps two, before he could carry out his plans. Marsaili was ecstatic. There was still a chance they could change the course of the future.

The morning Callum returned from the hunt, she raced to their secret spot on the faint hope he would be there. When she reached the top of the ledge and saw him looking out over the loch, her heart rejoiced. He turned toward her, face bronzed from the sun and dark stubble on his cheeks and chin. He was even more alluring than he had been four days before.

She had not so much as taken a step when he was upon her, arms encircling her, hands in her hair, and his lips capturing her mouth. "I missed ye," he said between kisses.

"And I ye," she replied as his lips traced a shivery path down her neck to her collarbone. "Tell me of the hunt," she urged, trying to silence the voice in her head that demanded she tell him of the earl.

He shrugged. "We killed a wild boar." He looked at her. "I dunnae care to kill animals."

"Truly?" she said, heartened to learn he had such compassion.

He nodded. "Aye, truly. But my father so shamed me for the weakness when I was younger that I forced myself to become an expert hunter. I dunnae mind killing near as much when it is for our food, but the sport of killing…" He shrugged again. "I dunnae have any desire for it. When I am laird of my clan someday, I will nae call for hunts for sport, only for need. Does that make ye think me weak?"

She pressed her body to the length of his and leaned her head against his chest. "I think ye perfect and strong."

"Would ye wish to wed a perfect, strong man who dunnae care to hunt unless it is necessary?"

She looked up at him, her heart stuttering. "Are ye asking me to wed ye?" Her hopes and fears crashed within her.

"Aye," he replied, his eyes growing dark as the ancient trees that surrounded them.

Happy tears welled in her eyes as joy, wonder, and love overtook her.

He pressed kisses to her nose, her forehead, and her lips. "I will need to travel home and speak with my parents first, but I kenned the moment I met ye that ye're the woman for me. What say ye?"

She wanted to say yes, but she still needed to tell him of the earl. "Ye dunnae really ken everything about me," she said, her voice softly wavering.

"It's true we have only kenned each other for fewer than two fortnights, but I have learned ye," he said. "Ye dunnae like winter, but summer. Ye prefer the night to the day, as ye love gazing at stars. Ye kinnae swim, either, I think, aye?"

"Aye," she said with a nod. "How did ye ken that?" She had thought she hid it well.

"I will tell ye." He took her hand, led her to the grass, stripped off his plaid, and laid it down. He motioned for her to sit. She swallowed the knot of desire that formed in her throat at the sight of his bare chest. Once they were both sitting, he lay back, crossed his feet at his ankles, and cradled the back of his head in his hands. "Come," he said in a most persuasive voice, "lie beside me and lean yer head on my shoulder."

She did so, soaking in his heat and his nearness. She felt utterly protected when he was close, which was a foreign feeling for her. "How did ye ken I could nae swim?" she asked again.

"Simple," he said. "Ye dunnae ever do more than dip yer toes in the water, and yer shoulders become tense as ye near the loch. Why is it that ye are afraid of the water?"

"My brothers," she muttered. "They used to push me under the water when I was younger and hold me there. The one and only time I managed to swim for even a brief moment, they caught me and held me under so long that I almost drowned. I was too scairt to venture back in after that, so I did nae ever learn to truly swim."

"Yer brothers deserve to be beaten," he said with a scowl, but then he smiled. "I will teach ye to swim when we are wed." His words held a powerful intensity of emotion.

Her heart clenched. She tilted her face up to his and felt something uneven brush against her cheek. Pushing herself up on her hands, she glanced down at his shoulder and found a short, jagged scar. "How did ye get this?" She traced the white line with the tip of her finger.

"From my first battle," he replied, then caught her hand and tugged her back down to him.

As she snuggled against him, she said, "Tell me of it."

"It was against the MacDonald clan. Their leader, the Lord of the Isles, has long attacked our clan ever since King David—or his advisors, really, since the king was but a lad at the time—gave Urquhart Castle to my father for services rendered."

"The MacDonald wanted the castle?" she asked.

"Aye," Callum said. "He wants to grow his power farther north, which includes our home. He's been attacking us since I was but ten summers."

"The king is crafty, aye?"

"Aye," Callum agreed. "He kept the MacDonald from getting too powerful, but he also did nae oblige himself to aid us. When he was older, the king told my father that he had too many other battles to fight and that if my father lost the castle, he did nae deserve it."

"Is this why yer father changed his allegiance to the Steward?"

"One of the reasons," Callum replied.

Their conversation continued for hours, past the nooning meal and into the evening as the sky turned purple and blue. She learned that he had one brother and that Callum was not particularly close to his parents. She discovered that he was a great hawker, and he promised to teach her the art someday.

As the hour approached supper, Marsaili's nerves grew; she had to tell him about the earl. She would not be missed in the great hall, as her father had instructed her not to come once the earl had departed, but Callum would need to make an appearance. She forced herself to swallow her fear.

"Callum," she began, "I want to wed ye, but ye need to ken that my father wishes to make me the Earl of Ulster's mistress, and when the man's wife dies, my father intends to wed me to him."

Callum's jaw tensed visibly, and his thick, corded arms tightened around her. "What gain is there for yer father?"

She told him quickly of the earl's brother possibly being named king of Scotland. When she finished, silence stretched between them, and the sickening feeling that he had decided she was too much trouble swept through her entire body.

He pressed his lips to her forehead and then said, "Dunnae fash yerself. My mother and father are cunning. More so than I have ever cared for, but in this, it may serve well. Surely, some sort of alliance between our two clans can be formed."

"Nae unless yer father has something of great value to

offer my father," she said bitterly. "I fear if ye wish to marry me, we may need to do so without my father's consent, and ye must accept that it may well bring his ire to yer clan's doorstep."

"I accept it," Callum vowed. "I will see what can be done and return to ye as quickly as I am able. Whether I take ye away in the dark of night or by the light of day remains to be seen, but ye will depart here with me. This I vow."

The tenderness of his gaze released her of all fear. "Callum," she said, her voice husky with love and desire. "I wish to consummate our commitment."

Possession flared in his gaze. "Are ye certain?"

"Aye," she said. "Nae ever have I been more certain of anything in my life."

His hands slid up her arms, bringing her closer, and he whispered his love for her in her ear. His hot breath sent gooseflesh racing across her sensitive skin. He lifted her on top of him so she was straddling his thighs, and then, ever so gently, he explored her stomach, her back, her breasts, making them instantly heavy and tight. They both shed their clothes, all the while touching and kissing. Her heart raced with eager anticipation, and at one point, he pressed her palm to his own racing heart.

He laid her back on his plaid, spread her hair around her, and worshipped her in a way she had not believed was possible. With strokes of his tongue and his fingers, he made her cry in pleasure and pain, and then beg for him to enter her and make her his. She could see the effort prolonging his own pleasure was requiring. His jaw was locked, his brow damp, and the corded muscles of his arms strained. He slid into her slowly to make them one.

He paused for a moment and looked in her eyes questioningly. "Are ye hurt?"

She smiled at his concern, his kindness, and his tendre for her. There was a small pinch of pain, but it was easing already. "Please, Callum. Truly make me yers."

He began to move within her, and the pain was re-placed by a slow-building pressure that grew until she felt she would be undone at the seams. She screamed out her pleasure, clinging to him, and his entire body tensed atop her as he cried out with his own release, his warm seed filling her.

They were bound by this night, this act, and their love. Nothing would part them now.

One

1361
Scotland
Three years later...

The dagger in Marsaili's hand felt like freedom. Pressing it to her evil stepmother's fleshy neck filled her with a sense of empowerment. Marsaili shifted her weight forward onto the balls of her feet so she'd be harder to throw off balance if Jean decided to fight back. Never again would she be the dog for her father and Jean to abuse. Marsaili was the fox—sly, wily, and impossible to catch. Or at least she hoped so since her father's men hunted her *and* her MacLeod half brother, Iain, had sent a man after her, as well.

Nearly three years earlier, she'd discovered that Jean was not her true mother, and Helena and her brothers had been her half siblings. Never had she been more relieved about it than at this moment. She detested Jean, and she had detested her sister and Campbell brothers until the day they had all met their makers. She detested her father, as well, but unfortunately, he still lived—and his blood flowed in her veins—whether she liked it or not.

Her father, no doubt, wanted to find her so he could finally fulfill the plot he'd concocted three years prior to marry her to the Earl of Ulster. She'd managed to evade her father's clutches for a long period by taking shelter and refuge with the MacLeod clan, whose laird she recently discovered was her half brother Iain. But her father had lured her out of that protection carefully and methodically by revealing to her that the child she'd borne from one night of passion with Callum Grant was not dead as her father had claimed. The child had survived the delivery, and her father had merely sent him from her.

Pain briefly gripped her heart as she thought of her bairn. Rage quickly followed for how she had been deceived by her father, and her anger at Callum, the deceiver, flared, as well. He had made vows to her that he had broken, and the result was that he had never known she was with child. That child, her child—not Callum's, *hers*—had garnered her a year's reprieve from being sent off to become the earl's mistress. Well, that and the fact that the earl's wife had not died as quickly as the earl had hoped, and she had refused to leave his side. Yet, Marsaili had known that her reprieve would come to an end at some time, so she had plotted to escape once her son was born.

"Marsaili," Jean hissed, startling Marsaili back to the task at hand. "We can make a bargain."

"I dunnae make bargains with devils," Marsaili growled. Her mind raced, considering all her options and all who hunted her. Broch MacLeod, one of Iain's fiercest warriors, was the warrior also tracking her. She would have turned to him for aid when she realized he was trailing her, but she was uncertain if she'd find a friend or foe. He had been a friend for two years, as had her four MacLeod half brothers. The only person she was certain remained her friend was her half sister, Lena MacLeod, now Lena MacLean. Before Marsaili had ever learned that she was half-MacLeod she had known Lena, as she had been married to Marsaili's brother Findlay. Lena was loyal, even though Marsaili had been forced to betray the MacLeod clan. She was uncertain if her other siblings—and most importantly, Iain—would be so understanding. She had betrayed King David, who was not only Iain's friend but a man to whom Iain had sworn political allegiance. Marsaili knew that Lena had written to Iain on her behalf to explain the situation, but Marsaili had no doubt Iain intended to drag her back to the MacLeod stronghold to take responsibility for her actions. But she could not go back to Dunvegan yet.

She tightened her grip on her father's prized dagger, which he displayed in his bedchamber but never used. More the fool was he. Having taken it renewed her courage. It had faltered when she'd returned to Innis Chonnell Castle under cover of darkness. She had lived nearly her entire life in her father's home, and it had been sheer torment. This was the last place she'd ever thought to willingly come back to, but here she was. It was by choice, but only because she'd not seen another option.

"Yer father will have yer head for taking his most prized possession," Jean snapped.

She attempted to back away, and Marsaili nudged the dagger a bit deeper, pricking Jean's skin and eliciting a hiss from her stepmother. "We both ken that's nae true," Marsaili replied with a snort. "He needs my head on my body. I doubt the earl is so obsessed with me"—as the man *was* obsessed, which was surely goaded on by her father— "that he would be willing to wed me headless."

"Ye, ungrateful wench! Ye—"

"Shut yer trap, Jean," Marsaili commanded, unable and unwilling to stop the grin that pulled at her lips. She'd wanted to say that to Jean for years, but she hadn't dared before, for fear of retribution. There was no fear now. It had been replaced by a hatred so strong that her throat burned with it.

"Where is my son?" she demanded, the words hollowing her gut. *Her son.* Joy bubbled in her belly, but a swift tide of fear, loss, and regret stopped the warm feeling. She still could not believe that the child she'd birthed was actually alive. Her heart pounded so hard that her fingertips pulsed where she pressed them against her father's weapon.

Her father. He didn't deserve to even be thought of as such, but her blasted mind continued to do so. He was the Devil's spawn, that's what he was. Any man who would lie to his daughter and tell her that her son had died simply because he wanted to be able to use her in marriage was despicable. She ground her teeth against her wandering thoughts. The lack of sleep over the last sennight was weighing upon her, making it hard to keep her mind on task, yet she had to do so. She knew she didn't have much time before her father's men overtook her. She was mayhap a day's ride ahead of them, but if they found her, she'd never escape.

Time was passing quickly. "If ye dunnae tell me where ye and Father sent my son, I'll slit yer throat," Marsaili rasped.

"Ye dunnae have the stomach for murder," Jean snarled.

Marsaili answered with a flick of her wrist that sent the sharp blade sliding across her stepmother's neck lightning-quick. Jean gasped and her hands flew to the surface cut, but Marsaili swiveled the blade to dig the point back into Jean's flesh.

"That was a warning," she growled, swallowing down a wave of bitter disgust that filled her mouth when Jean's warm blood trickled onto her fingertips. "Ye are wrong about me, Jean," Marsaili said, meaning it. "I may nae have had the stomach for killing before I fled here, but I have the will to kill ye now. And nae just ye, do ye ken me? I'll strike down anyone who stands in the way of me getting back the son ye stole from me. Now, where...is...my...son?"

The desperation and anger in her own voice sent goose-flesh up her back and prickled her neck. She didn't want to be this person. She didn't want to be violent. She didn't want to be a woman who betrayed her honorable brothers, men who had come to mean so much to her, but her father had left her little choice.

Jean shook her head. "I dunnae—"

Marsaili pressed the dagger deeper. "Dunnae spew yer lies to me."

Jean gasped. "I'm nae lying. The *Ceàrdannan* had been traveling near the castle when ye gave birth, and yer father sent the bairn with them. Told them it was a castle castoff from a kitchen wench."

Despair made Marsaili's knees weak. She hadn't thought she could hate her father more than she already did, but she had been wrong. The black rage she felt toward him in this moment frightened her. Her father had sent her newly born child with the Summer Walkers. They were a people without a clan, without any allegiance but to themselves and their leaders. They did not believe in possessions; therefore, they had no homes and traveled constantly. How would she ever find her son?

Tears clogged her throat and shot an ache to her thumping heart. She had no one to turn to for help, least of all Callum. He was the child's father, but he had betrayed her in the worst way. He'd stolen her heart and she'd given him her body, and in return, he'd given her a bairn. Unbeknownst to him, of course, which was entirely the Devil's doing. She'd learned she was with child *after* he had left with a vow to return for her as soon as he spoke to his parents. She had not known, however, that he had been promised to another since childhood. In the two fortnights they had spent together, he had never once mentioned it, not even when she had told him of her father's plot to marry her to the earl.

She pushed thoughts of him away as an anxious feeling stirred deep in her gut. She'd learned not to ignore those feelings. She glanced quickly at the window. She'd made a critical error in determining how much time she had before daybreak. It had been dark when she'd slipped into the castle, but the sky was already lightening, and once the inhabitants of the castle stirred, it would be near impossible to escape unseen. A tremor of fear coursed through her.

Her father would be crazed to capture her. King David still did not have a legitimate heir, and the earl's brother, John of Gaunt, might still be named heir presumptive to the Scottish throne if David were to die without one.

Even as her father continued to secretly support the Steward, he still wished to forge an allegiance with the earl and, subsequently, his brother. She could not imagine why the earl still wanted her. Perhaps he had created a fantasy of her in his twisted mind. "Ye can tell my father that even if he hauls me back here, I will inform the earl I am nae an innocent. Father will nae ever use me."

Jean smirked for a long, silent moment. "Simple, foolish girl. The earl kens ye had a bairn and have lain with a man." Marsaili hissed in a breath of surprise, which made Jean's smirk grow. "He had yer chambermaid reporting to him about ye, and the blasted, loose-tongued clot-heid wrote that yer belly had swollen with child."

"Brianna?" Marsaili croaked, thinking of the chamber-maid who'd been found drowned the morning after Marsaili had given birth.

"Aye." Jean averted her eyes, and Marsaili feared that her father had killed Brianna or had one of his guards do the deed. She pinched the skin between her brows, trying to sort out what Jean was telling her.

"I dunnae ken. If the earl kens I'm nae an innocent—"

"He dunnae care," Jean snapped, looking at Marsaili once again. "He has the fever for ye and will have ye as his."

Marsaili felt her mouth drop open. "I'll nae marry that man, nor become his leman. Ever."

"Ye will," Jean said. "If ye ever wish to see yer bairn again."

Marsaili stiffened. Even if she cooperated with her father, he wouldn't tell her how to find the Summer Walkers—if he knew at all. Jean's smirk grew wider. Jean knew it, too!

Marsaili wanted to scream, but she dared not for fear the guards who roamed the castle halls would hear. Instead, she flipped the dagger in her hand and used the hilt to knock her stepmother on the brow, in the very spot her father had long ago knocked Marsaili when she had displeased him. Her father's treatment of her had taught her two valuable lessons: never stand too close to him once he had been angered, and all it took to knock a person to sleep was a hard hit right above the eye with just the right curve of the weapon after the hit.

Jean crumpled to the ground and her stepmother's eyes fluttered shut. Marsaili gazed at Jean for a long moment before stepping over the body that was blocking her path to the door. She threw the door open and halted, her heart dropping into her stomach. Her stepmother's personal guard, Torquol, stood there. His gaze widened in recognition and then flew past her to where Jean lay prone on the floor. Marsaili tried to dart to the right of him to escape, but his hand clamped on her arm as he easily took her dagger from her.

"Marsaili Campbell," he said, his mead breath washing over her and making her stomach twist. "I see yer trouble-making ways have nae changed."

Two

Callum stepped into the inner courtyard of Urquhart Castle, the Clan Grant stronghold and his home. He swept his gaze around the courtyard, noting the Grant flags flapping in the wind. They were tattered from three long years of sieges by the MacDonald clan, as well as the Gordon clan. The flags were not the only battered parts of his home, though. The land to the west that had once been rich and green for sheep to feed was now bare from the constant galloping of war horses. The stone walls of the towers had chinks in them from the catapults used to try to breach the castle, and the defensive walls were peppered with large dents from the battering rams. In some places, the light of day even shone through. The walls needed to be repaired, but that required coin, and he had precious little of it.

Callum rolled his shoulders in an attempt to alleviate the knots that seemed to be a permanent part of his body. The roaring din of his clansman chattering as they proceeded from the castle, woods, and courtyard to the shore of Loch Ness below was a swift reminder that these people relied upon him for protection. The task was a great one, especially given the number of good warriors they had lost in battle over the past three years. He scanned the water of the loch, which shimmered almost silver in the bright sun, and his chest tightened as his gaze settled on the incoming birlinn carrying the Earl of Ainsworth to Urquhart.

"Callum, I hope ye remember well what has happened to us because ye broke yer vow to wed Edina Gordon," his mother said, coming up beside him with his younger brother, Brice. Callum stilled. He'd long ago accepted it as his due penance to be reminded daily that his actions had plunged his clan into war, a war that had gotten his father killed.

Beside his mother, Brice scowled and opened his mouth as if to protest. Callum discreetly shook his head, relieved when Brice clamped his jaw shut. Callum had long ago given up trying to make his younger brother understand the guilt he felt for their father's death. That was why he endured his mother's constant reminders, but he would not endure Brice and Mother fighting.

As if she recognized she'd won a moment to continue to speak as she desired, she waved to her companions, hovering respectfully a few feet away, indicating they should continue onward toward the steep path that led down the jagged cliff to the water. "Lady Coira will be expecting to see ye at the shore for her arrival at the tournament."

"I ken well Lady Coira and the earl will take offense if I'm nae waiting to greet them like an obedient hound," he replied, casting his eyes up to the blue sky in a bid for peace and patience.

His mother clucked her tongue. "Ye'd nae be in this position if ye had swallowed yer pride and wed Edina as yer father and I had agreed."

"Again, Mother?" Brice burst out, despite Callum narrowing his eyes at his brother. Brice shrugged, as if to say he was sorry for not listening. "I kinnae imagine that Callum could ever forget why ye believe we are in this position."

"Why I *believe* he is in this position?" Their mother's face purpled with anger. "Why I *believe?*" she repeated, her voice pitching high.

"Aye, why ye believe," Brice snapped. "Ye conveniently forget that ye and Father wanted Callum to wed Edina to simply gain allies. And neither of ye seemed to have a care that the lass was nae true to the upcoming union, nor was she pure."

"Sacrifices had to be made," their mother barked. "Callum could have taken Edina in hand and controlled her once they were married."

Their mother was right on that point. Callum also knew his love for Marsaili Campbell had kept him from agreeing to renew his broken vow to marry Edina. Then his grief over losing Marsaili before they'd ever had the chance to start a life together had held him firm in his refusal.

His gut clenched, as it always did, when he thought of Marsaili, of sitting in the great hall of his home arguing with his parents, telling them he would not wed Edina despite their insistence. He recalled acutely the moment one of their servants had handed his mother a sealed letter. Callum could still see her opening it, her gaze flying to him before revealing the contents of the letter: a proclamation that the Campbell's beloved daughter Marsaili had drowned. *Drowned.* She had drowned the day after he had left her with the promise that he would return to wed her.

The message had been short and impersonal, but of course, it would have been, as the Campbell had been unaware of Callum's love for Marsaili. He had been home for a month before the letter arrived, and he had been delayed in returning to Marsaili because of the Gordon's immediate sieges after Callum had refused to honor the promise to wed Edina. His mother and father had held firm that he must relinquish his foolish infatuation and mend things with Edina, which the Gordon had said would restore peace between the clans, especially since Edina had lied to her father and told him Callum had gotten her with child.

Callum had refuted the claim, but the Gordon refused to believe it. His own parents had claimed to believe him, but they also believed the Campbell would not agree to a marriage alliance with them when he could have one with the powerful Earl of Ulster. And they certainly had not wanted to draw the Campbell's ire by telling him that Callum had taken his daughter's innocence. They had robbed Callum of ever knowing if the Campbell would or would not have agreed. But later, when Callum had sent a call out for aid to fight the Gordons and the MacDonalds, the Campbell had shown he was not a friend.

"Look what yer pestering has done, Mother," Brice growled, bringing Callum back to the present. "Callum looks dazed."

"I did nae do it! Ye did!" his mother screeched.

"Enough." Callum looked from his mother to his brother and back again, his patience wearing thin.

His mother sniffed as if he'd injured her feelings. He didn't know whether he truly had or if she was acting. She was a strong, ambitious woman, yet she had loved his father, and Callum could vividly recall her grief when Father had died. He'd been stabbed through the heart by the Gordon laird during a siege on Urquhart Castle two fortnights after Callum had returned from the Gathering.

The memory of his mother's wails upon learning of his father's death made him hold in much of what he wanted to say to her. It was a fact that his refusal to marry Edina had ultimately plunged his clan into war with the Gordons. "Rest assured, Mother. My guilt about Father's death and at how our clan has been ravaged is nae ever eased." His mother nodded as if pleased by the confirmation. He took a long breath, searching for the calm that had eluded him all morning. "I ken well we need the Earl of Ainsworth, as he needs us. I will marry the cold Lady Coira—"

"Ye will thaw her once ye're married," his mother said in her practical tone.

He held his mother's stare. Her refusal to believe that he did not care to have Coira's affection always amazed him. He suspected it was how she avoided feeling any guilt for her own mistakes in life. "I dunnae care to thaw her," he said, biting out each word. In two months, he would take to wife a woman as cold as the northerly winter winds; yet, that was why he had finally decided he could marry her to save his clan. Her ambivalence toward him actually allowed him to accept the inevitable. He did not have to feel guilty that she would want his heart, when he knew well that Marsaili had taken it with her to her grave. God's blood, he had not wanted to think of her today, on the day that he would greet his soon-to-be wife. It seemed an utter betrayal to Marsaili's memory and the love he had held—still held— for her.

"This union benefits both clans, Son," his mother said, her voice more of a coo now that she was about to get what she wanted.

He nodded, for she spoke the truth. The Earl of Ainsworth had approached Callum a year ago about marrying his daughter. At first Callum had thought to decline, but a ride around his clan's ravaged castle and a particularly vicious siege by the Gordons, during which Callum had lost twenty good warriors, made him think again. His coffers were so low that he could ill afford to repair Urquhart, and he still needed to gain more warriors. He could no longer delay a marriage union to get an alliance.

He was lucky to have received an offer of an alliance at all. After his father died, he'd sent out a request for an alliance to those his father had considered friends, and not one of them, including the Campbell laird, had answered the call. Callum had then turned to King David, ready to pledge the loyalty his father had taken away and given to the Steward, but it was not that simple. The king did not trust Callum because he was his father's son, and King David had refused even to hear Callum's pledge, let alone offer him aid. Only recently had the king agreed to allow Callum to come to Edinburgh to speak with him. It had taken two and a half years of paying a penance fee to the king to achieve. Callum could not be certain what would happen when he saw the king. He may well leave Edinburgh still in disfavor. His clan had no one to turn to—except Ainsworth.

The earl wanted an alliance with Callum, as well, because Urquhart blocked the path that the MacDonalds needed to take to get to Ainsworth's home, which the laird desired to claim. MacDonald wanted to gain power closer to England. Ainsworth needed someone loyal to help fight off the MacDonald, and someone with a personal stake in keeping MacDonald away, like Callum, would fight the most fiercely against their common enemy.

"I love ye, Son," his mother said, squeezing his shoulder.

"Aye," he acknowledged immediately, knowing she did but also realizing her affection had many strings attached to it. And one of them was Callum agreeing to the union with Coira. His mother's motivation was not only to strengthen the clan but to receive the chest of gold that the earl had promised the Grants upon the marriage, which would bring great wealth to the clan—and to her.

"Ye will nae even think of Marsaili Campbell ever again once ye and Lady Coira have met in the marriage bed."

He didn't respond. There was no way he could without starting a quarrel. His mother was wrong; yet, in her heart, she believed she was right. He had no notion why she had mentioned Marsaili, unless she sensed him brooding the past couple of days—or more likely if Brice had said something to her about it. Brice had a problem holding his tongue. For Callum's part, he rarely talked of Marsaili, and when he did, it was never to his mother. He had loved the woman. In truth, Marsaili was the only woman he had ever loved—*would* ever love—but she had left this world and was never returning. And as laird, he had an obligation to marry Coira for the well-being of his clan. Besides, he had to atone for choosing his heart's desire over the good of his people the last time around.

"Callum, we should make our way down," his mother said.

He wasn't ready. He wanted another moment, just one, before he walked to the shore and put his past behind him for good.

Brice's shrewd blue gaze seemed to register Callum's unspoken thoughts. "We'll join ye shortly, Mother. Callum wanted to instruct me on which men to have guard his future wife while she is here for the tourney."

"I hope that is all," his mother said, giving Callum a pleading look.

"Dunnae fash yerself. I *will* marry the lass when the time comes."

She nodded, causing once-shiny black strands of hair,

now dulled by age, to slip from behind her ear. She twisted the locks around her finger. "I'm nae fashed," she replied, her lips puckering for a moment. "I ken ye realize that if ye had nae broken yer first vow to Edina, yer father would still be alive and we would nae be in such dire need."

"It amazes me how ye always manage to fit that re-minder into conversation several times a day," Brice quipped.

Callum held up a silencing hand to his brother and looked to their mother. "All will be fine," he said, willing it to be so.

"Ye will follow?" she persisted.

He nodded. "I'll be at the shore before their birlinn reaches it."

She offered a triumphant smile before walking away and disappearing down the slope.

"Ye ken," Brice said, "she has convinced herself ye will fall under Coira's spell."

"Does Coira have a spell for me to fall under?" Callum asked, eyeing his brother.

Brice scowled. "How should I ken? She is yer future wife."

"Aye, but ye just said—"

"I simply referred to her beauty," Brice interrupted, red-faced.

"Ye always have had an eye for the lovely lasses, but a pretty face will nae make me forget my past."

"Ye talk as if ye dunnae like Coira. Do ye believe her a bad person? She is simply tart-tongued."

Callum chuckled, recalling Coira once flaying Brice for flirting openly with her maid when they had visited her home. *Tart-tongued* was putting Coira Ainsworth's disposi-tion in a kind light. Still, he understood why she likely behaved as she did. "I dunnae believe she is a bad person, Brother. She is but a game piece moved on a board by her father, and she dunnae care for it. I can hardly berate her for feeling what I myself felt about wedding Edina."

"Och," Brice growled. "It infuriates me how ye are accepting this fate."

Callum smiled at his brother. Being younger had offered Brice a certain freedom that Callum had never had, though he briefly had tried to take it and failed. He was not fated to choose his wife; he had to marry for duty. It was not how he had wanted it—truly, he'd done his best to avoid it—but it was the way of it. Coira had told him she did not wish to wed him, either, because in him, she saw a man who would never love her. And she had been right. He had been unable to deny it, so he could not begrudge the cold way she treated him.

"Ye dunnae have to marry her, Callum," Brice said.

"Ye ken I do," Callum replied. A bird soaring through the air caught his attention, and he was struck with a very clear memory of something Marsaili had said not long after he had met her. She had been sitting by the water's edge, staring up at a bird in the sky with a wistful expression on her face, and said, *I wish I could fly away as birds do.*

That was how he felt in this moment.

"A pretty face may nae make ye forget the Campbell lass," Brice said, shifting beside Callum, "but it can make the joining more pleasant."

"We will join only once, to seal the marriage."

Brice gaped at Callum. "Ye kinnae mean that. Ye're nae a monk, Brother. And ye need an heir. What if ye dunnae get her with child during that one joining?"

"She kinnae have bairns," Callum said, revealing to his brother something he had not told anyone else, including their mother.

Brice's eyes widened. "How can she ken this?"

"She was married before, and they had nae conceived. After her husband died, she wanted to discover if she was the reason she had nae had children, so the medicine woman who examined her told her that her womb would remain forever empty, and a seer confirmed it."

"God's blood," Brice muttered. "Ye must have bairns. Ye're laird. Ye need offspring that will one day take yer place."

"Ye will have bairns, and *yer* son will be laird."

"Ye speak nonsense. Surely ye want yer own bairns."

"I dunnae, Brother. Now leave the subject be." The softness that had once dwelled in him, the part of him capable of tender emotions for a woman, the part of him that had imagined having bairns with Marsaili—children who would look like her—had died when he'd learned she had. He wanted none of it now.

"Ye're nae dead, Callum," Brice said low. "Ye live, like it or nae."

He glanced sideways and met his brother's worried gaze. He wanted to snap a command at him to stop speaking. He could—it was his right—but he simply nodded when confronted with the evidence of Brice's concern. "Aye, I'm well aware that I'm nae dead."

"It just occurred to me what ye're doing," Brice said, making Callum groan.

"Do ye ken," Callum grumbled, "that ever since the day ye were born, ye have been noisy? Ye came out wailing, and once that stopped, ye started jabbering, and ye have nae ceased."

Brice grinned. "Dunnae try to sway me from my thoughts with affronts. I've seen ye use that deceit enough times to ken what ye are doing. Now, I thought ye were marrying Coira only because of the blame ye place on yerself for Da's death, and certainly because we need the ally, but I see now 'tis nae so simple."

"I dunnae care to hear yer views on why I'm doing what I am doing," Callum growled.

"And I dunnae care that ye dunnae wish to hear it," Brice shot back. "Ye are marrying Coira because ye ken that with her, ye will nae ever have to risk feeling for a woman again."

"I dunnae ken any such thing, because I dunnae waste my time thinking upon trivial matters such as my feelings. I plunged our clan into war and cost Da his life when I broke my vow to wed Edina. I have a duty," he thundered, "and I'll see it through."

Brice opened his mouth, but Callum shook his head. "I'd nae if I were ye," he said, his anger now barely controlled. "Ye have said yer peace, and I let ye, but if ye say one more word, I will hit ye square on that mouth ye kinnae seem to keep shut."

"Ye ken yer temper has bested ye because I'm right."

Callum clenched his jaw on retorting. He rarely lost control, but Brice's words, the day, and the impending arrival of a woman he did not wish to wed had him on edge. His brother was correct that he never again wanted to feel the pain of loss. His grief had nearly drowned him when Marsaili had died. But he didn't fear that he would feel such pain again, because he would never feel for anyone as he had for her. Loving Marsaili, plunging his clan into strife for her only to lose her before ever truly having her, had left him keenly aware that his choices carried long-lasting, sometimes irrevocable consequences. He felt a thousand summers older than the twenty-seven he was, and he prayed he was wise enough now to never forget that.

Brice clamped a hand on Callum's shoulder. "I'm sorry, Brother. I see I pushed ye too hard. We can talk more of this when ye are ready to really listen."

Callum grunted and responded by starting toward the path to the loch. Brice fell into step beside him as he made his way down the jagged embankment. He could have taken the stairs, not far to the west, but he welcomed the burn in his legs from his muscles working to keep him from sliding and the tightness in his lungs from the clipped pace. It took his concentration, which was a welcome reprieve from the thoughts in his head.

"I ken ye heard me," Brice said, terseness underlying his tone.

"I heard ye," Callum snapped. "Now ye hear me. I'll nae talk more of this. Ye raise the topic again at yer own peril. Do ye ken me?" He stopped and turned to Brice. He could not afford—God's bones, the clan could not afford—for his brother to ruin the arrangement with Ainsworth. When Brice gave him a stubborn look, Callum's temper spiked. He knew his brother meant well, but when he looked at his brother, Callum saw the same naive fool he had once been, believing the good of one outweighed the good of many. "If ye push me, Brice, as laird, I will have to punish ye for failing to obey."

Brice's lips pressed into a thin line, but after a minute, he smiled. "Ye ken ye sounded just like Da when ye said that."

"Good," Callum said, meaning it, as he reached the shore. "Da was a strong laird."

"Da was ruthless and scheming," Brice replied. "As is Mother."

"Be that as it may, if I had relented to their demands to

wed Edina, he would be alive and the clan would be much stronger."

"Ye have shoved how ye felt for the Campbell lass so deep within ye that it seems all ye can recall is yer guilt. Ye have forgotten the feelings that led to yer choices."

"I do nae forget," Callum growled. "I only wish I could." With that, he turned from his brother and made his way down the seagate stairs.

Bright light cracked the darkness of the dungeon. Marsaili scampered up from the cold, slick floor, squeezing her eyes shut against the light. From her stiff limbs and the way she could hardly tolerate the light, she figured she'd been down here at least two days—no more than three. Her stomach growled with gnawing hunger, and she rubbed at it while slowly cracking her eyes open. Oh, how she detested the penance cell.

She could just make out the shadowy figure of a hooded woman. Marsaili's eyes watered as she willed them to adjust. It wasn't Jean—of that much she was sure. If Jean were this near Marsaili, the evil woman would have taunted her. She would have been crowing at how Marsaili had been caught by Torquol and dragged to the dungeon. Marsaili swallowed, her throat so dry it felt as if she'd just tried to get down a mouthful of dirt. When had she last had something to drink? Day one or two down here? Two, she thought, but who knew if that was truly correct. Her thoughts were swimming in her head like slippery fish that didn't want to be caught.

"Is my father here?" she croaked. The question elicited fear and anger inside her. She wanted to see him only to spit in his face, but if she was close enough to see him, any hope of escape was lost. Though, it seemed rather lost already.

"Nay," a woman answered in a tart, amused voice. "Lucky for ye, I'd say. Would ye nae?"

Marsaili sucked in a shocked breath. "Maria?"

"Aye," the Campbell medicine woman, who once had been her friend, answered in a hushed tone as she moved toward the cell, unlocked it, and stepped in to take hold of Marsaili's elbow. "Can ye walk?"

"Depends on where ye're leading me," she said, guarded. As the room started to sway around her, she reached back, glad her hand met with the wall. It was slimy and she wanted to draw away, but she refused to fall on her face and she could not be certain her legs were going to hold her upright on their own.

The woman sniggered. "I see yer time away has nae made ye any friendlier."

"I'm friendly when I ken I'm amongst friends," Marsaili replied, catching a faint trace of something that smelled suspiciously and enticingly like bread. Her mouth instantly began to water. "Do ye have bread?"

"Aye," Maria said, pitching her voice lower. "For my friends." Sarcasm dripped from her tone.

"I'm sorry," Marsaili said, lowering her voice as Maria had done. "It's just the betrayals are stacking up faster than I can count them. I dunnae ken who to trust."

Maria squeezed Marsaili's shoulder. "I was sent down here by Jean to tend yer wounds," she whispered. "She wants ye up above in the great hall shortly. Yer father's men, the ones who were supposed to be accompanying ye here, have arrived, as well as the Earl of Ulster's men." She motioned toward the door. "I overheard Jean say the earl is demanding ye be delivered to him at once."

Marsaili's skin crawled at the thought. "So are ye simply here to tend me?" It seemed she could trust Maria as she once had, but she needed to be certain.

"Nay, though yer head surely needs my care. Ye must have hit it quite hard whilst ye were away because I clearly recall helping ye escape once before. I also clearly recall ye saying ye would nae step foot in this castle ever again."

Marsaili snatched the bread that Maria was now dangling in front of her face and shoved it in her mouth. In between chewing, she said, "I was compelled to come back."

"Nothing on Earth will compel me to ever come back here again when I leave," Maria announced in a quiet tone.

Marsaili swallowed the bread and swiped a hand across her mouth to rid it of crumbs. "Are ye finally leaving?" She had begged Maria to come last time, but the woman had stayed because of her sister.

"Aye," Maria replied, linking arms with Marsaili. "With ye."

Marsaili was glad to hear it, yet she had to know what had changed. "What of yer sister? I thought ye could nae leave because of her."

"I could nae, but she married a Grant"—Marsaili flinched at the mention of Callum's clan—"nae long ago," Maria continued, oblivious to the havoc she had just wreaked inside Marsaili. She had never confided to Maria what had occurred between her and Callum. She wanted to, but she had been waiting to share her secret when he returned for her, but soon after he left, Helena had told her that Callum was promised to wed another and had been for years. Helena had been thrilled, sure that was why Callum had not succumbed to her charms, and Marsaili had been devastated and confused. Both emotions had given way to anger and betrayal when she hadn't heard from Callum again. Her father had immediately discovered that she was with child, and from then until the birth, her mind had been consumed with fear. After the birth, grief had consumed her.

"Anyway," Maria said, "my sister departed. I was hoping to be allowed to join the Grant clan, but I wanted to give her time to settle into her new married life before she asked her husband to go to the laird and make a request on my behalf." Maria shrugged. "I've nae heard from her yet, but I'm departing with ye anyway."

"What if the Grant laird denies yer sister's request?" Marsaili asked, thinking of how Callum had deceived her so long ago. Perhaps his father was as terrible a laird as his son was a person.

"I dunnae think he would. I've heard naught but good things about Callum Grant."

"Callum G-Grant?" Marsaili sputtered.

"Aye, ye recall him, I suppose, from the time he was here for the Gathering."

"Aye." Her face heated with shame of the truth she needed to admit. It was rather daunting having to tell someone she had given her virtue and her heart so foolishly, but she needed help. She had no notion how to find the Summer Walkers and her son, or even how she would know her son if she did find them. Not only was Maria a healer but she'd always seemed wise to Marsaili and she had always been kind. Her husband, who had been a warrior, had been killed by Marsaili's father for refusing to obey orders to turn women and children from her father's land after their husbands, fathers, and sons had died in battle for the Campbell. "He's laird now?"

"Aye. Has been for near three years."

Marsaili frowned. "Near three years, ye say?"

"Aye," Maria added, her words suddenly sounding rushed. "We'll talk more later, aye? When we are free from here? There is a guard outside. I'll tell him I need to tend ye in the healing room, and then we can take ye to Jean. He's been ordered nae to let ye out of his sight. But once we're in the healing room, I'll offer him a drink, which will be laced with a sleeping draft."

"What if he will nae drink it?"

Maria shrugged. "Then I'll hit him over the head with my candelabra. It's good and heavy, and should put him straight to sleep."

Marsaili shelved that bit of information for the future. "Then what?"

"Well, then we slip out of the castle, through the woods, and to the trails that lead us away from here. But as ye were compelled to come back here, I suppose ye seek something, and I would like to ken what."

Maria started to walk toward the cracked door, but Marsaili pulled her back. "I came here to find my bairn," she blurted.

Maria turned toward her, mouth agape. "Did ye just say ye have a bairn?"

"Well, he'll be closer to a wee lad now."

"I dunnae ken what ye're saying…"

"Nay, ye would nae," Marsaili mumbled. She quickly and quietly told Maria everything—of falling in love with Callum, of his promise to marry her, and of his lies. Marsaili's ears burned as she spoke of him not returning, of her sister Helena discovering that he was promised to wed Edina Gordon, of her father learning she was with child and making her hide the truth from everyone, and of his plot to wed her to the Earl of Ulster.

"I had the bairn, and I thought he had died at birth. My father and Jean," she said, nearly choking on her rage, "they told me he had died. I did nae ever consider that they would lie to me. I should have... I should have kenned my father would still be plotting to marry me to the Earl of Ulster."

"Oh God, Marsaili," Maria whispered.

Marsaili nodded. "He had so much thick brown hair when he was born," she said, tears stinging her eyes as the memory came to her. "And blue eyes. I wonder if his eyes are still blue. I have to find him, Maria. Jean says he's with the Summer Walkers, but I dunnae ken where they are, nor if I'll even ken my own child if, or when, I see him."

Maria clutched Marsaili by the arms and hugged her fiercely. "I've some notion of the path the Summer Walkers take, and I can tell ye exactly how to ken yer son."

"What?" Marsaili gasped, biting her lip when Maria motioned for her to lower her voice.

Maria cast her gaze to the door, where Marsaili could now clearly see the silhouette of a man standing guard. "I know the leader of the Summer Walkers. They travel almost the same route every summer, and as for yer bairn, I...I branded his foot. I'm certain now that the bairn was yers, and had ye told me of him, I would have helped ye." She gave Marsaili a stern look, but then she squeezed her hand. "Though I do ken why ye might have felt ye could nae."

Marsaili nodded but then frowned. "How can ye be certain that ye branded my son's foot?"

"Jean brought a bairn to me one night, freshly birthed and swathed in peasant rags. She told me he belonged to yer chambermaid, and that the woman had begged Jean to get rid of it because of the shame she'd bring her family since she was nae married. Ye ken as well as I do, Jean would nae ever do anyone a favor unless it somehow benefited her."

"Aye, I ken it," Marsaili said, bitterness curling within her at Jean's lies.

"I'm sorry to say I did nae question that yer chambermaid would have gotten herself with bairn. The woman had joined with near half yer father's guard."

"I did nae have any notion," Marsaili replied, thinking of Brianna who'd always seemed so sweet to Marsaili but then had betrayed her confidence.

"Jean had seen the Summer Walkers camping near the castle," Maria continued, "and she told me to take the bairn to them. I branded the bairn on his right foot with an X in case Brianna changed her mind and decided she wanted her bairn, er—" Maria gave Marsaili an apologetic look "—yer bairn back. I'm sorry, Marsaili. I'd nae ever have done Jean's bidding had I kenned the bairn was yers. Ye hid the fact that ye were with child verra well."

"Aye," Marsaili replied, thinking back to how scared and lonely she had been.

"The next morning Brianna was dead, and Jean told me the silly woman had drowned herself. Jean said to nae ever speak of the child, as it would just bring more shame to Brianna's family." Maria shrugged. "I had liked Brianna, so I kept my silence until now. That bairn was the only one born that month. The boy I branded must be yers."

"I have a way to ken my son," Marsaili whispered, her heart racing.

"Aye," Maria said. "If we can find him. Come, we must leave. Remember the plan?"

"Aye," Marsaili replied, following Maria to the slightly ajar dungeon door. "Godfrey of Antwerp," Maria called in a sweet voice as she strolled into the dark hall, gripping Marsaili by the arm. "Marsaili dunnae have the strength she needs for the journey to the earl's home."

"What can be done?" the man asked, looking to Marsaili. "Ulster will be furious if I delay bringing her to him."

"I thought as much. I have done all I can in the dungeon, but if ye aid me in taking her to my healing room, I have some restorative medicine that should see her through the journey and have her well by the end of it, so she may ease the earl's grieving pains."

When the guard, Godfrey, looked as if he was going to protest, Maria tugged the bodice of her gown low while murmuring, "The dungeon is so hot, is it nae?"

Godfrey's gaze fastened to Maria's bosom. "Aye. Ye will be quick about it in the healing room, will ye nae?" he asked, unable to pull his gaze away from Maria's chest. Marsaili rolled her eyes at Maria, whose lips trembled with mirth.

"Oh, aye. I'll be so quick, ye'll nae even ken anything is occurring," she promised, quirking her mouth at Marsaili. "If ye'll just take hold of Marsaili's right arm?"

Godfrey did as she had asked.

The journey from the dungeon to the healing room was a short one, as it was situated just to the right of the top of the dungeon stairs. No other chambers were nearby, so it was unlikely that anyone would hear Godfrey if he made noise when falling, nor was Marsaili worried that they would fail to overcome the man. Between her and Maria, they certainly could accomplish the task. Her greatest concern was getting out of the castle unseen and then putting enough ground between them and her father's men to escape capture.

As they entered the healing room, Maria paused right inside the threshold at a table that had a candelabra on it. She waved Godfrey in while she released her hold on

Marsaili, catching Marsaili's eye for the briefest of moments. Marsaili gave a slight nod to let Maria know she was prepared.

"If ye'll just help her sit on the chair," Maria instructed, "I'll get ye some mead."

"I dunnae want anything to drink," Godfrey answered, voice unbending.

"As ye wish," Maria murmured.

Marsaili's heart raced as Godfrey led her to the chair. When they were almost there, she said, "Ye may release me now. I'm feeling much better."

Godfrey gave a clipped nod and relinquished his hold on her. The moment he did, she cried out, "Oh my," swayed on her feet, and crumpled forward to her knees. Immediately Godfrey's hand came to her shoulder.

"My lady, are ye—"

The loud crack of the iron knocking against the man's skull resounded in the room.

"Watch out!" Maria called. As Marsaili scrambled to lunge out of the way, Godfrey's falling body brushed past her, and he fell forward and hit the floor with a hard thud.

She sucked in a jagged breath as she scampered back and then upright. Maria was standing beside her, heaving breaths, her hand still clutching the candelabra, before Marsaili had even fully regained her balance. They stared at the fallen man in silence. His face was turned to them, eyes closed and mouth parted with a line of drool already starting to run from his lips. A bright trail of blood from the cut on his head trickled across his cheekbone and dripped off his chin.

"Do ye think he's dead?" Marsaili asked. She'd never killed anyone, and she prayed Godfrey was not the first. Though the man had intended to take her to the earl, he was only doing his lord's bidding.

Maria's answer was to nudge the man in the shoulder with the tip of her shoe. When he did not move or make any sound, she bent over him and pressed her fingers to his neck.

"What are ye doing?" Marsaili asked.

"Seeing if his heart still beats."

"Does it?" Marsaili tried to catch her breath while waiting for the answer.

"Aye," Maria said with a satisfied nod. She stood, brushed her hands down her skirt, and then dashed across the room to a table littered with herbs. "Help me," the woman said, gathering the herbs into her hands and putting them in a leather satchel. "We may need these."

Marsaili hurried to Maria and shoved several handfuls of the herbs into Maria's bag. "We have to flee," Marsaili rushed out, her gut knotted with tension.

"Aye." Maria glanced around the room. "I wish we could take bundles, but we kinnae chance being seen with them. It would cause suspicion."

Marsaili nodded. "At least the cold nights of winter are behind us. Do ye have any weapons in here?"

Maria offered a sly smile before drawing up her skirts. She took a dagger from a holder strapped to her right leg. "Ye can have this one. There's also one on my left leg."

Marsaili took the dagger with a smile, lifted her own skirts, and put the weapon in the empty holder tied around her calf with a bit of rope.

"Are ye always prepared to carry a weapon?" Maria asked with a snigger.

"Aye. If only I always had a weapon to carry. I'm certain a lot of what has befallen me could have been avoided that way. Come. We'll take the woods to the west of here so that we dunnae have to enter the castle again."

"Agreed," Maria said, and without any more talk, the women departed the healing room and headed for the dark tunnels instead of the stairs. Marsaili had always avoided the tunnels when she lived at the castle because they were filled with mice, spiderwebs, and snakes, and today was no exception. Mice scampered across the ground as they ran, and she broke through more than one spiderweb. By the time they exited the tunnel, webbing clung to her face, her hair, and her arms. She shuddered, pausing to pull it off her when Maria suddenly clutched her.

"Down!" Maria hissed. Marsaili started to ask why, but then she heard men's voices.

They both dropped to their hands and knees, and crawled quickly toward a tree. Just as they hid behind it, two of her father's guards rounded the corner from the direction of the stables. Once they passed and were out of sight, Marsaili and Maria ran for the woods, and just as they reached the thick brush, one of her father's men stepped out of the copse of trees, tugging up his pants.

She didn't recognize him, and by the grin he gave her, he didn't know her, either. "Maria," he slurred, obviously having imbibed in too much drink, "who is the fetching lass ye have here, and where are the two of ye off to?"

Maria smiled, tugging her bodice low as she had before, which drew the man's gaze and offered Marsaili the opportunity to discreetly lift her skirt and retrieve her dagger as Maria spoke to the guard.

"So," Maria finished, drawing out the word, "we are heading to pick those rare flowers."

The guard's brows drew together. "I kinnae let ye enter the woods alone. I'll attend ye."

"That will nae be necessary," Marsaili said, which got

the guard to turn toward her. At the exact moment he did, she knocked him above the eye with the hilt of her dagger, but the man did not crumple as she had hoped he would. For one breath, he appeared shocked and then anger swept his face. He reached for his sword, and as he did, Maria, who had moved behind him, hit him over the head with her own dagger. He fell to one knee, sword in hand, and though it turned Marsaili's stomach to hurt him, she knew he would foil their plan of escape if she did nothing. She knocked him over the head once more, and he fell forward into the dirt.

She and Maria exchanged a long look as he lay there motionless, and with a thumping heart, Marsaili dropped to the ground and started trying to roll him toward the thick brush to hide him from the other guards.

"We must make haste," Maria said, joining Marsaili in her efforts.

"Aye," Marsaili answered with a grunt, and together, they moved the guard into the brush and covered him with leaves.

Once they were finished, they made their way over the jagged rocks and weaved through the twining branches at a clipped pace. They didn't talk, the only sound between them the unison of their breathing until a wolf's howl filled the night, setting both women into an all-out run. By the time they reached the edge of the loch that surrounded the land her father's castle was built on, her side pinched fiercely. Behind them, the howling had increased to a cacophony of lethal noise.

Marsaili motioned toward the dinghy. "Get in!"

Maria glanced from the secured dinghy to the woods. "The wolves are coming!" she cried. "We have to swim for it."

Marsaili's heartbeat exploded as she lunged for the rope tied to a tree stump at the water's edge and began to sever the bind. "I kinnae swim," she said. "Leave me if ye must."

Within a breath, Maria was beside her sawing at the same spot. Just as the rope broke, the first wolf burst through the woods onto the crest of the hill, and then another, and another. The women pushed the dinghy, heaving, until it slid into the water. They scrambled in, took up the oars, and swiped them through the water furiously.

"Wolves can swim!" Maria cried.

"Aye," Marsaili said grimly, putting all her strength and her will to live into rowing. Halfway across the water, the wolves howling grew louder, causing her pulse to increase to a dizzying speed. The women worked to put distance between themselves and the wolves, but Marsaili feared that even if they reached land first, the wolves would simply trail and overcome them. She glanced behind her to see where the wolves were, and as she did, an arrow flew across her vision and lodged into one of the beasts. Another arrow followed, and another.

Marsaili feared taking her attention off the wolves, but she had to know who had shot the arrow. She had no friends in these parts, save Maria. She faced forward, as Maria gasped, to find five men standing on the bank at the other side of the loch. She couldn't see their faces, but one man gripped a wooden pole that had a piece of material flapping from it. It fluttered several times in the wind before she got a good look at the emblem. She sucked in a sharp breath. "God's bones. It's the Black Mercenaries…"

Maria paled, as tension pulled her mouth into a stern expression. As she continued to row, she spoke softly. "We go from an enemy baring their teeth and who would eat us alive, to an enemy with no morals and who will nae even blink at using us."

Marsaili nodded. She knew about the Black Mercenaries. They lived in the woods, or so it was said. No one knew for certain, as the men seemed to appear like mist from the sky and disappear much the same way. One minute they were there, and the next they simply were gone. They had fought for King David in his quest to take control of Scotland ever since he had been released several years prior from being held prisoner in England, but some of the Mercenaries had also fought for the king's enemies—the Steward and the King of England. They had no loyalty to a king. Their only loyalty was to coin. She had no notion why they might be near her father's home, nor did she want to know, but she feared she and Maria were about to discover why, whether they wanted to or not.

In taut silence, Marsaili and Maria paddled the brief distance remaining to the shore. There was nowhere to run. They could not return to the woods, so they had to go forward toward the five men awaiting them on the shore. Before the dinghy even banked, a tall man, built like a solid tree with hair cropped so short that Marsaili could only see it because the blackness of it seemed to shimmer beneath the skin of his scalp, leaned over, gripped the front edge of the dinghy, and brought it to a shuddering stop. Gray eyes pierced her before shifting to do the same to Maria, and then the man seemed to hold the two of them in his gaze at once.

"Ye have just made my task much easier and my pockets much fuller." He grinned, but it was mirthless and twisted with a downturn of contempt. Then his gaze, probing and cold, settled on Marsaili. "Ye have an enemy, Marsaili Campbell, and I've been paid generously to see ye punished for yer folly."

Marsaili's heart thumped viciously against her ribs. "I've many enemies," she said, pleased her voice sounded so calm when a storm of fear raged inside her. "Ye're going to have to be specific, Lord...?"

"Ye can call me Lucan," he said, yanking the boat forward so hard that she fell backward into Maria. Before they could untangle themselves, Lucan snatched her dagger out of her hand and had Marsaili firm in his grip. A shorter man with limp red hair and a long hawkish nose did the same to Maria. Lucan lifted Marsaili off her feet, plopped her on the ground, and before she knew what was occurring, he was winding binds around her wrists. She looked over to see Maria receiving the same treatment. The other three men had already turned away and were walking through the woods toward horses that Marsaili could see tethered some distance away.

Marsaili yanked back on her wrists to no avail as the man had bound them so tightly the rope cut into her skin. Immediately, the blood seemed to gather at the site and pulse. If she was kept like this long, she feared she would lose the use of her hands. "Who—"

"Euphemia Stewart," he answered before Marsaili even completed her question. "Seems ye and yer sister, Lena MacLean, made quite the enemy."

Marsaili frowned, casting her thoughts back to when she had gone with Lena and her husband, Alex, to the Steward's home. Marsaili had been desperate to find out where her son was, but the only way her father would tell her was if she discovered what castles the king had planned to raid and when. She'd barely spoken to Euphemia while she had been at the Steward's home, though Marsaili had not been overly friendly when they had spoken. The only thing Marsaili could even think of that might have prompted Euphemia to desire revenge was Lena doing something to the woman and Euphemia striking out at Marsaili simply because she and Lena were sisters. It must have been a well-placed blow by Lena for Euphemia to send this Mercenary after her.

"I did nae do anything to that woman!" she shouted.

He snorted. "I dunnae care if ye did or nae. My concern is for the coin I'll receive once I've done as she's bid."

"Ye're despicable!" Marsaili snapped.

"Aye," he said with a wink. "And if ye dunnae forget that, we will rub along just fine until I give ye away."

Marsaili gasped, jerking back reflexively. "Give me away?"

"Aye. That's the thing about crossing someone twisted like Euphemia. She will nae be satisfied just to have me kill ye. She wants ye to suffer for a long time." He laughed, as if he had relayed something humorous. "Come," he said, yanking her farther forward. "We have a tourney to attend, where I'll be finding the perfect man to lose ye to."

"Ye mean to wager me and purposely lose?"

"Aye, ye're rather quick. And I'll choose the most despicable man I can find, too."

Marsaili shuddered. She glanced at Maria and back to Lucan. "Release Maria. Ye came for me, nae her."

Lucan's answer was to grab Marsaili by the waist and hoist her onto his horse. He then motioned for the warrior who was holding Maria to do the same thing. "I consider yer friend a gift, lovely lady, and I'm nae a man to reject such a thing." With that, he tapped his horse's flanks and set them on the way to trouble.

Three

The flap of Callum's tent opened just as he tilted up his leather pouch to take a drink of mead. He swallowed the liquid as Brice strode in, a fierce scowl on his face.

Brice set his hands on his hips. "We've a problem."

"What is it?" Callum asked, turning the pouch down to voice the question.

He'd been competing in the tournament for five days now, and today had been especially brutal. But every battle he won earned them much-needed coin, and it kept him so occupied he didn't have to spend much time with Coira. Her constant complaining defied belief and had become increasingly harder to tolerate with each day that passed. She also had stirred up trouble with the kitchen lasses. It seemed his future wife was cold but jealous. She'd tried to rid the kitchen of all the young lasses she considered pretty because she did not want them serving him. He'd had to intervene and tell her, in no uncertain terms, that he was the only one who held the power to dismiss a servant.

"Has Coira done something else?" he asked.

"Nay," Brice replied, but his pacing did not set Callum at ease.

"What then?" Callum inquired.

"Cedric Ainsworth won two women as a purse in a

passage-of-arms contest. The man who put out the call to fight him wagered the women instead of coin."

Callum frowned. That was unwelcome news. Not only was the Earl of Ainsworth's son known to treat women cruelly but Callum disliked the practice of wagering women. He forbade it in his own clan, though he knew it went on in some others and often among men with no clan allegiance. "Where is Cedric? I want to speak with him."

"I thought ye might say that." Brice paused a beat. "Now, ye ken we kinnae anger him or we risk the alliance with the earl."

"I ken it," Callum said. The Earl of Ainsworth had proven to be a fine man, honorable even, but it had become apparent since he had arrived here with Coira and Cedric that the earl indulged his son, ignorant to the fact that the man was immoral. "The women who were wagered, what do they say?"

"I dunnae. Cedric took the women to his tent for a rest before he faced his next opponent. He refused me entry to speak with them."

As laird, Callum could demand entry to the tent, and he could even dispute Cedric's "winnings" if the women protested it, but it would require treading very carefully. If it came down to it, he could simply take up the challenge that Cedric had issued. He felt confident he could beat his future brother-in-law, but it would make the prideful man angry. Yet, if he ordered Cedric to release the women, that would make the man angry, as well, and he likely would refuse to comply.

Callum picked up his sword, having learned long ago to always be prepared. "I'll speak with him and see how best to sort this."

"Ye'll be fighting," Brice replied with a shake of his

head. "I'm certain of it. Ye must make it seem that one of the women he's won has captured yer fancy, and ye can bid him to wager them both. He's nae a man who would expect ye to be true to his sister. Trust me."

"Ye've thought this through," Callum commented, impressed.

Brice nodded. "Aye. As I came to find ye, I tried to determine the best way to free the women without Cedric kenning what ye were really doing."

"The only problem with yer plan is Coira. She dunnae want me, yet she dunnae want me to so much as look at another lass. I believe she may fear I will lie with another lass," Callum said, exiting the tent to a bevy of noise. The grassy plain to the east side of his home was filled with tents for the warriors who had come to compete in the tourney his clan hosted. Banners hung on poles in front of tents, fluttering in the wind, and identified which tents housed which clans.

"Mayhap she only has acted cold because she senses ye are nae open to caring for her," Brice said, falling into step beside Callum.

He said nothing, just kept weaving his way through the narrow passages between the rows of tents. The smell of cooked meat filled the air, making his stomach growl. He saw his mother to his right, and he offered an obligatory wave. She stood near the earl's tent, and Callum tensed at the prospect of seeing Coira. When they were well past the hill, he felt his shoulders relax.

Brice elbowed him. "This response is exactly what I mean. Ye scowl at the possibility of seeing yer future wife. At first, I felt sorry for ye, but now I'm feeling sorry for her."

Callum made a derisive noise. "Ye have too much time

to sit around contemplating my life, let alone Coira's. I want ye to start training the men every morning with me. It's quite apparent I have nae given ye enough duties." He looked at his brother and raised a brow. "Now, let's make haste. I'd rather get this done and ken the sort of trouble I face."

"Get off me!" Marsaili snarled, kicking out and connecting her foot with Cedric's gut. They were alone in the tent now, as he had ordered one of his men to take Maria to the place where he would fight any man who answered his challenge, to use her as an enticement as part of the prize. Marsaili, he had declared, he would keep for himself. She shuddered inside. She would not live like this, nor would she allow Maria to do so.

The journey to the tournament had been fast, bumpy, and hard, but at least the Black Mercenaries had a code of honor and did not use any woman they were to deliver for coin. It was a twisted sense of honor, but it had served to protect her and Maria from being ravaged. Now there was no protection. Upon arriving at the castle—she still had no idea which clan owned it—she'd asked Lucan where he had brought them, but he'd ignored her as he sought out the most despicable man he could find, just as he'd said he would.

It had all happened so fast, her head still spun from it. She needed food and sleep, both of which she had obtained little of over the past few days. Anguish for Maria, herself, and her son filled her chest, and as if Cedric could sense her weakening state, he shoved her foot away and pressed himself on top of her, covering her mouth with his. She did the only thing she could think of and bit down as hard as she could on his tongue, which had plunged inside her mouth.

He rose up with a roar and swiped a hand across his mouth, smearing blood over his lips. "You bitch!" he bellowed and pulled his hand back to hit her.

Fear sent a surge of strength through her, and she scrambled off the pallet and to her feet. She turned to flee only to knock into a hard, unrelenting, immovable wall of warm flesh and bone. Tears sprang to her eyes as she unseeingly brought her hands up to pummel the chest of the man who blocked her escape. He had to be one of Cedric's guards.

"Ye kinnae keep me here!" she screamed.

Strong hands captured her wrists and deftly stopped her blows. A sob of despair tumbled from her lips. "Release me," she begged, pulling on her wrists to no avail.

"Shh, lassie," the man whispered, even as Cedric began to yell. "Dunnae fash yerself," the stranger said under the roar of Cedric's temper.

"Leave go of my woman," Cedric demanded.

For a moment, there was a small glimmer of hope that the man holding her would be honorable and come to her aid, but he released her and her hope plummeted. And when the stranger said, "Dunnae get churlish over a wee wench," despair threatened to overcome her. She could ill afford the weakness of such an emotion. She thought of her son, and anger burst forth.

"I'm nae a wench, ye blackhearted swine," she growled, looking up into the man's face. Shock hit her hard as her gaze met the soulful brown eyes of Callum Grant. Her lips parted with a jagged breath.

She gasped, her chest tightening with a storm of confusion, memories, and emotion. In the space of a breath, she careened wildly from disbelief, to anger, then to happiness, and back to seething anger. "Ye!"

For a moment, Callum simply stared at her, his own lips slightly parted. His fingers, still encircling her wrist, tightened as his chest rose with a sharp intake of breath. A crease appeared between his thick, dark brows but smoothed immediately when Cedric spoke. "Do you know my prize?"

"I'm nae yer prize!" Marsaili snapped, turning her head to glare at the odious Englishman.

When she felt Callum suddenly release her, she turned her attention to him once more, but he was looking at Cedric. "Nay, I dunnae ken the lass."

Marsaili's jaw slid open again. She knew three years had passed since they had seen each other, but a lifetime could have gone by and she would have known Callum Grant, even if age or warfare had ravaged him. He knew her, the foul beast! The only explanation was that he did not *want* to admit he knew her. For the second time in her life, Callum Grant had managed to humiliate her so much that she wished she could disappear. To make matters worse, the betrayal that had nearly killed her soul pounded at her once more.

Damn Callum. She had never planned to seek his aid in finding their son, let alone tell him of the child. He was a liar and a betrayer, and she could not trust that he would allow her to keep the child. Still, it was like liquid fire beneath her skin to know that if she had wished to ask for his aid, he obviously never would have given it. She drew herself up to her full height, which felt rather pitiful at the moment, given she only came up to Callum's shoulder.

"This is Marsaili Lamont—"

"Lamont?" Callum interrupted Cedric. "Are ye married?" His brow knitted, and a vein in his temple was suddenly pulsing.

She pressed her lips together. She was certainly not going to explain to Callum Grant how it came to be that she was perfectly fine going under the false name given to her by that clot-heid Lucan because he hadn't wanted any trouble. Yet, he was boring a hole into her with his penetrating stare, and she did not get the feeling he'd let the question go unanswered.

"That's an odd question," Cedric replied, saving Marsaili from having to answer. "She's not married, just a wench from a nameless family—no clan affiliation." Callum narrowed his gaze upon her, but before he could say anything, Cedric went on. "Curtsy to the laird of the Grant clan, wench."

She stood stiffly, her mind and her body refusing to curtsy to a man who had lied to her and used her. For one moment, confusion flickered in Callum's dark-brown eyes. She was angry he had denied knowing her, but also glad. When she escaped Cedric—because she fully intended to do so—she would not have to worry about fleeing Callum, as well.

"Curtsy!" Cedric ordered again. He clamped his hand on the back of her neck and shoved her head forward. Pain shot from the point of contact to her eyes and made her hiss.

"Dunnae handle the lass so roughly," Callum said. Though his tone was even, there seemed to be a tension underlying it. When Cedric released his hold on Marsaili's neck, she glanced to Callum, but his expression was unreadable. However, another man moved into the tent behind Callum, and his eyes glittered in obvious anger.

"What brings the Grant brothers to my tent?" Cedric demanded.

"I came to see how ye were faring against yer challengers in yer passage of arms."

Cedric grinned and then smacked Marsaili on the bottom. She swung around and raised her palm to slap him in the face, but he captured her wrist with a chuckle. "I won this spitfire." He yanked her to his chest and slanted his mouth over hers. She tried to turn her face but to no avail, so with her free hand, she raked her nails down Cedric's cheek.

Immediately, he broke the kiss with a growl and reared back to hit her. She flinched and tensed, but the hit didn't come. Callum had caught Cedric's wrist from behind, and when Marsaili glanced at Callum's face, the rage twisting his face shocked her. "I'm afraid I dunnae wish to stand here watching ye hit this woman, Cedric."

"She needs disciplining," Cedric said, his eyes narrowed on Marsaili.

"Mayhap, what she needs is a gentle touch," Callum returned, releasing Cedric's arm. Deep in Marsaili's mind, unwanted memories of the night of passion she had shared with this man returned like so many unfulfilled dreams to nearly suffocate her. He had been gentle, and patient, and an expert at making her feel pleasure.

Cedric released her wrist and turned toward Callum. "Well, she's mine, so I'll do with her as I please. I'll simply wait until you have departed."

The mere thought made Marsaili shudder.

"Have ye bested everyone who has challenged ye?" Callum asked.

"Yes. I wish you had accepted the challenge, so I could have bested you, too," Cedric boasted.

"It would take more than coin to get me to fight ye, Cedric. I dunnae wish to anger yer da by defeating ye," Callum said with a wink.

Cedric's hands curled into fists. "Don't concern yourself with my father," he snarled. "If you were to win, I'd deal with him, so there would be no need to worry about losing him as an ally."

"Nay," Callum said, glancing behind him. "Brice will fight ye, though."

Callum's brother did not hide his feelings nearly as well as Callum. Surprise settled on his face. "I will?"

"Aye," Callum said jovially—almost too jovially. True, she did not truly know the man, nor had she ever, but his lightheartedness seemed forced. Cedric's annoyed face revealed no sign that he sensed something being off as she did. Callum patted his brother on the shoulder. "Brice has taken a liking to the other wench ye won, and he wishes to fight ye for her instead of coin. What say ye?"

Cedric laughed. "I'll fight you, Brice Grant, but you'll not win the woman. And I'll only fight Brice if you agree to battle me, as well, Callum. You're the only one I truly believe to be close to my equal."

Callum quirked his mouth as if in thought. "I already told ye I dunnae wish to take yer coin." As the words left his mouth, his dark, penetrating gaze settled on Marsaili, and faint amusement swept over his face. "Mayhap if ye wish to wager the hellion?" he suggested, motioning to her as if she were some sort of good to be bartered at the market. Fury had her curling her own fists. What was this ruse he was about, and why was he about it?

Cedric chuckled. "Very smart of you to instill a leman to produce an heir before you wed my barren sister."

A soft gasp escaped Marsaili and caused both men to

look at her. God's teeth, she wished she had not made a sound, but what the devil did Cedric mean when he said Callum was to be married? He was supposed to be married already! Had Edina passed? Cedric frowned at Marsaili, but she could not make herself care when her mind whirred with the shock of learning Callum was unmarried.

Callum winked at Cedric. "Let us nae tell yer sister, aye?"

Marsaili swallowed her disgust.

"Of course," Cedric said smoothly.

"Excellent." Callum's gaze flickered to her once more, but his dark eyes were hooded, like a hawk, unreadable. He abruptly turned away toward Cedric. "A man needs a leman to give him pleasure as wives never do."

Beside Callum, his brother looked as if he were just barely holding in words. Or was it laughter? Marsaili clenched her teeth so hard, she felt a stab of pain and feared she'd cracked a tooth. Callum was despicable! Never would Marsaili allow him to touch her, and never would she tell him of their son.

"I'd rather be under the dirt in my grave with worms crawling in my eyes than let ye lay hands on me, ye *lan dhen cac*, poor excuse of a man!"

"I don't believe the wench likes you, Callum," Cedric mocked.

"I believe ye're correct, but that tends to make things rather interesting in my experience," he replied, turning his attention to her.

"Exactly what I believe," Cedric crowed. "Come, then. Let us see what you and your brother can offer me as sport in hand-to-hand combat."

Marsaili was furious with herself for being so shocked that a man who had lied to her and used her would not blink an eye at trading her with another man as if she were a piece of cloth. Callum had no morals, and he was probably not married because Edina had been smart enough, unlike Marsaili, to see the sort of man he truly was.

"Do you have a favor for me, wench?" Cedric said, reaching for her breasts.

She smacked his hand away. "If I had a dagger, I'd plant it in yer heart—and then his," she spat, motioning toward Callum. "That is the only favor I have in mind for either of ye. So beware: whichever of ye is the victor, ye'll nae be able to rest easy at night if I'm forced to lie by yer side."

"Such threats!" Cedric chuckled, looking amused as he gripped her arm and dragged her past Callum, out of the tent, and into a thick throng of people.

Four

allum could not order his thoughts, nor could he form words to answer his brother, who'd now asked him twice what was wrong with him. Confusion and disbelief swirled in his mind as he strode several paces behind Cedric and Marsaili.

Marsaili.

It could not be. She was dead.

He squeezed his eyes shut for a brief moment, sure that she'd be gone when he opened them, nothing more than a figment of his imagination. But when he opened his eyes, she was still there, in the flesh and as familiar as a woman would be if a man had committed every detail of her to memory. Yet, there was something different about her with the time that had gone by.

He rubbed his suddenly aching chest as he weaved in and out of the crowd, acknowledging people who spoke to him with a simple nod. Out of the corner of his eye, he saw Brice give him a confused look as they continued the progress toward the arena of grass where they'd both fight Cedric, but Brice did not ask him again what was ailing him. Callum locked his gaze on the source of his troubles—Marsaili Campbell, *not* Lamont. He had no notion why she was going by that name, but he intended to find out as soon as he won her and got her alone.

Desire and yearning flowed through him at the thought of having her to himself, touching her, kissing her, learning what had happened, and—"God's teeth," he swore under his breath, halting to take a deep breath and gain control. He could question Marsaili, but that was it. The touching, the kissing, the wish to take her in his arms and feel her welcome him into her body and heart once again would never be—*could* never be. By God's grace, she was still alive, but that did not change the future before him. Her father had been his enemy since the day the Campbell had refused to offer aid to Callum's clan, and now the Earl of Ainsworth was Callum's only hope for an ally to stand against the MacDonalds and the Gordons.

"What the devil is the matter with ye?" Brice demanded, cutting into Callum's thoughts.

Callum motioned toward Marsaili, who was twenty paces ahead with Cedric, the man's grimy hand still locked around her arm. Hot rage poured through Callum. He was going to enjoy beating Cedric into the ground. It was the least he could do for Marsaili after the way the man dared to speak to her and handle her. Callum had the strong desire to kill Cedric, but that certainly would cause them to lose the earl as an ally.

The good of the clan comes first.

The muscles of his heart seemed to grow taut like a bow as he stared at her. She was *alive.* It seemed impossible, yet there she was, just across the clearing with her long mahogany hair he had dreamed many a night of running his hands through. Presently, her locks were not shiny and tumbling in inviting waves around her shoulders as he remembered them to be. Her hair was dull and matted in clumps around her dirt-smudged face. Her blue eyes still shone brighter than water glistening in the sun, yet now they seemed lit with anger. Her body had changed, as well. Her hips had become a bit rounder, and his fingers twitched to grip them. Her breasts appeared even fuller than they had been before, her voice huskier, and when she spoke, desire shot from his head to his groin.

He was uncertain of much, but the fact that she still possessed the ability to incite yearning within him just by being near was not in question. Never had a woman enticed him as she did. His father had always said that every man had one weakness that had the potential to fell him, and Callum had nary a doubt that Marsaili was his.

"Callum," Brice growled and elbowed him hard in the side. "Ye're standing there gaping, nae responding to a word I say, and ye look as if ye just saw someone rise from the dead."

"Aye," Callum said with a nod, unable to tear his gaze away from Marsaili. If Cedric so much as pulled, yanked, or raised a hand to her again, Callum feared he'd kill the man with his bare hands.

"What in God's name do ye mean, 'aye'?" Brice asked, exasperation heavy in his voice.

Callum forced himself to look at his brother. "That woman, from the tent—"

"The one Cedric won? The wench—"

"She's nae a wench," Callum bit out.

Brice frowned. "The lass—"

"The bonny lass," Callum inserted, inwardly cursing his fool tongue when his brother's lips parted with surprise.

"Aye," Brice agreed. "She's bonny, but she does need a good washing afore I'd—"

"Dunnae ye dare utter any foul insinuation about what ye would do or wish to do with her." Callum's heart seemed to be working four times as fast as it had been one breath ago. Blood rushed so loudly in his ears, it sounded like the roar of crashing waves. "That is the lass I plunged our clan into war for," he said in low tones, though they were not standing close enough to anyone for them to hear.

Brice's eyes widened, and he looked back and forth between Marsaili and Callum. Then Brice motioned Callum to follow him. Callum nodded, and his brother strode to a tree across from where Cedric had stopped. The man handed Marsaili off to a guard who was also gripping the arm of Marsaili's companion, a silver-haired, green-eyed lass. Callum frowned. She looked too young for the odd color of her hair.

"I wonder how yer lass—"

"She's nae my lass," Callum interrupted, though the denial made his gut knot.

"Well, she was, and the only reason ye gave her up is because ye thought she was dead," Brice growled. "Do ye mean to tell me that ye will deny yerself the lass now that she's here in front of ye like a gift from God? She has risen from the dead."

Callum glared at his brother. "She did nae rise from the dead, and ye ken it. 'Tis plain to see that her father lied about her death." The question was why, and was it at her request?

"What will ye do?" Brice asked, jerking Callum's attention back to the present. Brice was stripping off his plaid to prepare to fight. Callum did the same, as an opponent could grab it to aid them in bringing the other off his feet. Callum turned to lay his plaid behind him and nearly groaned at the crowd that was gathering. He had hoped to fight this particular battle without Coira knowing about it, but he would simply have to explain to her that he could not stand by and allow any woman to be wagered like a belonging.

"Did ye hear me?" Brice said. "I asked what will ye do?"

"I'll win my fight, as ye better. And then once we have sent Cedric on his way, I'll have ye attend Marsaili and her companion safely home. I dunnae ken how she ended up here, but I dunnae believe anyone from her clan is here to attend her." He heard himself talking so matter-of-fact, but inside, he felt like the waters of a storm-ravaged loch. His thoughts dipped and tumbled. Had Marsaili's father lied because she'd asked him to? Or had he learned of their affection and become enraged because of his plan for her to marry the Earl of Ulster? Or mayhap something altogether different had compelled the lies.

Brice frowned. "Ye honestly think it will be that simple to rid yerself of the woman who has haunted ye for years now?"

Callum sighed. "I think it will be complicated," he answered when Brice nudged him. "But I will make it simple. I must do so for the clan."

Brice sniggered. "I think it will be rather entertaining to watch how this unfolds."

"I'm glad ye're amused," Callum said irritably.

"Brice Grant, I'm ready to best you," Cedric mocked from across the field.

"Dunnae lose," Callum instructed. "Remember, the fewer complications the better. I dunnae want to have to haggle with Cedric over that silver-haired woman."

"Dunnae fash yerself," Brice told Callum, which caused wariness to rise inside him instead.

Brice was being too cocksure. He practically strutted to the center of the field to meet Cedric. Around the men, jeers and cheers resounded from the still-gathering crowd. Someone tapped Callum's arm, and he glanced to his side to find Coira.

"What is this?" she demanded, her green eyes narrowed.

"Brice accepted yer brother's challenge," he replied, hoping Coira would not press the matter further.

"What is the purse?"

"A woman," he said. "Why dunnae ye make yer way to the great hall for supper?" he suggested.

She plunked her hands on her hips. "Can you not keep your brother out of trouble?" she accused, referring, he supposed, to Brice's penchant for embroiling himself in situations with lasses.

"Nae this time," he answered honestly. "Yer brother led him there."

"Mayhap you need to punish your brother for being so gullible," she snapped.

Callum gritted his teeth. "As *I* am laird, that is for me to decide."

Coira snorted. "The woman looks like a whore, as does the woman over there with the dark hair. Perfect play toys for Cedric."

Callum's gaze immediately shot back to Marsaili, who was side-by-side with her companion. Her head was turned in conversation, and he took a moment to devour her beauty.

"Callum," Coira said shrilly, yanking his attention back to her. "I don't care for the way you stare at that dark-haired whore."

"She is nae a whore," he growled, fixing his gaze on Coira, though all he truly wanted to do was look at Marsaili.

"Are you familiar with her?"

"Nae exactly," he said, which was technically the truth since he honestly did not know Marsaili anymore. She could have changed drastically in three years.

"I wager she's Cedric's whore," Coira said triumphantly.

He restrained the urge to slap his palm over Coira's venomous mouth. "She's nae," he said evenly. "Cedric won the woman in a wager."

"Well," Coira said with a barbed laugh, "if she was not a whore already, she will be made one soon."

His temper snapped. "The lass will nae be made a whore because I will gain her freedom by fighting Cedric and winning her, and—"

"You will not!" Coira cut in before he could say that he would set Marsaili free, no matter how much the idea of doing so twisted him into knots. Coira pointed at him. "I forbid you to fight for her freedom."

"Ye dunnae have the right to forbid me to do anything, Coira," he snarled, glancing once more to Marsaili, who now stood with a defiant tilt to her chin and her arms crossed over her chest. His chest tightened. He refused to feel any guilt, even as his long-dormant desire stirred. He would not act on his desire, and he would have fought to free any lass that had been wagered unwillingly.

"I have a right as your future wife," she proclaimed. "You may not take a leman and produce a bastard! I refuse to allow it!"

"I am nae doing any such thing. I am simply fighting to free a lass who has been wagered against her will. I'd think as a woman that would please ye."

"It does not," she said with a dark scowl. "I don't know this woman, nor do I care about her, and I don't want anyone whispering that you do."

"Coira, if we are to be married, ye best heed me now. I will nae ever allow ye to order me about, and I will always do what I can to help others, bonny lass or nae."

"Bonny lass!" she gasped, indignation sweeping over her face. "Have your fight," she snarled, drawing the eyes of the people around them, "and free that whore"—she was raising her voice and his temper—"but you will set her from your home immediately, or I will consider that you are breaking your sacred promise to wed me and be true to me. Then you will have yet another enemy, for my enemies are my father's enemies," she threatened.

Callum didn't doubt that. Though her father had used her in marriage once already and was about to use her again, the man demanded she was treated with respect, though he clearly did not care that she did not want to marry Callum. He suspected that the earl felt that disrespecting his daughter or son was disrespecting him, and it would make him appear weak.

As Callum intended to free Marsaili immediately anyway, and he would never do anything further to put his family and clan in harm's way, he said, "I will set the lass free because that is what I was planning to do already, *nae* because ye are threatening me."

"I'm going to tell my father of your treatment!" she cried out, then turned and stomped away.

Callum did not even bother to watch her depart as his brother's fight was starting. She'd likely go to her father, and there'd be trouble to contend with later—or at the very least, apologies to be given—but he'd deal with it then. Right now, the only thing that mattered was freeing Marsaili. Then he would have Brice see her home, or wherever she would be safest. But before that, he had to talk to her. He had to know what had happened, why he'd been told she was dead. It changed nothing, of course, yet somehow it mattered whether it had been her or her father who had sent word of her death. He was a fool either way, for if it had been her father's doing, it would only make parting with her again that much harder. If it had been her doing, and she had decided those years ago that she did not wish to be with him, then he had cost his father his life and caused his clan years of strife for a woman who had not felt what he had: an attachment so strong and true that he had forsaken his honor and his family for Marsaili's heart.

Five

" I hope he goes down as fast as his brother did," Marsaili muttered under her breath as she stared at Callum, who was striding to the center of the field.

"Ye dunnae mean that," Maria replied. "Ye may detest the man, but from what I've overheard from the people talking around us, he and his brother are considered verra honorable and Cedric is reviled. I've a bit of hope that Laird Grant will set ye free if he wins ye, but I've nary hope Cedric will free me."

"I'll free ye somehow," Marsaili assured Maria. "We can tell him of yer ties to yer sister, who is now part of his clan."

"Nay," Maria said. "I will nae bring trouble to my sister and her new husband. Dunnae say a word."

"Ye're certain?" Marsaili asked, staring at Callum.

"Aye," Maria replied.

Marsaili nodded as she continued to watch Callum. She told herself it was because she wanted to see him felled, but the weight of the lie pressed on her chest. She rubbed it absently as she gawked.

Damn the Scot, he was even more handsome than she had remembered, and with every piece of his clothing removed but his braies, which clung to his hips, she didn't even have to rummage around in her memory to pull up a mental picture of how Callum's body had looked as if it were made of stone.

"God's teeth, that Scot is a sight to behold," Maria murmured. "Are ye certain ye dunnae wish to tell him of the son the two of ye share?"

Marsaili nodded. "I'm certain. I dunnae trust him. I kinnae be sure he'd nae take our bairn from me, and I'll nae chance it. The woman he is to marry is barren; our son will likely be his only heir. I fear he might take him from me and give him to his new wife to raise."

"Ye have good reason to fear and keep yer secret, then," Maria agreed.

Marsaili heated simply watching Callum circle his massive shoulders to loosen them before the fight. With each roll, his muscles rippled. It disgusted her that she still felt such desire for a man who had used and betrayed her. Suddenly, his gaze locked on her, sharp and assessing.

She boldly returned his stare, refusing to be cowed. Was he trying to ascertain how she had ended up here, as the possession of a man like Cedric? What story would she tell Callum if he won her in this fight? Did he think himself so compelling that she would lie with him again like a fool?

She vowed never to allow him to touch her again. But as she considered Cedric and Callum, she had to admit, she preferred Callum to win her. He, at least, seemed to possess the barest hint of honor—but only the barest. Mayhap he'd not force himself upon her as Cedric would undoubtedly do. The thought of being ravaged made her skin crawl.

Callum broke eye contact with her as Cedric approached him, and she keenly felt the loss of his gaze on her—too keenly. She could not fall under his spell again. The horn blasted, marking the beginning of the fight, and she sucked in a sharp breath as Cedric swung first, his fists almost connecting with Callum's chin. But Callum ducked down at the last possible second and came up fast with a jab to Cedric's stomach. She could see the man gasp, but he recovered quickly, swinging out with his left hand. This time, his fist slammed into Callum's jaw. His head jerked to the left, but with a quick shake, he rebounded, delivering two jabs to Cedric's face. Blood immediately gushed from the man's nose and leaked from his lip.

He swiped the blood away and kicked out at Callum's knee. Callum jumped back, evading the move. With a roar, Cedric lunged at Callum, and the two men went down in a tangle of arms and legs. Suddenly, Marsaili saw a flash of steel, and as she realized that Cedric intended to win the fight by cheating and using a dagger, she cried out to Callum, "Careful! He has a weapon in his right hand!"

A shocked murmur rose from the crowd as Callum rolled away from Cedric just as the man brought his dagger down very near Callum's neck.

"Coward!" someone from the crowd yelled, and shouts of Cedric being treacherous started all around her.

"Why is nae anyone intervening to stop the fight?" she cried out as she turned to Maria.

Marsaili winced at the sight of Callum's brother, Brice, beside Maria. When had the man come to stand there?

He studied Marsaili for a moment, as if he was trying to decide if he was going to answer her. "We dunnae stop the fight because to do so would make it appear as if Callum needs us to help him."

"But the fight is nae fair!" she shouted.

Callum jumped backward when Cedric swiped the dagger out at him, and Marsaili's breath hitched.

"Much in life is nae fair," Brice replied, an odd tension in his voice. "Dunnae fash yerself for Callum. He has nae ever lost a one-on-one battle."

"I'm nae fashed," she snapped, though her heart was racing and her breath was ragged.

"Ye appear to care for him still," Brice said in low tones, shocking her.

"He told ye about me?"

Brice gave her an uneasy look but nodded.

She could only imagine how Callum must have boasted of the conquest. She ground her teeth, then glared at Brice. "Just because I dunnae wish to see a man killed dunnae mean I care for him," she whispered furiously. Yet, a breath later, when Callum knocked the dagger out of Cedric's hand, then brought the man to his knees, there was no repressing the relieved exhalation that escaped her. "He won," she said, both glad and fearful at once. Yes, she had rid herself of Cedric, but she still needed to escape Callum, and she'd prefer not to have a conversation with the man at all if she could help it.

She glanced around the grounds, now nearly bereft of people despite being littered with tents. Night was almost upon them. Many of the people who were not gathered around this fight had obviously already made their way to the great hall for supper. Her best hope of fleeing would be now. If they could get Brice to move away from them...

She turned to somehow let Maria know her intentions, but as she did, Cedric's guard strode up to them and grabbed Maria by the arm. "Come on, wench."

"Ye kinnae take her!" Marsaili protested, aware she had no way to stop the man.

"She's Cedric's property," the man snapped, and when he jerked on Maria's arm, Marsaili lunged at him and bit down hard on his arm. He released Maria with a howl and reared his arm back to strike Marsaili, but before he could, Brice hit the man. Then all hell broke loose.

It was the perfect distraction for them to flee, and without a second thought, Marsaili grabbed Maria's hand. "Come! We must away!"

In one breath, Callum was bargaining with Cedric for the purchase of the woman with Marsaili, which had only been made possible by threatening to tell the earl of his son's dishonorable actions, but in the next breath, fighting between his men and Cedric's broke out and he was roaring commands to cease fighting, as was Cedric. Once their men finally obeyed and Callum glanced around, he realized that neither Marsaili nor her companion were anywhere to be found.

Fear and anger sprung within him. "Cedric," he demanded, "did ye order yer men to take the lasses?"

The confused frown Cedric gave Callum was answer enough.

Brice pointed. "I saw the lasses run that way, but I was tied up with this one." He shoved at Cedric's man, who shoved back at Brice.

"God's bones," Callum growled, as he motioned to his brother. "Come with me." With that, he took up his sword from where he had set it by the tree, and then he set off running in the direction Brice had pointed.

He led his men through the rows of tents, thankful it was so close to supper that most people were in the great hall. But the hour also meant darkness was descending quickly and would make it harder to find the women. He had no notion why the lasses would run from him, but what he did know with a stomach-twisting certainty was that tournaments had a tendency to attract men with little-to-no morality, men like the one who had wagered Marsaili and her companion away. Many of those men, who may well have lost their money in wagers and fights today, would be angry and on the road home. And others, who had traveled far to reach the tournament, might just now be nearing Urquhart and might see two women alone in the woods as their right to use for their own comfort.

Callum paused at the crest of the hill where he could head to the shore, the loch, or the woods. When he had known Marsaili, she had not known how to swim...

"What are ye doing?" Brice asked in panting breaths beside him.

"Trying to decide which way Marsaili would have gone." Just as he finished his sentence, a scream tore through the night from the direction of the woods and black fright swept through him.

Marsaili!

Her voice had long been committed to his memory. Every instinct he possessed to protect others sprung to life, and he took off in the direction of her voice without a backward glance or explanation to his brother.

⁂

"Ye son of a devil!" Marsaili screeched, reaching frantically behind her to try to gouge Godfrey's eyes. But her efforts were fruitless. The Earl of Ulster's man, the very one she and Maria had knocked unconscious to escape Innis Chonnell Castle, simply tightened his grip around her neck and cut off her air so she would stop fighting.

"Are you going to behave, lass?" Godfrey demanded.

Marsaili jerked her head in a nod as best she could. Godfrey released his hands from her neck but slipped a solid, immovable arm under her breasts, preventing her from moving. Her feet dangled from the ground, locked as she was in the tall man's embrace, but for the moment, that was likely a good thing. Tiny dots of silvery light peppered her vision, and she feared she would faint.

"You've caused me quite a bit of trouble forcing me to track you like this."

"Good," Marsaili spat, glancing down at Maria's still body. "If ye've killed my friend, I vow I'll kill ye in return." More the fool was she for not having secured a weapon before racing away from the Grant hold. She'd been so anxious to put distance between her and Callum that she'd not properly thought things through. It was a mistake she'd never make again.

"I gave that hellion a thump on the head, and that is all. But if you continue to fight me, it will get a lot worse for her."

Marsaili gritted her teeth against responding. She feared he'd carry out his threats without delay.

"My orders from the earl are simple: bring you to him immediately and not irrevocably harmed. I've got leeway there, you see." Godfrey sneered and squeezed her so hard that she hissed in pain. "Now, I'm going to set you down, and you are going to do exactly as I say."

Marsaili nodded as she quickly thought about her options. Despair rose in her as Godfrey set her down and turned her toward him. "Hold out your hands. I'm going to bind you."

"Oh, please!" she begged, trying to delay. "I vow I'm done fighting. I—" She took a deep breath. "I'm tired and hungry, and will go willingly to the earl's castle."

"That's a right smart choice you've made, lass."

She nodded, eyeing the dagger protruding from the

holder at his hip. If she could grab it and stab him, she could put enough distance between them to escape, if she did not wound him sufficiently to fell him. But then what? She'd have to get aid for Maria.

"Marsaili!" a man's voice—Callum's voice—roared through the night.

Gooseflesh swept over her body, and her heart raced. When Godfrey turned to look toward the dark woods and the direction from which Callum's voice had come, she lunged forward, grabbed the hilt of his dagger, and swung it up to stab him. He turned toward her like a flash of light, and his hand came up to deflect the weapon. She jerked to the right, intending to plunge the dagger into his heart, but she sank it into his shoulder instead.

"You she-devil!" he roared and leapt for her, but she scampered back, stumbling over some gnarled roots sticking out of the ground. She screamed as she fought to maintain her balance, steadied herself, and then took off through the thick branches toward Callum's voice. He would help her and Maria. He had to.

She shoved tree limbs out of her way as she blindly ran, unsure if she was even heading toward Callum. Behind her footsteps pounded. "Callum!" she cried out. "Callum, where are ye?"

"Keep calling me," Callum answered, his voice loud and clear. "Lead me to ye. We're coming."

"Ready yer weapon!" she yelled, running, tripping, and falling to her knees. Wood cut into her palms, but she ignored the pain and scampered to her feet once more. Behind her, Godfrey's footsteps pounded closer. She ran through a thick bramble, thorns tearing at her sleeves and slicing the skin of her arms and hands. When she came out the other side of the thorny brush, she smacked into Callum and almost fell backward at the force of the impact.

"Callum," she sobbed, reaching out for his arms and clinging for one breath, not caring for a moment that he, too, was her enemy.

"Shh," he demanded harshly, and before she knew what was occurring, he shoved her behind him as Godfrey broke through the bramble with a roar, sword raised high. Callum sprang forward and sent his blade straight through Godfrey's heart. The man teetered for a moment before he crumpled to the ground.

Marsaili clenched her teeth against the horrid gurgling sounds Godfrey made, and then he fell silent. She began to shake violently, her teeth clanking loudly. Behind her, twigs snapped, and aware of how defenseless she was without a weapon, she scampered toward Callum's side as a man appeared like a mist from the darkness. In the moonlight, she could barely make out his face. When she realized it was Callum's brother, her legs shook even more, but this time from relief. Immediately, she became aware of Callum's heat and his masculine smell.

He turned to her. "Are ye unharmed?" he asked in a voice that sounded truly concerned.

For a moment, she could not speak. She had dreamed of seeing him again for so long. At first, the dreams had consisted of his begging her for forgiveness and giving her explanations for why he'd lied, which were always understandable even if unacceptable. In her fantasies, he would cup her face and kiss her while whispering his love. Later, the dreams had turned to ones where she would see him and be a fine and beautiful lady. His regret for forsaking her would be plain on his face. Never had her dreams consisted of her on the hunt for their child, because she had long ago gathered all her will and used it to not think of the dead bairn for fear the thoughts would drive her mad.

But now, standing before the man she had loved and whose child she had borne, she longed to tell him that they had a son who was alive. But he was a deceiver, not someone she could trust, no matter how honorable he might appear. He was, she realized in that moment, as cunning as her father. The realization filled her with a bitter sense of irony: she had given her heart to a man just like the very one she detested more than anything on this earth.

"Marsaili?" Callum asked, and then to her utter shock, his hands were cupping her face. "Are ye hurt, lass?"

She shoved his hands away and turned in the direction she thought Maria was in. She got no more than five steps before Callum grabbed her by the arm and swiveled her toward him. His brother stood just behind him. "Release me!" she demanded of Callum. "Maria was felled. She needs me!"

He released her at once but fell into step beside her with his brother behind them. "Are ye injured?" he asked again.

As she strode through the woods, shoving branches out of the way, she said, "What concern does a liar and a user have of how another fares?" Sweat dampened the hair at the base of her neck, her stomach tightened and roiled, and she realized with frustration that she was waiting, almost hopefully, with bated breath, to hear what he would say.

"None, usually," he said, answering after a long pause. His voice sounded odd, resigned, she thought with confusion. He inhaled an audibly long breath. "However, guilt of my past actions compels me to now be concerned."

All the anger and resentment she had stored within her released like a rushing river. "Ye can keep yer guilt. I dunnae need nor want it," she snapped, while ducking under a low-hanging branch. "What I will take is two daggers for myself and Maria, if ye please, and a bag of coins to travel."

"Ye kinnae travel without men to guard the two of ye," Callum said. The unbending tone he used ignited her anger further.

"I can, and I will!" she rebutted. "And if ye will nae give me weapons and coin, then I dunnae have further need to speak with ye."

"Marsaili," Callum said, halting her once again by gripping her arm. Exasperation and what almost sounded like a plea was in his voice, "I kinnae allow ye to set out without protection. I dunnae ken how ye came to be at my home and wagered away to a man like Cedric, nor do I ken who the man I killed is and why he was after ye, but ye are in danger when traveling with no companion other than a woman. Ye need an escort to wherever it is ye are going."

"Release me," she demanded, frustrated that his touch on her arm stirred feelings of desire that she'd rather forget.

He did so at once, and she slowly turned to him, gasping at how close he was. He must have taken a step toward her without her hearing it. She tried to put distance between them, but the brambles stopped her. She craned her head to look at him, very aware that his presence was every bit as commanding and overwhelming as it had been three years ago when they had first met.

"Quit following me," she demanded, his answer a snort and his brother's a snigger. She ground her teeth as she continued to stomp through the forest. Twigs and dry leaves snapped underfoot as she went. After a short bit, she started to worry that she could not actually find her way back to Maria. She stopped and called to her friend, but no response came.

From behind her, Callum said, "I can locate her for ye."

She absolutely did not wish for his aid, but she did not see another choice. Maria could truly be hurt. "Then get on with it," she barked, not caring how ungrateful she sounded. The man deserved her ire.

He and his brother moved past her and bent low to the ground. She could not see what they were doing, but she heard them.

"Up ahead," Callum said.

"Aye. And to the right," his brother went on.

"Ten paces."

"Give or take a pace," Brice replied.

Both men stood and started walking. Marsaili had to triple her strides to keep pace with them. But within a few minutes, they led her to Maria. Marsaili dropped to her knees and gently shook her friend.

"Oh!" Maria moaned. "My head. It feels as if it might split in two."

Marsaili hovered over Maria and rummaged through her satchel. "Tell me what to give ye."

"A pinch of the brown leaves," Maria instructed, her voice barely above a whisper. "Where's Satan's son?"

"Dead," Marsaili replied.

"Ye killed the Grant laird?" Maria gasped.

Marsaili winced, and from behind her, she heard Brice chuckle and then say, "Did ye hear that, Brother? They refer to ye as Satan's son."

"Callum lives," Marsaili snapped. "I thought ye were referring to Godfrey. Callum killed him."

"I presumed ye would manage that," Maria chided.

"I would have," Marsaili insisted as she handed Maria the brown leaves from one of her medicine pouches. "But the man jolted when I tried to stab him, and I hit his shoulder instead of his heart. Come on, then. I'll help ye up."

"Nay," Maria replied. "I feel dizzy from the hit to my head. I need to be carried to a bed for sleep."

"But—"

"I'm happy to oblige." Brice stepped forward, bent down, and scooped up Maria. Before Marsaili could form a proper protest, he was striding away. She stood and brushed her skirts, aware that Callum was looking at her. She could not see his eyes upon her in the dark, but she could feel his gaze, just as she always had before.

A tingling began in the pit of her stomach, and something intense flared through her. God's bones, the man was disturbing to her in every way. She hated him, yet it was painfully obvious to her that her attraction to him had not dulled, despite his betrayal. She didn't want to contemplate what that said about her nature, for she would not give in to such base desire again. She needed—and wanted—to flee him immediately, yet she could not go without Maria, and Maria obviously needed rest. Plus, if it could be managed, it would be wise to gather some provisions for the road, weapons, and coin. She'd not ask him for these things again, as she'd done in the heat of her earlier anger, so she needed to discover a way to get them. First, though, she needed to ascertain if he would be amenable to her and Maria staying at his home for a few days.

She cleared her throat. "It seems Maria and I may need shelter for a few days while she recovers." She refused to ask, but if he offered...

"Of course," he said immediately. "I'll have bedchambers readied for ye."

"If ye think to make me yer leman—"

"I dunnae," he said stiffly.

"But ye said—"

"I lied in an effort to release ye from Cedric's possession without causing strife for my clan."

She snorted. "I see ye are still an expert liar."

His answer was stony silence, which for some reason unnerved her more than if he had given a sharp-witted response. "Will nae yer future wife dislike me ensconced in yer home?" she asked, shamefully wishing to needle him.

"She dunnae have cause to worry; therefore, she dunnae have true reason to dislike my sheltering ye and yer friend. I have given my vow to Coira to marry her, and I will nae break it."

Hurt streaked through Marsaili, which she masked by saying, "As if a given vow makes a difference to ye, ye foul beast. As far as I can perceive, it's a habit of yers to make vows to women and break them. Did ye nae promise to wed Edina Gordon? Oh wait," she growled, sensing her anger was getting the better of her but simply not caring. "Ye pledged yerself to three women. I forgot to include myself. Unless Edina died before ye could wed her?" She honestly had not heard a mention of Edina and Callum since the day Helena had told her of their promised union.

When Callum stared at her in unnerving silence, she said in a purposefully sarcastic tone, "I suppose if Edina Gordon died, then the breaking of that particular vow was nae yer fault—well, the marriage part anyway—as ye did break the vow with me. Ye ken, the part that says ye *will be true*."

"I ken," he said, his voice rigid. "I have to wonder"—he sounded almost angry now—"why ye are so vexed with me. One minute ye say ye dunnae need or want my guilt, and the next ye seem angry, as if ye were betrayed by me somehow."

"I—" She clamped her mouth shut, belatedly wishing

she would have kept it closed and controlled her anger. She tried to think quickly of a plausible explanation for her behavior. "I must admit that even though I used and lied to ye at the Gathering, I did nae care to find out ye had done the same to me."

He frowned. "Ye used me? Ye lied to me? Do ye care to explain?" he asked, his tone full of disbelief.

She shrugged, her stomach dropping to her slippers. "Ye did nae mean a thing to me. Ye were but a game I played to entertain myself. I forgot ye the day ye left."

"I see," he said evenly. "Well, ye certainly were an accomplished liar when I met ye at the Gathering, then."

How dare he act self-righteous! He was the one who had lied, but she supposed he now thought she had lied, as well, which was what she wanted. "Aye," she drawled, a physical ache rolling through her. "I suppose that's why we were drawn to each other—one deceiver recognized the other."

She heard his ragged intake of breath. How strange that it disturbed him so to be called a liar when he had admitted it himself. "I—" He paused for so long that she decided he had changed his mind about finishing his sentence, so she started to walk away.

Suddenly, she found her arm in his grip. He whirled her around to face him before she could protest, and then he pulled her so close that they were merely a hairsbreadth apart. His warm breath fanned her face, and the heat his body radiated enveloped her. "I wish I could have forgotten ye. Ye have haunted me as a ghost would."

"A ghost?" she asked, a strange, warm, delicious heat spreading from where his hands now gripped both her arms to her entire body.

"Aye," he replied, the word a rumble from his chest.

"That is a strange compliment to give. I have nae ever been compared to a ghost. I believe to call me an enchantress would be a much finer compliment." Her heart beat viciously at his nearness.

"Ye are certainly that," he bit out, "for I find I still desire ye even now."

"Desire all ye wish, but ye will nae ever have me."

"Nay," he agreed, sounding almost desolate, but that could not be. "I will nae have ye, but, God's bones…" With that, he pulled her to him and his mouth captured hers in a ravenous kiss that stole her breath.

She could not think beyond her leaping senses. It was as if a part of her that died had just been resurrected against her will. Her heart hammered, and a pulsing knot formed in her stomach as his tongue gently slid into her mouth and his heat invaded her. Her limbs ached to touch him, and she found her fingers suddenly tangled in his thick, wavy hair. His tongue swirled around hers, inviting her to let down her guard, encouraging her to forget. She felt like clay to be molded by only his hands. He left her lips to kiss her neck, her cheeks, her nose, her forehead. His hands cupped her face, uneven breaths flowing over her.

"*Mo chridhe,*" he whispered.

It was as if she had been dropped into an icy loch where she was pricked with painful reality. With a cry, she shoved away from him, angry at herself for her weakness and angrier still at him.

"Yer heart," she ground out, pleased her words vibrated with rage. "Dunnae tell me I am yer heart!" She was about to say he did not have one, but she bit down on her treacherous tongue until the metallic taste of blood filled her mouth. She itched to slap him, but she refused to reveal how he had once hurt and humiliated her. Instead, she shoved past him with a growl and marched blindly into the woods, not caring at the moment whether she reached his castle or not.

Six

She hated him. Her voice revealed it, even if her words did not. Her words confused him, actually. He pushed branches aside that Marsaili had let swing toward him— purposely, he was certain—as she charged angrily through the woods. Mayhap she simply felt guilty upon seeing him about changing her mind and not wishing to marry him. But that explanation did not even make sense. She had said they had lied to each other, but he had not lied to her about how he felt, and he could have sworn she had not lied to him. He was a fool when it came to her, though, as he had been since the day they had met.

As they passed the stream where he often watered his horses as he was leaving on a trip, he blinked in surprise. He'd been so lost in his own thoughts, he'd not realized the lass was headed in the wrong direction. "The castle is the other way," he called out, positive she'd not be pleased to hear him speak and even less happy to learn she was going in the wrong direction.

"I'm nae a clot-heid," she snapped, then turned and marched past him in the other direction. Her chin was tilted stubbornly, and her gaze shot daggers at him as she passed by. They'd have to talk before they reached the castle because once they were there, it would be impossible to do so without prying eyes and ears around, and he wanted answers, though that was foolish, as well. He should let the past die.

As she strode ahead of him, back straight, and shoulders stiff, he knew she needed a moment longer—or more likely a lifetime longer—before her anger would cool, but he did not have a lifetime to wait. But a few minutes would hurt nothing. His eyes were drawn to her backside. In the tattered dress she wore, he could see the curve of her perfect bottom. His fingers twitched with a flood of memories of cupping that round bottom. Desire instantly hardened him, and he jerked his gaze to the safer area of her shoulders.

Except even that was not safe. A recollection of feathering kisses along her creamy shoulder heated his blood. He thought of the kiss from moments before, and he tasted her then, sweet like honey. God's bones, it had been foolish to kiss her. He'd stood there looking at her, with her mahogany hair in wild disarray, her blue eyes lit like a fire, and her full mouth stoking a flame that had never died in him, and all the yearning, aching, and longing he had worked daily to repress had overcome him. He'd forgotten how powerful the emotions were. They had become like a dull pain that was simply part of his day-to-day life, but with her there, in the flesh, stubborn, prideful, and so breathtakingly lovely, the feelings for her he held within him threatened to drive him to his knees. And he'd wondered if mayhap he'd spun memories that were more powerful than the reality of her. One kiss, and he could know. One kiss, and he could forget her.

But he would never forget her. That one kiss had proven his memories of her, and her ability to elicit desire in him, perfect. She stopped suddenly at the fork in the woods and glanced to the left and right. When she started to go left, he said, "The castle is to the right."

She surprised him by swinging toward him. "Why did ye kiss me?"

It would be useless folly to tell her the truth. "The memory of ye overcame me," he said, getting as close to the truth as he dared.

She narrowed her eyes and crossed her arms over her chest. "Do nae kiss me again while I am at yer castle," she said in a threatening tone.

"And if we are nae at my castle?" he replied, unable to quell the urge to banter with her, even after what she had revealed about using him and not caring for him.

Her eyes widened and then grew flinty. She poked him hard in the chest. "What we did together will nae ever be repeated. Do ye ken me? Dunnae try to force yerself on me."

"Might I remind ye that I did nae ever force myself on ye. I am not so dishonorable."

"Ye lied to me," she bit out.

He frowned. "Did ye nae say ye lied, as well?"

She bit down on her lip. "Aye," she said slowly. "I did say that."

He was struck suddenly with the feeling that she was hiding something. Perhaps it was simply his male pride that had been wounded, or perhaps since he hid the truth himself, it was making him doubt her. But the doubt tugged at his mind. "Tell me," he said slowly, watching her carefully, "are ye the mistress of the Earl of Ulster now?"

Vivid, unmistakable hurt flashed in her eyes and twisted his insides. Her lips pressed into a thin, white line, and for a moment, he thought she would not respond. "Nay," she whispered, the pain in her voice like a lash against his skin. She *was* hiding something from him, and he had to know.

Years of mourning her and loving her demanded he know. Reason be damned. Self-control be damned.

"If ye were simply entertaining yerself with me, why ye did nae become the earl's mistress?"

"I...I kinnae say," she responded, her voice tight and most definitely fearful.

"That's a shame," he said, struggling to keep his own voice from revealing the depths of his feelings for her. "I will hear the truth from yer lips, and ye will nae leave my home until I do."

"What?" she gasped. "Nay! Ye kinnae keep me here." The panic rioting in her voice confirmed that she had been—was still—lying to him.

He took hold of her arms, his blood racing through his veins. "I will keep ye here until I believe I have the truth." He heard the coldness, the utter finality in his tone. What he was doing was folly, but he would at least have the truth, if he could not have this woman. And she was hiding it from him. He would wager his life upon that.

When she tried to wrench free, he gripped her tighter. "I have a verra comfortable tower I can lock ye in for months and months." He would not, of course, but she did not know that.

"Callum, nay! Ye must nae do such a thing."

"Tell me the truth," he replied. "Nae spun lies."

"Ye tell me the truth," she bellowed, tugging and pulling to be freed. "Did ye ever feel bad about the lies ye told me? Was Edina here and waiting for ye the day ye came home from the Gathering? Did ye tell her of yer unfaithfulness? Is that why ye are nae yet married?"

"Ye cared for me," he heard himself say. The things she had said before had been to protect herself, to hide that she had cared. He was at once grateful to know and made miserable by the revelation.

"Aye," she growled. "Are ye satisfied to ken ye hurt me?"

"Marsaili, nay!" He could not allow her to believe that. "I did nae ever want to hurt ye."

She turned her face from his. "I was young, foolish, and naive, and I believed the things ye told me. I am nae such a fool now."

Frustration gripped him in an iron hold. He felt he would explode with it. She had cared for him. She had. Maybe she had sent word that she was dead after believing he was promised to another? He wanted desperately to tell her that he'd not acted dishonorably toward her. He wanted to explain how he had broken with Edina before traveling to Marsaili's home and meeting her. He could tell her how he'd returned to Urquhart with every intention of obtaining his father's blessing to marry her. He could relay how he'd chosen her over his clan's needs. But what good would it do for her to know he'd plunged his clan into war for her, lost his father because of his choices, and that he and his clan still suffered greatly for his selfish choices.

It would not serve her to know these things. They could not wed. He needed an ally, and her father was his enemy. The truth burned his mouth like fire. It clawed his throat, desperate for release. He would need to take care to guard his words and emotions when Marsaili was around him, but he intended that to be as little as possible while she was at the castle. "I did not believe it honorable to marry her after what had occurred between us," he said, forcing himself to not say more.

"Dunnae expect me to praise ye because ye discovered a sliver of honor within ye," she bit out.

"I'd nae ever expect it," he replied. "But it is that sliver of honor which compels me to insist ye take the protection I can offer."

She pursed her lips. "I dunnae need yer protection," she growled.

"Nay?" He cocked an eyebrow. "Ye seemed to need it nae long ago when the English swine was chasing ye. And exactly who was that swine?" Callum asked, all his questions coming to him at once.

"That is nae any of yer concern," she snapped. "Now release me, if ye please."

"Shortly. I'm afraid I need a few more answers, whether ye wish to give them or nae. I must ken if more people will be pursuing ye and bringing more strife to my home." He needed to know in order to protect his clan and her.

A long silence stretched, in which she inhaled several times as if to speak but fell back into silence. He was trying to think of how else to force her to tell him what he needed to know when she said, "The man ye killed was Godfrey of Antwerp, knight to the Earl of Ulster."

Possession and denial hit him, and fury almost choked him. "So ye *are* the earl's leman?"

"Nay, ye swine!" She wrenched back, and he released her, feeling a great war within himself to hold her close, keep her as his, but it could not be.

"Tell me what has occurred," he demanded, realizing as he did that such demands pulled him further into her world when he was required by his fate to stay out of it.

"I have managed to avoid becoming his leman with cunning," she replied, her voice flat. "My father pursues me, unwilling to relinquish his plot to tie himself to the brother of the possible future King of Scots, and the earl, it seems, refuses to relinquish his wish for me, as well."

He wanted to tear the Earl of Ulster apart limb from

limb, and he wanted to do the same to her father. The Campbell was without honor. "I will protect ye."

"Nay," she said, her tone fierce and hard as any man's he'd ever heard. "I am nae yers to protect. Ye should concern yerself with yer soon-to-be wife."

"I have nae forgotten Coira," he said tightly. "I will have my brother see ye to safety. Tell me, if ye will, what cunning kept ye from the earl's bed?" He found he was desperate to hear what her life had been since they had parted.

"Clever cunning," she said, her voice hard as stone.

She was going to answer as little as possible, he understood this clearly now. Perhaps not knowing what had happened was best. Yet, the need to know if it had been her or her father who had sent false word of her death, burrowed into his head and would not leave go. "Did ye ever speak of us to yer father?" he asked, unable to stop that one question.

"Nay. Of course nae. That would have been quite foolish on my part. It is not as if I wanted my father or anyone else to ken that I had dishonored myself by joining with ye." Her words were like a well-placed dagger in his heart. That she viewed herself as dishonored made his insides twist into knots. He'd done this to her, and he could not undo it.

"Dunnae ye need to make haste to supper?" she bit out suddenly, eyeing him. "Is nae yer future wife awaiting ye?"

"Aye, she is." And she could wait a bit longer, too. "Where will ye go when ye depart here?"

Distinct wariness came into her eyes. "To Dunvegan Castle," she answered slowly.

"The MacLeod hold?" He frowned. He knew the MacLeods were enemies of her father, so it was odd that she knew them at all, let alone sought them out. "Yer family's enemies?"

"My *father's* enemies, nae mine. I call them friends."

"How? How did ye even come to ken the MacLeods?"

"It dunnae matter. I did, and that is all ye need to ken."

Jealousy he had no right to feel gripped him. "Are ye going to a particular MacLeod? A man?"

"Aye," she said, giving him a cool smile.

He wanted to deny her leave, but it was not his right to do so. She was not his. She would never be his. Yet the idea that someday she would be another man's wife stirred something primal within him. "When ye and yer friend are ready to travel, I'll have my brother attend ye."

"That will nae be necessary," she replied without hesitation.

"I insist." He sensed suddenly that something was amiss, though it could just be that she wanted to rid herself of any association with him as quickly as possible.

She nibbled on her lip for a moment, then finally nodded. "That's verra generous of ye, considering the MacLeods are nae allies of yer clan. Dunnae ye fear that ye will be sending yer brother into danger?"

"Nay," he replied. "I will send word ahead that he is travelling with ye so that they will grant him safe passage."

"A good thought," she said, but her voice was strained and the worry that pinched her face made him aware that she was lying. The only thing was, he had no notion why.

Seven

"Maria," Marsaili hissed, shaking her sleeping friend. "Maria, please." Maria simply had to wake up so they could flee!

The door to Maria's bedchamber creaked open, and Marsaili glanced up as a woman strolled in. She was fine boned, eyes keen and a deep shade of brown. Marsaili hissed in a breath. The woman had eyes the exact shape and color as Callum's. She pushed her thick, peppery-brown hair behind her ears as her gaze traveled slowly over Marsaili and then came to rest on her face once again.

"I'm Lorna Grant, Callum's mother. I'm also the healing woman here," she said in a haughty tone. "Shaking yer friend will nae do any good. I gave her a sleeping draft. She'll nae be waking for a while." The woman's eyes darted to the door as if expecting someone.

Marsaili frowned at how odd Callum's mother was behaving and at the fact that she had given Maria a sleeping draft, which would prohibit them departing as quickly as Marsaili had hoped.

She stood and offered a curtsy. "I'm Marsaili Lamont," she said, using the false name. She could not chance giving her name and having it lead her father to her. She would get to her son, no matter the lies she had to tell to do so.

"Save yer lies," Callum's mother snapped. She stepped

fully into the room and shut the door behind her with an ominous click. "I ken well who ye truly are," she said, her voice cold and exact. "Brice told me when he brought yer companion to me to care for. Marsaili *Campbell*," the woman said. Disdain seemed to trace her words. "Imagine my dismay and my surprise."

"I'm afraid I kinnae," Marsaili said as she backed up a step. She sensed danger, and she never ignored her gut.

"Ye are the woman responsible for my husband's death."

Marsaili frowned. The woman was daft. "I did nae ken yer husband," she said evenly, though her palms tingled and her belly was tight with worry.

"Aye, that's true enough, but ye are bathed in his blood, nevertheless. My son could nae be swayed to marry as we had commanded after he met ye, and his stubbornness brought the Gordon clan to our doorstep wanting vengeance. My husband died fighting the Gordons when they raided our land—"

The information shocked Marsaili, yet the woman's words also confused her. "Yer son made his own choices," Marsaili interrupted. "He did not break his vow to wed Edina Gordon for me. He did so to ease the burden of shame he carried for his dishonorable actions."

The woman's mouth parted, and her eyes widened. "Ye have talked to Callum, aye? Ye must have. He was much delayed returning to the castle. I saw him rushing to the great hall to sup with his soon-to-be wife."

Marsaili felt her nostrils flare on the news that Callum had kissed her and then rushed off to appease Coira. The man had not changed at all. "I spoke with him," she managed through gritted teeth.

"And yet ye dunnae see," the woman said, her tone

contemptuous.

"I dunnae see what?" Marsaili demanded, her temper banishing the fear she had been feeling.

Obvious anger flared in Lorna's eyes. "Ye speak of my son's dishonor when ye swim in yer own," she hissed.

Mortification burned Marsaili's cheeks, neck, and chest. Callum had told his mother what had occurred between them. He had to have for the woman to say such a thing to her. "I'm nae ashamed of what I did." She had been in love, and though she regretted her choices now that she knew she had given her heart and body to a man who had not loved her, she refused to feel shame.

"I'm nae shocked," Lorna spat. "Ye are just like yer father. He dunnae have any honor, and neither do ye! I dunnae ken how ye ended up here to be wagered away, and I dunnae care. Ye kinnae stay. Callum is to marry, and I'll nae allow ye to ruin this chance for him again."

Marsaili drew in a slow, fortifying breath. "I dunnae have any intentions to stay and ruin yer son's plans, so dunnae fash yerself. As soon as Maria awakens, we will depart."

"I dunnae believe ye," the woman rasped. "What deceit is this?"

Marsaili stiffened. She was used to feeling unwanted by her own family, but it chafed to be so disliked by someone who did not even know her.

"I speak the truth," Marsaili bit out. "I dunnae need nor want yer son."

"God's bones," Callum's mother whispered, clearly shocked. "Ye do speak the truth." She glanced to the door, then back at Marsaili. Indecision seemed to flutter across her face, then she said, "Wait here. I, er, I'll fetch ye some daggers for yer journey. Ye should nae be traveling defenseless. Evil men lurk about."

"I ken," Marsaili muttered.

Lorna whirled toward the door and hustled out of the room as if a wolf were snapping at her heels.

When the door clicked shut, Marsaili slumped into the chair beside Maria. Her head and her heart ached terribly, and exhaustion threatened to overcome her. Why had Lorna acted as if Marsaili had somehow wronged Callum? *He* had been promised to another when he had wooed her. *He* had lied! *He* had made her fall in love with him. *He* had never come back for her as he'd vowed he would. But it seemed he had family who loved him.

And what did she have? A father who had lied to her, robbed her of her child, and was trying to use her for his gain. All the emotions she had long ago caged inside her fought their way to the surface. When the door creaked and started to open, Marsaili scrambled to her feet, hastily swiping at her cheeks. She did not want Lorna to see her weakened, but as the door opened farther, she nearly cried out in fright. Looming in the doorway was Lucan.

Her stomach clenched tight in fear that she refused to show. "Missed me?" she asked, trying to sound playful.

The Black Mercenary chuckled as he pointed a dagger at her. "Aye," he drawled, his gaze sweeping over her and a leer twisting his lips. "I believe I did." He rubbed a rough finger over her cheek that made her skin crawl. "I wish I could say I came for ye to make ye mine, but alas…"

She barely contained her sigh of relief, which he must have sensed because he sniggered. "I did nae. I've been given a new assignment in regard to ye, my pet."

"How nice for ye," Marsaili snapped, glancing toward the door. Any minute now, Lorna should be returning, and hopefully, the woman had a weapon. "Why are ye here, then?"

"Well," he said, scratching at his stubble with the blade of the dagger he held, "I was amazed, then pleased to hear some English knights discussing a lass they were to find for their lord, the Earl of Ulster. It seems the leader of their party, a Godfrey—" A smile twisted his lips. "I believe ye ken him. Actually, I believe ye killed poor Godfrey. I stumbled upon a dead body in the woods when I was making my way back here to retrieve ye."

"Aye, I killed him," she lied. "Just as I'll be killing ye when ye least expect it."

"I like a lass who's nae afraid to threaten," Lucan said in a voice that revealed his fondness for dark deeds. "As I was saying," he continued, sounding amused with himself, "I overheard them mention the earl was rather eager to have ye brought to him. It seems he's quite taken with ye. I thought to myself, 'Lucan, a rich earl would likely pay ye a great sum to bring the wench to him.' So I killed the English guards, and here I am."

The matter-of-fact way he spoke of murdering the Earl of Ulster's men swept icy fear through her. She swallowed, her palms tingling. "So ye came here to take me to the earl, and what? Bargain me away to him?"

"How astute ye are, Marsaili."

Her mind raced as she contemplated how she would get away. She didn't see a way, unless Lorna's return distracted Lucan enough that she could get around him and both she and Lorna could flee. "How did ye manage to get into this castle?" she asked, wishing to delay.

He chuckled. "That," he said, slowly drawing out his words, "is a story I'm afraid I was paid generously nae ever to repeat. But I'll tell ye this, my sweet, have a care before ye ever choose one man over another again."

Marsaili frowned. She had no notion of what Lucan was speaking. "I dunnae—"

Lucan lunged at her, taking her by complete surprise. He clamped a hand over her mouth, turned her face directly to his, and knocked her over the head with the hilt of his dagger so hard that everything went black.

Eight

Sitting upon the dais with Coira and Brice, Callum tried to concentrate on the conversation the two of them held, but it was useless. His mind was occupied with thoughts of Marsaili. She had cared for him. He was certain of it. And the knowledge made the ache in his heart that much worse.

A chuckle from Coira startled him, and he turned to see a genuine smile lighting her face. It seemed a strange sight, given he'd never seen her smile that way, made stranger still by the fact that Brice was smiling in return. A shaft of guilt went through Callum that his brother had made the effort to become acquainted with Coira when Callum should be doing the same. Clearly, Brice found some redeeming quality in Coira, even if it was just her ability to carry a conversation.

"What are the two ye talking about?" Callum asked.

When they both launched into an explanation at the same time, they laughed, and then Brice said, "After ye, my lady."

Coira, who sat on Callum's right, gave Brice a faint smile before turning her attention to Callum and telling him that she and Brice had discovered they had a mutual love of horses. As she launched into a long explanation of the horse she was training, Brice joined the conversation again, and

Callum's attention drifted almost immediately to Marsaili and the MacLeods. Who was she going to see there? He had no right to be jealous, but he was. He wished he could press her more about it, and about how exactly she had managed not to be sent to the earl yet. But again, it was not his right to press her on anything, truly.

"You are not listening to me," Coira said.

Brice, who was to Callum's left, gave him a disapproving stare, Callum presumed for his utter lack of decorum toward his future wife. It was almost amusing that his brother, who had tried to convince him of the folly of Callum marrying Coira, now championed her cause. Then again, Brice was honorable, and that fact compelled him to believe that since Callum was committed to marrying Coira, he needed to behave accordingly. Callum agreed, but it chafed him to be called to task by Brice, so his answer to his brother's disapproval was a glare.

Coria had not been the lively conversationalist before Brice had entered the great hall. She'd sat in sullen silence. Admittedly, Callum understood he was not good company and did not exactly invite conversation. He knew well he needed to make more of an effort to be attentive to Coira. "I apologize," Callum offered, but even as he said the words, he was wondering why Marsaili had not come to the great hall yet. "Ye did say Mother was fetching Marsaili, aye, Brice?"

Brice scowled at Callum but then answered. "Aye. They should have been in here by now. I'll see what detains them."

Brice tilted his head toward Coira in an obvious hint to Callum, and Callum nodded, forcing himself to focus on her. "I am listening to ye."

"Finally," she grumbled. "I have not told my father of

your earlier treatment, but if you keep overlooking me, I just may."

"What is it ye wish to say?" he forced himself to ask, though honestly, shamefully, he did not truly care.

"What did you do with that woman from earlier?"

"What woman?" he asked, being purposely obtuse. He did not wish to talk of Marsaili with her.

Her face darkened. "The whore. I heard you won the fight."

Callum took a long breath to gain control before speaking. "Listen well," he said, his blood pumping hard through his veins. "I'll nae allow ye to speak in such a way of a woman ye dunnae even ken. Marsaili Lamont is nae a whore."

Coira's eyes narrowed. "Now *you* listen to *me*," she said in a quiet but firm tone. Callum clenched his teeth but nodded. "I did not care that you only wished to marry me because you needed my father as an ally, as I am being forced to marry, yet again, so my father can stop the MacDonald from taking our land, as well. And when I discovered that you would not ever have soft emotions toward me, it did not wound me as much as it could have." Her expression, which had been rigid, softened, as if she were weary of being angry. "I watched you whenever we were around each other, and I saw that you did not have eyes for any other women, either—not just me. I did not know whether you just did not fancy women or a woman had once taken your affection and you did not have any left to give."

The last words were said in a whisper, but they were so close to the truth that they hit him like a powerful blow. "And now?" he asked, straining to keep his calm.

"I don't know who this woman is you fought to free,

but I do recognize the possessiveness in your eyes, I hear an affection for her in your voice." Her tone was accusatory and wounded, and he understood at once he had hurt her. "I'll not abide you making this woman your leman. I'll not raise any bastard that you have out of our union as my own. I want her out of this castle immediately. I am to be your wife, and if you don't have any affection to give me, so be it, but you'll not be giving any to another."

He scrubbed a hand across his face, his mind turning. He'd thought her simply cold, but she had been reacting to how he'd been when around her. He felt guilty for the indifference she had perceived in him, but he could not force emotions that were not there, nor could he allow her to think she could order him about. He cast his gaze out over the crowded great hall, where many of his clan were merrily chatting and eating. They were his responsibility. Knowing this, knowing his alliance could be in jeopardy, he *should* simply say what Coira wanted to hear, but it would be a lie and dishonorable.

"I am to be yer husband, ye speak the truth," he said, not touching on the subject of how he felt. "And as such, I will be true to ye when we are wed, but hear me now, Coira. I do nae take orders from ye or any man, do ye ken me?"

"I do," she snapped. "You will not do as I have asked. You will not rid this castle of that woman! I am but a pawn, used by my father and not even wanted by you!"

She stood, and as he thought to reach for her, Brice appeared in the door. Callum let Coira depart the dais as he focused on his brother. Brice met her midway in the center aisle. They faced each other for a moment, and then Brice said something as she swiped at her cheeks, nodded, and then left the great hall. Callum rose as his brother strode toward the dais.

"What's occurred?" he asked before Brice even came to a halt.

Brice scowled at him, which surprised Callum. "I'm nae certain. I found Mother in the healing room. She's been knocked on the head."

"What?" Callum shoved out of his seat, his pulse racing. "Ye left her there? What of Marsaili and her friend?"

Brice shook his head. "Maria is there, awake now. She came to while I was helping Mother to her feet. Maria is a healer herself and is caring for the cut on Mother's head. Marsaili was nae in the room. I sent men out to search for her and then came straight here to tell ye."

Callum nodded and moved to depart, but Brice gripped his forearm. "I was against ye marrying Coira, but if ye are determined to do it, she deserves yer respect. If the clan suspects ye have affection for Marsaili, that ye place her above Coira, they will give Coira less respect. I think we judged her too quickly, Brother. She has good qualities."

"I dunnae doubt it," Callum replied. "But we kinnae seem to rub along well."

Brice frowned. "Perhaps it would be best if ye let me deal with Marsaili."

Callum's body tensed at the suggestion, his mind rebelling against the notion. His brother had only made a point that Callum himself had considered, yet he could not agree. "I will decide what shall be done and by whom after I have spoken with Mother and find Marsaili."

"Be careful, Brother, that ye dunnae accidentally shame Coira. Ye are too honorable for such actions."

Callum nodded, knowing his brother spoke out of concern. "It is good of ye to try to learn her, though I ken ye believe I am doing wrong by this union."

Brice nodded. "Aye, I do believe the union is nae good for ye, but if ye will nae be swayed, then I will ken her and give her respect."

"I will take a care for Coira as well," Callum promised. "Now tell me, what does Mother say happened?" he asked striding toward the door. He gave the signal for his men to stand down as they had been trained well and clearly were aware that there might be a problem. He did not want to sound an alarm before knowing if one was necessary.

When the door closed behind them, abruptly silencing the cacophony, Callum swung toward his brother who had yet to answer him. "What does Mother say?" he demanded.

"She says Marsaili hit her on the head because she caught the lass about to flee with stolen daggers and coin."

"Marsaili would nae have left Maria," Callum said in disgust. "If she'd wanted to flee, she would have tried to do so in the woods rather than return here, to a castle armed with my men, to wait for her companion to be able to depart. Mother is lying."

"Aye," Brice agreed. "Any notion why?"

Callum motioned his brother to start walking, and they fell into step side-by-side, making their way down the passage toward the steps. Callum paused at the steps that led down to the healing room. "Nay. I've nae told Mother who Marsaili was to me, so—"

Brice cringed, and then his cheeks flushed. Callum groaned. The only time his brother ever turned red was when he felt bad about something he'd done. "Tell me ye did nae reveal who Marsaili truly is to Mother."

"I'm happy nae to tell ye," Brice said slowly, "but I fear ye'll only be even more vexed if I keep it a secret."

"God's bones, Brother," Callum muttered, taking the stairs three at a time. "Did it nae occur to ye that Mother would nae welcome kenning that the woman I broke my first promised union for was actually alive and in our home?"

"It occurred to me," Brice shot back.

Directly outside of the healing room's closed door, Callum grabbed his brother by the forearm. "Ye thought to purposely stir trouble?" he accused.

"Aye," Brice replied, holding Callum's stare. "Ye are making a grave mistake marrying Coira. Ye dunnae have any tender feelings for that lass, and she dunnae have any for ye."

"I am grateful for yer concern, Brother, but stay out of it," he ordered. "I dunnae want to speak to ye about this again."

Brice scowled. "Fine."

Callum made his way into the small healing room, which smelled distinctly of mugwort and anise. Maria was crouched over his mother but straightened at the sight of him, her green eyes narrowed and her mouth pressed into a thin line. The woman's silver hair was in a tight coil atop her head, and the few strands that had escaped, she shoved back with her hand, then motioned to Callum's mother.

"*She* is a deceiver," Maria announced.

Callum flicked his gaze to his mother, who sat up with a look of outrage on her face. "Callum, I command ye nae to let this woman speak to me this way!"

"Sit down, Mother," he ordered when he saw her sway on her feet. He looked for signs of serious injury and saw none—just a bump and small cut on her right temple, and the faint traces of a purple bruise that would surely darken. He walked over to her, kneeled, and caught her gaze. "So ye came into the room and Marsaili was in the process of fleeing? Is that what occurred?"

His mother nodded. "Aye, that is exactly what occurred. She had two daggers in her hands and a pouch full of coin. I tried to stop her, and she hit me on the head."

He had to clench his teeth momentarily on calling his own mother a liar. "She hit ye with a dagger?"

"Aye!"

"So Marsaili held a dagger in each hand along with the leather pouch?" Brice asked, standing directly behind Callum.

"I..." His mother nibbled on her lip for a moment, as if considering her words before speaking them. "Aye."

Callum scooped up the leather pouch sitting beside his mother. "Is this nae yer pouch?"

"Aye. She must have stolen it from my room."

"She's verra fast to have found yer room in the short time from when I left her and when I watched ye depart to go to her," Brice commented.

She looked away. "Aye, she must be verra quick," their mother mumbled.

"She'd have to be," Brice said. "And she'd require the ability to vanish like a ghost."

Callum frowned, and their mother whipped her gaze back to Brice. "What do ye mean?"

Brice squatted beside Callum and picked up the longer of the two daggers on the floor. "This is my dagger," he said. "And it was in my chamber when I left for the great hall. And I went to my chamber after I left ye to wash before supper. Unless the lassie can make herself unseen, she did nae come to my chamber and take this dagger, which means someone else did, *Mother*."

The news didn't surprise Callum, nor did his mother's eyes popping wide or the tense look that crossed over her face. Silence stretched the room, and Callum chose to let his mother squirm in her seat for a moment and think seriously about how she wanted to proceed.

"Tell me truth now, Mother," Callum ordered. "I'm sorry to have done things in the past to make ye so verra fearful that I'll make a greedy choice now, but ye dunnae need to fash yerself. I will nae ever put my desires above the needs of the clan again."

His mother stared back at him, her hands twisting together furiously in her lap. Suddenly, Maria shoved past him, snatched his mother by the arm, and hissed, "Listen carefully, old woman. If ye dunnae spit out the truth, I'll curse ye!"

His mother gasped. "Ye'll curse me?"

"Aye," Maria replied, her eyes shining bright. "I spent some time in the company of some *ban-druidh,* and I ken well how to deliver a curse that will haunt ye for the rest of yer life."

Callum couldn't tell whether Maria was being truthful or not, but his mother had gone white as snow. She wrenched her arm free. "She wanted to leave!" she wailed. "And I wanted her to, as well." His mother swung toward him. "Callum, Son, I could sense she would ruin everything for ye, for our clan, so I, er, I demanded she depart, and she said she was only too happy to do so. But she refused to without weapons and coin."

Regret for all that had occurred, all that could have been for him and Marsaili, assaulted him. He clenched his hands by his side, struggling to keep his emotions within. "Why, then, would she hit ye on the head if ye brought her what she asked for?"

"How am I to ken the woman's mind?" his mother wailed.

Something in her demeanor, perhaps the way her eyes

kept darting about, made him certain that she was not offering the entire truth. "Consider this: if I discover ye are lying, I will break ties with ye. I will set ye away from me and ban ye from the castle to dwell in a cottage on the outskirts of my land to live out yer life alone and miserable."

His mother's hand fluttered to her neck. "Ye would banish me over a lie intended to protect ye? One born out of love?"

"Lies are nae born of love, Mother," he bit out, his conscience niggling at the fact that he had not told Marsaili the truth of his feelings for her. But that was different. It did not endanger her to be ignorant of it, and he could not change their future anyway. "If ye are purposely putting Marsaili in peril—"

"Enough!" his mother shouted. "When I came to bring her the daggers and coin, I found her struggling with a man."

A cold knot formed in his chest, and his hand went directly to his sword. "The man hit ye?"

His mother nodded. "So I kinnae say what happened to Marsaili," she mumbled, her tone defensive.

"Mother," he clipped, the urge to shake her senseless strong, "what did the man look like?"

"I couldn't say," his mother muttered.

Callum studied her. She was perfectly still, yet her eye twitched as if she was using great effort to repress things. "Mother, ye are lying."

Her nostrils flared, and very slowly she said, "I believe he had a shaved head and gray eyes."

"Lucan!" Maria cried out. "Yer mother just described the Black Mercenary who seized us, brought us here, and wagered us away."

"Ye were stolen?" Callum growled, realizing belatedly he never had gotten Marsaili to reveal how she had come to be here. "How did the man manage to breach the Campbell hold and snatch the two of ye?" It was an important question, as it seemed the man had also slipped into Urquhart Castle unnoticed.

"He took us when we were nae in the castle," Maria said.

"For what purpose?" Callum asked. "Had he intended to travel here for the tournament but did nae have coin to wager so he thought to use the two of ye?"

"Nay. He was hired by the Steward's wife, Euphemia, to take Marsaili."

Callum frowned. "What grudge does the Steward's wife hold against Marsaili?"

Maria shrugged. "Marsaili said the only thing that she could think of was that her sister, Lena MacLeod—"

"MacLeod?" he interrupted in surprise.

Maria gave a firm nod of her head. "Lena and Euphemia were—or rather, *are*—enemies, as Euphemia had a past with Lena's husband, Alex MacLean."

"MacLean?" Callum knew the laird of the MacLean clan and liked him well enough. "I did nae ken he had married, nor did I ken Marsaili had any sister other than Helena, especially nae one who was a MacLeod."

"Helena is dead," Maria said, her voice devoid of emotion. "Lena, the sister I speak of, is Marsaili's half sister, and the laird of the MacLeod clan, Iain, is her half brother, as are his three brothers. They share the same mother but nae the same father. The Campbell is still, unfortunately, Marsaili's father."

"God's blood," Callum muttered. There was so much he did not know about Marsaili. Had she withheld all of this from him purposely, or had she learned it after their time together? He didn't know her well enough to say. It struck him then that, perhaps, he had never really known her. Perhaps he had only thought he had.

Maria's eyes narrowed to slits. "Ye knew her as well as she knew herself," Maria said, her tone reproachful and unforgiving. He flinched that his thoughts had been read so clearly on his face. "'Tis she who did nae ken who ye truly were. She thought ye honorable, and that mistake has haunted her."

"What do ye mean?" he demanded, even as his thoughts turned to how to track this Lucan and rescue Marsaili.

"'Tis nae my story to tell," Maria said. "Ye'll need to be asking her."

"I will," he answered. "When I find the man who took her."

"Callum!" his mother said, clearly dismayed. "Ye kinnae mean to leave here to search out that woman!"

He barely repressed the harsh reply on his tongue. "I intend to do exactly that. Marsaili was a guest in my home; therefore, as laird she is my responsibility to keep safe."

"Let yer brother try to find her," his mother begged.

"Nay," Callum barked. "Brice will stay here and keep the castle safe. I will go after Marsaili, as I am the one our enemies will ultimately look to and think that I could nae even keep a lass safe in my own home."

"Ye will jeopardize yer impending marriage!"

Brice gave him a look that Callum was unsure how to interpret. He knew his brother was against his marrying Coira, yet he also knew that Brice believed that if Callum was going to go through with the union, he ought to leave taking care of Marsaili to Brice. Callum agreed in his head, but his heart would not allow him to turn away from

Marsaili. He had loved her body and soul, and he had to ensure that she was safe. "Brice will make a reasonable excuse to Coira for me. All will be well with the union."

"Callum, ye will destroy the union," his mother wailed.

"Nay," he replied. His departing would anger Coira, but Brice had a silver tongue. He would make her understand. There was no possible way Callum would leave Marsaili to the fate of a Black Mercenary, nor would he send his brother out against such a foe. Brice was a good warrior, but Callum was better. He was a better tracker, as well, and time was critical. "Do ye have any notion why Lucan would have returned for Marsaili?" Callum asked Maria.

She shook her head. "Nay. To receive coin from Euphemia, he was to wager Marsaili away to a man who would make her life horrid. Once that had been done, he departed, and even if he did hear that ye had won her, I dunnae believe he would have returned for her as his task was completed, regardless of what occurred after."

"Agreed," Callum replied, fear for Marsaili making it impossible to slow the rapid thudding of his heart. "Mercenaries care only about coin. For this man to return here, there had to somehow be gain for him." As the words left his mouth, a disturbing clarity overcame him. "Ulster..."

"Aye," Maria said grimly. "I had the same thought. Godfrey was nae alone at the Campbell hold to do Ulster's bidding. He had three other knights with him."

"They must have tracked Godfrey here or planned to meet here," Callum said.

"Aye," Maria agreed. "We'll make our way to Ulster's home and hopefully overcome Lucan and Godfrey's men."

"Nay," Callum replied. "I'll make my way. Ye will slow me down, and I kinnae have that." He had to save her. He would not be able to tolerate it if something happened to Marsaili.

Nine

After two days as Lucan's captive, Marsaili could hardly think past the hunger gnawing at her belly, the thirst clawing at her throat, and the burning of her eyes from lack of sleep. Lucan had given her small sips of liquid since taking her, and a few bites of bread and cheese, but not much else. And when they finally stopped for Lucan to rest, Marsaili forced herself to stay awake for a chance to escape.

She watched him as he built a fire, hoping that if anyone was coming to her aid, they would see the flames or even the smoke. Night had descended, smothering all light from the woods but a sliver from the moon and the orange flames that now danced in the shadows and cast a small beacon for anyone who might be looking for her. She doubted Callum or anyone else would be searching for her, though. The only people searching for her were ones she did not want to find her.

Callum may have shown that he still desired her, but he had never cared for her. It took the latter to risk one's life for another. Pity rose inside her, but she ruthlessly shoved it down. She would not allow pity. Her son was out there, and he needed a strong mother, not one who wallowed in her problems.

Lucan didn't speak as he worked the fire, but she'd grown accustomed to him not saying much. In their time together, he had communicated with her in mostly grunts and glares, except when he threatened her. When he finally sat down, he did so close to her, but not so close that he touched her.

He turned to her, eyes narrowed. "Dunnae make me come after ye this night. Ye'll regret it."

She'd come to hate the words *ye'll regret it*, which Lucan repeated every time he warned her not to do something. She didn't know if the threat meant he'd kill her in cold blood as he had the earl's knights or if it meant he'd beat her, but she did not intend to find out. If—no, when—she got loose, she wouldn't stay around long enough to learn.

She held up her right ankle, which he had tied to a tree, and then her bound wrists. "I believe ye've ensured that I'll nae be going anywhere this night."

"A wise choice," he replied, his tone ominous.

"As if it is a choice," she muttered as he closed his eyes.

She watched him, looking for signs of sleep and fighting her own drowsiness. The air had cooled, which helped keep her awake somewhat, but as tired as she was, it was not helping enough.

His chest began to rise and fall in a steady rhythm, but she could not say with a fair amount of certainty that he was asleep. She'd likely only get one chance to escape Lucan, and she could not afford to ruin it by trying to do so too soon. When her vision blurred with the need for her own respite, she started counting stars. When she reached 150, she heard Lucan snore. Immediately, she wiggled her wrists to try to loosen the ropes that encircled them.

"I like yer determination to escape me," Lucan said, causing her to yelp in fright.

Her pulse raced as she laid her hands in her lap. "I was nae trying to flee. My wrists hurt."

Lucan chuckled. "There's a lie, if ever I heard one," Lucan said. "Ye've spunk, lass. If I were inclined to take a wife, it would be one such as yerself."

The mere idea repulsed her. "I'm verra glad ye're nae inclined for such a thing, then," she bit out.

In the firelight, Marsaili could see both his eyes slowly open, and the mirth that had been in his voice was gone from his icy gaze. "Careful, aye. I'm a prideful man, and if ye wound it too greatly by making me think ye'd nae welcome the touch of a man such as myself, I may feel obliged to show ye what ye are missing."

"Ye would nae dare," she whispered, horrified by the thought of having his touch, or any other she didn't want, forced upon her.

"Nay," he said, sounding irritated at himself for admitting he was not such a loathsome creature as that. "I'd nae. I dunnae need to force myself upon a lass. There are many who wish for my touch."

"I find that hard to believe," she snapped.

He turned to face her. "Shall I show ye what it is a man can do for a woman?" he asked, his tone silky.

"I already ken what a man can do for a woman," she replied, trying to steady her racing pulse as fear beat wildly within her. "Men can use women, lie to women, and break their hearts."

"Women can do the same to men," he growled.

It occurred to her then that maybe she was going about things the wrong way. Maybe she should try to understand Lucan, get him to trust her a bit, and then escape him. "I dunnae believe there is a woman alive who could have pierced that cold heart of yers," she said softly. She held her breath, hoping he'd respond by telling her something of himself, something she could use.

"My mother hurt me," he said, sounding distracted. "She abandoned me when I was a lad of eight summers because she could nae feed herself and me, and she knew it would be easier to stay alive on her own."

Despite the fact that Lucan was a murderer who now held her captive, her heart squeezed for the pain such a thing must have caused him. "I'm certain," she said slowly, "that yer mother did nae wish to leave ye." Tears filled her eyes as she thought of the son who had been taken from her.

Lucan made a derisive noise. "I'm certain she did, as she told me so. Ye dunnae forget being told ye have been nae a thing but a burden since the day ye were born."

Marsaili's throat tightened. "I'm sorry, Lucan." She could hardly believe she had so much sympathy for a man who had stolen her—twice.

"Dunnae fash yerself for me," he said, his voice frosty once more. "I only tell ye this because I want ye to truly ken that I do what I must to live. I've been near starving in my life, and I'll nae ever be near starving again, even if I have to murder and take ye to some English lord to ensure I have enough coin. Ye can try to escape me, and ye may even succeed, but I'll come after ye, and then—"

"I'll regret it," she finished for him.

"Aye."

She had no doubt he meant it. "How would ye make me regret it, Lucan? Ye kinnac kill me," she said, matter-of-fact. "And if ye wound me, ye risk the earl nae wanting me anymore."

"Oh, I'd nae hurt ye," he said, rolling onto his back once more. "Well, nae so much that it leaves a scar. I learned long ago that the best way to hurt someone is to strike at who they love."

She thought again of her son, but Lucan did not know of his existence. He was safe. "I dunnae love anyone."

He snorted. "It did nae look that way when ye were kissing the Grant laird."

Marsaili gaped. "Ye've been watching me?"

"Nay, nae since I left ye to Cedric. After I discovered the earl had sent men for ye and I dispensed of them, I was making my way to the castle to collect ye and take ye to the earl. I was verra shocked to find ye in the laird's arms, but verra glad to discover he'd dispensed of Godfrey for me. It may nae seem it, but I dunnae actually relish killing. I do it because I must."

Her skin tingled with his words. He believed that. He truly did. And that made him very dangerous. She swallowed hard, an image of Callum floating in her mind. She had loved him with all her heart, and he had destroyed that love. Yet, that did not mean she would ever want him hurt, not truly. "Callum Grant stole a kiss from me. I did nae give it willing."

"Ye looked more than willing to me—until he called ye *mo chridhe*. Then ye turned wild, much like a woman scorned. I've been on the receiving end of that anger enough times to ken what a lass whose heart has been broken looks like."

"Ye're mistaken," she protested, fearful that her heart did still hold some attachment to Callum, her first and only love. She also feared that attachment would somehow cause Callum harm if she managed to escape Lucan.

"I'll kill the Grant laird if ye cost me my coin," Lucan said, firmly shutting his eyes and crossing his arms over his chest. "Keep that in mind."

"It dunnae matter to me what ye do to the Grant laird," she lied.

The only answer was that of the wind and the creatures of the woods. She sat there, tense, her stomach knotted and palms sweating. It didn't seem to be long before Lucan's snoring filled the night once again, but this time she waited for a long spell before she moved at all. First, she wiggled her wrists again to see if she could loosen the ropes, and much to her surprise, she could. The rope chafed her skin, causing it to burn, but she ignored the pain and struggled with her left hand until she finally got it free.

When Lucan grunted in his sleep, she froze, her heart nearly exploding. She locked her gaze on his chest, which continued to go up and down in long breaths. Sweat dampened her neck and brow as she bent toward her ankle and released her foot. She curled her knees in and slowly stood, her blood roaring in her ears. Lucan slept with both his daggers clutched in his hands, and his sword was sheathed along the length of his leg. She desperately feared that if she tried to take a weapon, he would awaken. If she managed to obtain a weapon and he woke up afterward, would she be able to kill him? She didn't think she had the stomach to murder him unless she was defending herself.

The only thing to do was get as far away as she possibly could. Decision made, she turned and crept toward the thick trees, hoping to lose herself in their canopy. When she entered the woods, she stilled and glanced around her. Urquhart Castle was to the east, and she thought Inverurie was to the west, where Maria had said the Summer Walkers would likely be. But if she headed toward her son, she would be abandoning Callum to Lucan's wrath.

Cursing, she turned toward the east. A branch snapped underfoot, and a roar resounded behind her. "Marsaili!" Lucan yelled, as she began to run. "I'm coming for ye, lass!"

Callum had just finished tethering his horse to a tree so he could take a rest when a man's voice bellowed Marsaili's name in the quiet night. Happiness that he had tracked them correctly, and so swiftly, yielded to fury that she was in danger. Callum withdrew his sword as he ran toward the yelling, but before he got more than two steps, Marsaili burst through the trees and collided with him. Instinctually, he caught her in his embrace, the touch of her warm skin filling him with powerful emotions that went well beyond desire.

"Callum," she gasped, "give me a weapon!"

Without question, he handed her a dagger while reaching to shove her behind him. But she slipped from his grasp, and as the Black Mercenary raced through the very spot she just had, to Callum's astonishment, she rushed toward the man with the dagger and thrust it in front of her.

"Marsaili!" he called out, alarm spiraling through every part of his body. He moved toward her, but it felt as if time—and he—had somehow slowed down. She stabbed the Mercenary in the chest, and then she screamed as the man reached out and grabbed a fistful of her hair, yanked her head back, and brought his dagger to her neck.

"Dunnae come closer," the man grunted at Callum while Marsaili screeched and kicked out to no avail.

Callum came to a shuddering halt, and Marsaili shouted, "Dunnae listen to him! He'll kill ye, but he'll nae kill me. I'm too valuable to him."

"Oh, I'll kill her," the man threatened. "To be sure, if ye take another step, I'll kill her."

"I'll nae take another step," Callum said and threw his dagger. The weapon lodged into the man's hand, and with a howl, he released Marsaili, who scrambled away from him and toward Callum.

As she did so, the Mercenary withdrew his sword. Without thinking, Callum shoved Marsaili down out of the sword's path and met the man with his own. Their weapons clanked and slid blade to blade with a screeching noise. Rage pumped through Callum's veins as he struck a blow to the man's right leg and then left. Lucan crumpled to the ground, reaching for his shins, which Callum had sliced across. As Lucan rolled onto his back, screaming in pain, Callum raised his sword overhead to deal the man a deathblow.

"Nay!" Marsaili cried, scrambling toward Callum and grabbing at his arm. "Dunnae kill him."

Breathing hard, Callum kept his gaze trained on Lucan. "Why? Why do ye wish to show him mercy?"

"He kinnae follow us," she said calmly. "Nae wounded as he is."

Callum glanced down at the man writhing in agony, then finally looked to Marsaili, who was but a shadow in the dark woods. "He will likely die here."

"Likely," she agreed, "but his death will nae be on our shoulders." With that, she pushed around Callum, kneeled down, and gathered Lucan's weapons. "I'm sorry yer mother abandoned ye," she said to Lucan. Callum blinked in astonishment. "Ye did nae deserve that. All children should ken their parents." She murmured the last sentence so softly that it took him a moment to discern exactly what she had said.

When she turned toward Callum, the moonlight hit her face, which glistened from the tears streaming down her cheeks. She brushed past him, two daggers and a sword crushed to her chest, leaving Lucan groaning on the ground.

Callum watched her, hips swaying attractively, despite her determined march. He was certain she would pause, turn, and offer some explanation, but when she started up the hill he had descended not long before, he understood she had no intention of saying anything else.

He turned to Lucan. "I'm letting ye live, though I doubt ye'll make it out of here alive. But hear me now. If ye do somehow live and think to come after me or Marsaili, I'll nae be so generous as I am at this moment. If ye try to take her again, or threaten her in any way, I will rip out yer heart with my bare hands."

"I look forward to ye trying," Lucan called to Callum's back, for he had already started after Marsaili.

He overtook her on the other side of the rocky ledge where a stream meandered through the thick woods. She didn't pause in her stride or acknowledge his presence. "Marsaili," he said, thinking she would surely stop.

"Aye?" Her tone was cool.

"Ye are going the wrong way. My home is to the north."

"I'm nae heading to yer home," she replied, quickening her pace.

"Do ye nae wish to return for yer friend before I take ye to Dunvegan."

She came to an abrupt stop. "Ye?"

"Aye. I've decided to take ye myself."

She gave him a wary look. "Nay. I dunnae have time to return for Maria."

He frowned. "To where do ye flee in such a rush that ye would leave yer friend behind?"

"She will ken," Marsaili replied and turned away to continue her flight. He grabbed her arm, sending the sword and one of the daggers she had been holding to the ground between them. Something inside him jolted with the contact, and he was fairly certain it was his heart. She did not try to pull away, but perhaps she sensed he would not let her go. His resistance to Marsaili was nearly nonexistent, and he could not afford for that to be so. His greatest defense would be to allow her to depart as she wished, but no force on Earth, even his position as laird, would compel him to abandon her when she was in such danger. The admission was dredged from a place beyond logic and reason.

Marsaili was strong, yet when faced with the enemies that were hounds on her heels, she was very vulnerable. And whatever secrets she was hiding from him, for he saw that she was in the depths of her gaze, they must have weighed on her most terribly to cry for a man who had seized her twice. No, Callum could not part with her. The best he could hope for was to keep his guard up and not allow himself to be drawn to her so much that he once again forgot his responsibilities. Yet, in order to help her, he needed to know the truth, or as much as he could persuade her to tell him.

"What the devil are ye about, Marsaili? Maria told me ye share the same mother with the MacLeods, and she mentioned that ye once believing me honorable cost ye much. I'd stake my life on the fact that ye dunnae have any intention, nor did ye likely ever, of traveling to Dunvegan Castle." An outraged look crossed her face, but it did so a breath after her eyes had widened to the size of saucers. "Dunnae bother to deny it," he growled. "Yer guilt shows in yer eyes. Why did ye tell me ye were going there to a certain MacLeod? And surely ye have nae been at yer Campbell home these whole three years? Where have ye been? Running from yer father? Did ye flee to the Mac-

Leods?"

She immediately cast her gaze from him and set out untying rope at her calf and moving it to her waist where she put her remaining dagger. "Ye dunnae have the right to demand answers from me," she said, the words rough, as if she'd ground them between her teeth before spitting them out. "I dunnae hold importance to ye."

A thousand denials came to his lips and froze there. Nothing he wanted to say was possible to do so without revealing how he really felt. There had never been a woman more important to him than she had been, and there never would be again. He wanted to reach out and caress her cheek, bridge the distance that his duty required he keep from her. But he could do none of that. He curled his hands into fists, his desire for her thicker than the blood in his veins. "I may nae have the right to demand answers of ye, but as yer protector, I'm taking the right, mine or nae."

"Ye're nae my protector!" she said, her horror at the notion all too clear.

He would have been offended, but he wondered suddenly if she, too, was still drawn to him as she had once been and was fighting it. God's blood, he was a fool to even ponder such a thing. It was more likely that she simply detested him and did not want to be around him because she believed him dishonorable. Yet around him she would be, whether she liked it or not.

"I am yer protector from this moment forward," he said.

"By whose authority?" she demanded.

"By the authority given by God to all honorable men when a woman foolishly means to put her life in peril," he growled, wincing the moment the belittling words left his mouth.

She whipped up the dagger that she had sheathed and pointed it at him. "Release me, or I'll stab ye."

"Ye would nae," he countered, though he was prepared to block a thrust of her dagger with his forearm in the event that he was misjudging just how vexed she was.

She blew out a frustrated breath, which allowed him to exhale his own pent-up one. "Release me, Callum. Ye dunnae have a claim on me."

Her words punctured his heart like so many well-placed arrows. "I dunnae, ye speak the truth, but I intend to see ye to where ye wish to travel, and I'll nae be parting ways with ye until I am certain ye are safe. So ye can tell me where it is ye truly are heading, or I will simply throw ye on my horse and take ye back to my castle where I ken ye will be safe."

"I imagine yer future wife would have a few things to say about that," Marsaili said, sarcasm heavy in her tone.

"I imagine she would," he agreed, not caring one bit in this moment.

"I kinnae return to yer home," she murmured, almost as if distracted by her thoughts.

He looked down at her, her brown hair in wild disarray, dirt and traces of blood from branch scratches smudging her cheeks. None of it mattered. Her beauty radiated from within and made him want to weep shamefully like a bairn. He swallowed, keenly aware the battle to resist her was raging already.

"Tell me where ye are going, and I will see ye there." And then somehow, someway, he would have to find the will to leave her there and return to his home, to the duty that bound him. "Will ye be safe there?"

"I dunnae ken," she said faintly. "But I must go anyway."

God's teeth, if she was his he would keep her safe forever. *If...* But she was not his. The most he could hope for was to deliver her into the hands of someone who had her welfare in mind and would strive to keep her from harm. He prayed it would be one of her MacLeod brothers, for if Callum had to hand her off to a man that might one day marry her or have her heart, it would rip him apart. "Could ye travel to Dunvegan when ye are done?" he asked hopefully.

"Nae now." Her gaze skittered to him and then away. "I will someday, and I hope the welcome is warm and nae frosty."

"Why would yer brothers nae welcome ye warmly?"

"I have done unforgivable things, yet my sister Lena has asked them to show me forgiveness, so we shall see what comes to pass."

He could not imagine her doing things that were unforgiveable. She was too good, her heart too pure. He swallowed thickly. "What things? Can ye tell me?"

She shook her head. "I dunnae wish to tell ye. I'll nae be revealing my secrets to ye ever again. Doing so once was a mistake; doing so twice would make me an utter fool. Ye lied to me. I told ye what ye would face if ye wanted to wed me, I told ye of my father's plot, and ye sat there and ye sat there, nae saying a word about yer own future. Ye were promised to wed another and ye joined with me! Offered vows ye kenned ye were nae free to offer!"

He felt he would explode with frustration. His heart hammered, a searing heat sweeping through him, and his blood roared in his ears. He curled his fists in an effort to hold in the truth, but it would not be held. It clawed out of him, out of the darkness that he felt without her. "I thought myself free," he said, the intensity of his emotions making his words sound choked and ripped from his throat.

"I dunnae believe ye," she hissed.

"I dunnae blame ye for that," he said, feeling almost numb from the pain. "I should have told ye of Edina when I met ye, of the promise that had been between us, but I was engrossed by what was occurring between ye and me. And I had told her I would nae marry her shortly before the Gathering. I intended to see that break through when I returned home."

"Oh aye?" she replied, the disbelief evident in her sarcasm. "Ye wish me to believe ye broke the promise to wed her before ye met me, then did nae wed her because of me, though ye did nae ever return for me?"

"I thought ye were dead!" he exploded.

"Ye lie," she spat.

"Why would I lie?"

"Because ye think to join with me again! I see yer desire for me. That," she growled, "I believe. The rest are lies ye weave, but I will nae be fooled again."

When her chin thrust out stubbornly and her eyes narrowed, he sought his mind for some final words to convince her, but he could think of none. He had given her the truth, though God knew he should not have, and she had refused to believe it. Given that he had to wed Coira anyway, he simply should have let the past die as he had told himself he would.

"Fine. Dunnae believe me. But I will see ye to safety. Where am I taking ye?"

"I'll tell ye, but only because I need an ally, a strong one, and at the moment, ye are the only one I have. So I kinnae afford to refuse yer offer, however much I wish to."

Her words made him ache. The depth at which he had hurt her by not returning for her, by withholding the broken promise to Edina, was clear. Her pain pierced him at his core, and the knowledge that he could not ease her hurt, felt as if it would kill him.

Ten

Marsaili gulped a deep breath and reached for a tree to keep herself upright. His revelation left her so shocked that her legs shook. Had he truly told Edina he would not wed her before he had come to the Gathering? Marsaili could forgive him and understand why had had not told her if he honestly had thought the deed done, but had he really thought he would return home, tell his parents of it, and be finished with Edina? And what of him saying he had thought her dead and that was why he had not returned for her? Why would he think her dead?

The need to ask him burned her tongue, yet he was now to wed Coira. That was a fact. It was also a fact that Coira was barren and could not give him an heir. Marsaili could not be certain he was telling the truth, or that she could trust him, so she still could not be certain he would not take her son if he knew of the child. Their son would be his only heir; she had to keep her secret.

"My horse is tethered over that hill," Callum said, pointing and interrupting the train of torment in her head.

"Lead the way," she replied, praying her voice did not sound shaky. She needed a moment to compose herself. His wary look almost made her laugh. If she'd not known it was because there was no trust between them, it would have been humorous, but the fact that the man who had been her first and only love was a stranger, made her sad. Still, she forced a smile, wanting to conceal how she really felt. "I vow I'll follow ye."

He nodded, turning in the direction he had indicated and setting out at a clipped pace, despite the darkness. As she followed, she tried to think how best to tell him that they were headed to find the Summer Walkers. She also needed a believable explanation for who their son was when they found him. Despite her anger and the fear that Callum would take her son from her, knots of guilt formed in her stomach. She would never have imagined keeping such a thing from him.

She came to a huffing stop beside him, where he was already untethering his horse. The silence stretched thick, heavy with the past that lay between them. Once the horse was freed, Callum turned to her. The darkness concealed his expression, but she could sense his frustration, as well as his curiosity.

"Well?" he demanded.

An idea of what to say came to her. "I travel to Inverurie," she said, glad that she had learned the path the Summer Walkers took from Maria before she and Maria had been separated.

"Inverurie?" he repeated, confusion in his tone. "That is on the other side of the Gordon's lands."

"Oh," she said, only just making the connection that they would have to pass through Gordon land to reach Inverurie. That would be dangerous for Callum given the Gordons were his enemy. "I did nae ken. It's too dangerous for ye to accompany me—"

"Nay. We will be careful. Why do ye make yer way to Inverurie?" he asked.

"Because," she said slowly, thinking carefully about

each word. It would be best to keep the deception as close to the truth as possible, "I vowed to my chambermaid on her deathbed to find the Summer Walkers, and I happen to ken that they convalesce in Inverurie for a short time before the summer solstice."

"Why did ye give such a vow?"

Marsaili cleared her throat. "She believes they have her bairn, a boy, who was stolen from her by her father."

"Why would her father do such a thing?"

The anger and incredulity in his tone increased her doubts. Was she misjudging him? Would he allow her to keep her child if he knew?

"Her father wanted her to marry a certain warrior, and he knew she would not agree, as she was in love with another, the father of the child."

"Well, where in God's name was the father of this child when it was born and then taken? He should have damn well been there and stopped such an atrocity."

She was glad for the darkness because tears pricked her eyes. His words mirrored the thoughts she'd had about him. She licked her lips, her palms tingling from vexation. "He died," she said, not wanting the story to be so close to the truth that he would recognize their story in it.

"I see," he replied and sighed. "So the father did nae want yer maid to have ties to the dead man that would make her nae marry the other warrior?"

"Aye, exactly."

He nodded and looked up at the sky thoughtfully. "We will pass my home on the way to Inverurie. Is time of the essence?"

"Aye," she said, forcing herself to keep her emotions under control. "The Summer Walkers are always gone by the summer solstice, which means we only have a fortnight to get there."

"Then we must make haste. I'd prefer to fetch some warriors, as we will have to travel through the Gordon's land, but we will travel by night and do so carefully. Making our way to fetch warriors could delay us too much." Callum swung himself onto the horse, surprising her.

"Take my hand, lass. We'll travel by moon for a bit before we rest for the night. I want to put distance between us and Lucan, as I dunnae have any notion if there are other Black Mercenaries afoot."

She'd not even thought of that. Lucan had originally traveled to Callum's home with other mercenaries, but when he had returned to take her the second time, he had been alone. Quickly, she grasped Callum's hand, his strong fingers closing around hers, and then she swung onto the horse with his help. She settled in front of him, trying desperately to put as much distance as possible between them while on the horse.

Even without touching him, his body heat enveloped her, and the memories of lying with him flesh to flesh stirred. To her horror, her stomach fluttered. She would have shifted forward, but there was nowhere to go. His arms suddenly brushed each of hers, and he leaned near to grasp the reins. His chest touched her back, and it was every bit as hard as she recalled. Her belly tightened with recollections of running her hands over his taut chest. His thighs flexed, squeezing closer to her legs, and she felt trapped in every sense of the word. She desired him as much as she had the day she had given herself to him, and she was disgusted with herself.

She concentrated on that irritation, as he said, "Get, Lightning." His warm breath caused gooseflesh to rise on her neck, her chest, her arms—everywhere, really. She tried and failed to repress a sudden shiver, born of yearning and not cold.

"Are ye cold, lass?"

"Nay," she growled, praying he'd not try to speak to her again. She desperately needed time to compose herself.

She sat tensely, but as the horse's pace increased and trees blurred by, the repeated thudding of Lightning's iron-shod hooves striking the hard ground almost soothed her. All the things that had happened—and that she had learned in the last few sennights—tumbled around in her head now that she had nothing to do but think. She'd tried to avoid thoughts of Callum as much as possible, but one question would not leave her be. He'd said he had thought her dead. But why? If it was true, who would have told him that? Her father was the most likely suspect she could think of.

God above, what if he was, in truth, as honorable as she had once believed? What if he had truly loved her? He could be honorable and have loved her, and still take her son from her, a voice in her head reminded her. He had said himself that he needed the alliance with the Earl of Ainsworth, and she knew Coira was barren. Her belly clenched at the thought of finding her child only to have him taken from her again. But she wanted to trust Callum. He had come to her rescue more than once now, but the risk seemed too great. She was not the naive fool as she had been three years ago. Lairds would always choose loyalty to their clan and protecting their clan over love.

The monotony of the motion of the horse, along with her lack of sleep, started to outweigh the questions filling her head. She fought to keep her eyes open, knowing if she fell asleep, she'd likely end up leaning on Callum, but in the end, she lost the battle.

Marsaili slumped against Callum, but he'd been expecting it. He'd watched her head bob to the right and left as she fought sleep, and he had suspected it would not be long until it overcame the lass. When it did, Callum was glad. He didn't even bother denying why. He pulled her closer to him, circled his right arm tightly around her ribs, and allowed her head to rest against his chest.

God's blood, it felt so right to hold her. Her soft, womanly curves not only stirred his desire but her delicateness made him even more aware of how very vulnerable she was and how much she needed a protector. And damnation, he wanted it to be him. Yet it could not be so. Who did that leave? He had to ensure she was under the care of someone who would keep her safe, yet the idea of handing her over to another man gutted him. Even if he took her to her half brothers, they would want to marry her off someday. His Marsaili... But she was not, yet in the deepest part of his soul, the space only she had ever occupied, she was his. She would always be his.

He tilted his nose toward her hair and inhaled her fragrance. His throat tightened with emotion, and when she shifted so that her bottom pressed more firmly against him, he had to clench his teeth to fight the wave of longing that washed over him. Did she feel anything for him still? God's blood! Why was he torturing himself with such ponderings?

As they rode, he thought about all she had been through in the very short time since he had discovered she was alive. And then he thought about her crying over the Black Mercenary and her statement that all children should know their parents. Considering it now, it made sense given she had learned that her mother was not who she had thought. He wanted to speak with her of her discovery and question her about her life, but to do so would be folly. He had to keep his distance. Even now, holding her close, pulled him in a little further. If he was not careful, he'd be in the same position he was in when he first had met her: willing to forsake his duties to his clan for her, the woman of his heart. If she could love him once more, if he could find a way to protect his clan, secure another alliance...

Frustration pummeled him. There was no other alliance available. Even if Marsaili loved him, even if they married, Callum would not want an alliance with her father, not that he would be given the opportunity. Not only had the Campbell proved himself to be dishonorable with all his actions but he was truly aligned with no one, seeking only to do things to put himself in the greatest position of power. The man could not be trusted.

Further, Callum could not, in good conscience, align himself with anyone who had pledged fealty to the Steward. He fully had come to believe King David should remain on the throne, yet as it stood, he was not even certain the king would accept his pledge this time. He had nowhere to turn. It didn't even matter that the MacLeod laird, Iain, was her half brother. He was the king's greatest supporter, and until the king accepted Callum's pledge of loyalty, Callum was an outcast to King David and all who supported him.

His heart and his head pounded equally hard. So many uncertainties, yet a whisper of a thought grew inside him, and with each strike of his horse's hooves upon the hard earth, the volume of it increased. The only thing he was certain of was that he loved Marsaili still and that he would be a shell of a man without her. He had no answers or solutions, and weariness pulled hard at him. But he rode on until his own eyes grew heavy, and when it no longer seemed wise to press forward, he found a well-hidden spot in the woods by a river bank where they could rest and then wash in the morning.

Marsaili snored as he dismounted with her in his arms, but when his feet hit the ground with a jarring thud, her eyes popped open. "Where are we?" she rasped, pressing a palm against his chest.

He looked into her blue eyes, laced with fright, and his chest squeezed. He wanted to be the man who tried to ensure she never felt fear. He wanted to be the man to protect her if she did. Without another solution to the alliance he needed, he could be neither of those things. Or could he?

Mayhap the answer was to choose uncertainty and *then* find a way. Was that not what made a man strong? The ability to rise up when everything around him pulled him down? Yet, how could he ask Marsaili to endure that uncertainty with him? Her brothers would likely marry her to a powerful man with many allies. The thought put knots in his gut. Oh, how could he face his clan and tell them he had once again broken an alliance that would have protected them?

"Put me down," she demanded, jerking him out of his own head.

He obliged immediately, though he was loath to do so. "I've stopped to rest."

"I ken that," she said. "Ye sleep over there, and I'll do so right here." She tapped her foot on a patch of grass.

It would be warmer if they slept side by side, but given that his resistance to her was weak at best, he nodded. "I'll make ye a pallet," he said, stripping off his plaid to hand it to her so she could use it to keep warm.

"Put that thing back on!" she cried.

He finished tugging his plaid over his head and squinted at her through the moonlight. "What's the matter with ye?"

She batted at his plaid and took a step back as if the thing would burn her. "I told ye I will nae be dishonoring myself with ye again."

He tossed up his hands in frustration. His plaid went flying from his fingers and smacked her in the face, where it settled. Her gasp filled the silence. "Ye threw yer plaid at me," she accused.

"I vow I did nae," he said, laughter now rumbling from him as he watched her tugging at his plaid, which was apparently stuck and still covered her face.

"Ye and yer too easily given vows," she grumbled as she reached her hands behind her back. The dark prohibited him from seeing what the plaid was caught on, and he started to move toward her to aid her when she said, "Dunnae ye dare come near me."

"I'd nae dream of it," he replied, forcing himself to stop.

She threw the plaid hanging over her face upward and tried—and failed—to get free of it. She growled and turned in a half circle while trying to grasp the edge of the plaid. "Are ye going to simply watch me all night?" she growled.

He could. He could watch her do such simple things as try to unhook herself for the rest of his life, it filled him with such happiness. "If ye say please, I'll aid ye. Though just so ye are aware, I was offering it so ye could keep warm. I was nae removing my clothes with the thought that ye and I would be joining."

"Oh." The embarrassment in her tone made him feel bad for her. "I'm sorry. I thought—"

"I ken what ye thought," he interrupted. He closed the distance between them, felt with his fingers to discover the plaid had gotten caught on the tip of her sheathed dagger, unhooked the plaid, and then held it toward her. "Dunnae let yer pride keep ye from using this to stay warm while ye sleep."

"What of ye?" she asked, not yet taking the plaid.

Thoughts of how her lush bottom had felt pressed against his hard groin would do to keep him warm, but he'd dare not say that. "I dunnae get cold easily. Take the plaid."

"Ye'll stay well away?"

"Aye," he said with a sigh. "Believe it or nae, I am able to control myself." Or at least he sincerely *hoped* he was when it came to her.

She finally took the plaid and wrapped it around her shoulders. Seeing her bundled in it put knots in his throat and his gut. He was fairly certain he'd had a dream where she had worn nothing but his plaid.

They stood face-to-face, unspeaking for a long moment. Marsaili suddenly cleared her throat. "Not that I believe ye, but if ye did tell Edina that ye did nae wish to marry her, what compelled ye to break yer promise? I ken it could nae have been me, as we had nae even met yet."

Callum stilled. He had never spoken to anyone of what had gone through his head that day. His parents had not wanted to know. All they had wanted to hear was that he would change his mind and do as they bid. "I saw her with another man in the most intimate way, but I kinnae lie, I was grateful to have a reason nae to wed her."

"Ye were?"

"Aye. I kenned that she was greedy and nae particularly nice, but my clan needed the alliance." Speaking of it out loud brought all the guilt he had been living with to the surface. "She still wanted the alliance. She was carrying another man's child and told her father it was mine, that I had joined with her."

She frowned. "But ye had nae."

He shook his head. "Nay, but it did nae matter. My parents demanded I keep the alliance. The Gordon even threatened war because he said I had ruined Edina and shamed her with my lies. When my parents realized I would nae heed their demands, they pleaded, but I still refused." The guilt swallowed him now. "I chose ye," he said, knowing with a pulse-pounding certainty that he wanted her to understand he had loved her. If he could not have her now, if he could not tell her of his heart in this moment, he would tell her what had been in it. "I chose ye over my clan. I loved ye, and for my choices, for my greed, I plunged my clan into a war that cost my father his life and has weakened my clan greatly."

Tears streamed down her face. "Ye loved me."

It was a statement. She knew. She understood.

"Aye," he answered. "With all my heart."

"And what of now?" she asked, her voice a broken whisper.

"I am laird, and I must make choices for the good of my clan."

"Ye will place what is good for yer clan above all...as I thought." She nodded. "We should rest."

Marsaili turned her back to him and walked a few feet away. He watched her settle on the grass, shaking his plaid over herself. He found a spot against a boulder. The ground was hard, but it made no difference. He suspected sleep would be a long time coming.

She shifted around restlessly, muttering to herself, which he found endearing. A few times, she leaned up on an elbow to push at his plaid. He had the overwhelming urge to go to her, pull her into his arms, and let her rest her head on his chest, but with each breath he took, he fought it. By the time, sleep finally claimed her, he let out a ragged exhalation, weary from the battle with himself. Just as Callum started to drift to sleep, Marsaili cried out, and his eyes flew open as he scrambled to her.

"The bairn! The bairn," she whimpered repeatedly.

He shook her to wake her, but she batted at him. "Marsaili," he tried, then tentatively reached toward her and brushed his hand across her forehead. She settled instantly and turned her cheek into his palm. Her need hurtled him beyond the point of return. With his heart beating hard, he lay beside her, offering her his warmth and his presence while she slept. But lying beside her put him at ease, too, and almost immediately, sleep claimed him.

Eleven

Marsaili awoke abruptly to rain, thunder, lightning, and Callum looming over her. She blinked the water out of her eyes and tried to clear her groggy mind.

"We need to seek shelter," he half shouted over the torrential downpour.

Before she could answer him, she found herself swept into his arms, her legs dangling, and her shoulder pressed against his chest as he strode through the woods toward what appeared to be a cave in the distance.

"Put me down," she gasped, vexed at the immediate heat that flared within her for this man.

"Nay," he returned, grim faced. "I'll nae take the chance of ye falling and hitting yer head on one of these rocks."

An odd warmth spread through her belly at his concern for her. She wasn't helpless, by any means, but it was nice to feel that someone was there for her, if only for a moment. It was not true, but she indulged in the fantasy for a few breaths.

When they got to the cave, she tapped him on the shoulder. "Now, ye may put me down."

He obliged by setting her on her feet. "Wait here," he commanded, tossed his plaid at her, and shot out of the cave before she could say anything.

With lightning illuminating the sky, she could track his

progress to the tree where his destrier was tethered. He turned, reins in hand, but as he did, lightning struck a nearby tree and cracked it in half. The horse reared, kicking its legs very close to Callum's head.

"Callum!" she shouted, fear gripping her.

He stepped to the side of the beast as its hooves struck the ground. He pulled sharply on the reins and then set a steadying hand on his horse. He leaned close and appeared to whisper in the beast's ear. Then he led his wild-eyed destrier through the pouring rain and into the cave. He tethered the horse to a small boulder and turned to her.

His hair dripped around his face, and when he reached up to slick it away, she found herself staring at his arms and the way his biceps moved. He was a powerful man, and not just physically. Everything about him commanded respect and notice. It always had.

"We'll have to wait out the storm here," he said, waving a hand around the cave. "It's too dangerous to travel in lightning."

"How long do ye think the storm will last?"

"I dunnae," he replied, glancing around the cave. "The winds are verra strong and the rain verra heavy. Hopefully nae more than a few hours, the day at most."

"The day!" she exclaimed, not wishing to be trapped in the cave that long with him, not when his words from last night rang in her head. He had loved her. She believed it. He might even love her still, but he had made it clear that this time he would choose his clan over her. Could she blame him? Look at what his previous choice had caused? His guilt had been clear in his voice and on his face.

"Well, lass, ye certainly ken how to make a man feel wanted," he teased. But she could do no more than stare at the two dimples that appeared in his cheeks. She'd forgotten he had dimples. Did their son? Did he have Callum's brown eyes or her blue ones?

Knots jumbled in her belly just thinking about the bairn. Really, he'd be more a young lad now at two summers. She turned from Callum, who was frowning at her, as tears pricked her eyes at the thought that she'd never held her son in her arms as an infant. And who had nursed him? Had he ever cried himself to sleep? Did he now?

A sob escaped her, which she tried to muffle by slapping her palm over her mouth.

Then Callum was behind her, so very close but not touching. "Marsaili?" The undeniable concern in his tone, almost undid her. "What is it, lass? What's vexing ye? Are ye afraid? I'll protect ye, dunnae fash yerself."

The emotions she'd been holding within her roiled. "Stop!" she barked, his concern shredding the invisible binds that held her together. "I kinnae—" She gulped. "I kinnae take yer kindness. I dunnae—" She shook her head, choking on her words. Gulping again, she continued, tears now streaming down her cheeks. "I dunnae ken what to think or what to do. Or what is truly right. I'm alone, all alone in this. I have to be strong." She pressed her lips together on saying more, on saying too much.

Suddenly, she was being turned around to face Callum. His hands felt like fire pokers on her skin. Or perhaps it was her? Was she feverish? Her heart pounded a desperate beat, and that same frenzied desperation sent her blood rushing through her veins to roar in her ears. Her stomach felt hollow, and as his gaze pierced her very soul, he said, "Let me help ye. Tell me what ye fear."

The truth clawed its way up, and she worried she'd not be able to hold it in, so she did the only thing she could. She rose up on her tiptoes and kissed him. Her heart lurched as he stiffened. He was going to push her away! But a growl seemed to come from deep within him, and he delved his hands into her hair to cradle her head and slant his mouth over hers. The kiss tore through every defense she possessed. It was violent in its passion and blissful in the way it seared her from the inside out.

Her hands had been clenched at her sides, but as his tongue slid inside her mouth and his heat consumed her, she could not hold back. She ran her hands up his thick arms to his shoulders and dug her fingers into the muscle there. Their tongues met, swirled, and retreated, as he ravished her mouth and her senses. Every memory she had worked so hard to repress flooded her. Each touch they had shared. Each kiss. The moment they had become one. She whimpered, when his lips found her neck, and then he stilled and jerked away.

She pressed her fingertips to her throbbing lips as she stared at him. He looked stricken, and in that instant, she knew he was thinking of his future wife. He was honorable. Maybe he'd not been—she honestly didn't know what she thought anymore—but he was honorable now or self-loathing would not be twisting his face.

"God's blood." He clasped his hands behind his head, inhaling a deep breath, and then swiped his open palms over his face. His whiskers scratched against his skin, and an acute memory flashed in her mind of those same whiskers tickling her inner thighs when he had long ago trailed kisses there.

"Marsaili," he said, his voice heavily laden with sorrow. "I should nae have kissed ye."

"Ye did nae," she said, hearing her own flat tone. "I kissed ye, and I'm sorry I did." When a scowl crossed his face, she rushed to continue. "I was swept up in feeling alone." That was true, though it was but a paltry sliver of the truth. She had been swept up by the longing for him that still raged within her. She had been taken by memories of what was and what would never be, but the greatest thing that had moved her had been her desire to confess the truth to him.

She could not chance it. She wanted to. God's blood, she did. She knew he was honorable and good now, yet it was that very honor, that guilt he harbored over having once chosen her over his duty to his clan, that made her hold her tongue. It was that very honor she feared would compel him to take their son from her and raise him to be his heir with his soon-to-be new wife.

As if he could hear her thoughts, he said, "I must marry Coira. I—God's blood!" he thundered, the words bouncing off the walls of the cave. The horse neighed, and Marsaili flinched.

"Dunnae make apologies. I did nae ask ye to."

"I ken ye did nae," he growled, glaring at her. "Ye dunnae ask anything of me, and yet I want—" His words jerked to halt.

He wanted what? She dared not ask, for fear he might say something that would have her spilling her secret to him. She could not take the information back once revealed. He clamped his jaw shut, and she was near enough to him that she thought she heard him grinding his teeth. Was that in an effort to stop speaking? She thought perhaps it was. Callum, she realized, had his own secrets he did not wish to reveal to her.

They stood in silence, which stretched to the point that Marsaili thought she would scream. When her stomach growled, she seized the chance to think upon something other than the secret she was harboring. "I'm famished," she announced, glancing toward the cave opening, where she could see the wind and rain coming down at a sharp angle—a sheet of white against the sky, now gray because dawn had broken.

"I'll get us something to eat and gather wood to start a fire."

"Ye gather the wood," she said. "I'll catch something to eat."

"Ye kinnae venture out there," Callum said. "Ye could be struck by lightning."

"So could ye," she shot back and stomped toward the entrance. She got one foot out into the rain when she was pulled back into the dryness of the cave.

"Lass," Callum growled, his hot breath tickling Marsaili's nose. "Stay put and let me hunt the food and gather the wood."

She yanked her arm out of his hold. "I'll nae sit here idle while ye risk life and limb for me. I am nae that sort of lass!" she fairly shouted. He glared at her, opened his mouth to argue, and then promptly threw back his head and laughed. "What?" she asked, poking him in his hard abdomen when he continued to roar with mirth. It took a few more minutes, but his laughter finally died to a quiet chuckle.

"Ye're most definitely nae the sort of lass to sit idle, but I'm nae the sort of man to allow my woman—I mean, to allow ye," he corrected mid-sentence, "to risk yer life for me. I'm yer protector, or have ye forgotten?"

"Ye are my temporary ally, nae my protector."

A long sigh rattled from him. "Ye're the most stubborn and most braw lass I've ever met. Stick close to me, aye? If ye dunnae, I'll throw ye over my shoulder and bring us both straight back into the cave. We'll be wet with nae a morsel for our bellies, and we'll lack a fire to warm our bones."

"I'll stay by yer side," she agreed, still reeling from the compliment he had given her. When he drew his weapon, she followed his lead and drew her own. He turned to her, his gaze impaling her. "Ye ken ye're a lass, aye? And lasses are supposed to let the man, the protector, lead?"

She chuckled. "I ken it, but I did nae ever have a protector until I was too old to need one. I learned good and well how to protect myself. And I did nae spend long enough with my MacLeod brothers to become truly accustomed to men who were sincerely interested in how I fared."

Callum scowled. "If yer Campbell brothers were alive, I'd kill them for how they made ye fearful. As for yer father, I vow—"

She pressed a finger to his lips. "Dunnae make yerself more of an enemy to my father than ye already are. He would happily destroy ye, and he has the warriors to do it."

His hand cupped her cheek, his jaw twitching as if touching her pained him. She started to pull away, but his hand moved to the back of her neck lightning-quick and held her there. "Ye're gutting me, Marsaili." The word was cracked, and it strummed with untold agony.

She inhaled a sharp breath. "I'm nae intending to."

He nodded, not speaking for a moment, simply staring at her. Finally, he said, "I thought I kenned ye." His voice held awe. "And I did, but just the tip of ye." The tic in his jaw had grown ferocious. "Ye deserve to be protected always."

Hot longing pierced her. She wished the past could be wiped clean, but such things were impossible. With that in mind, she untangled herself from his hold, noting that he did not stop her. He looked like he was at war with himself, and oddly, it gave her the strength to put space between them.

When he took out his dagger and started out of the cave, she was glad to be given something to concentrate on besides the impossibility of the situation in which she found herself. They walked silently through the pouring rain side by side, weapons drawn. Callum killed a rabbit before she'd even seen it. As she watched him make quick work of skinning it, all she could think was that he should know their son and their son should know him. Fear and guilt raged within her, battling for dominance.

"Will ye gather some brush?" he asked over the din of the rain pelting the now raw, red earth. She nodded, eager to be of use. "I'll get the wood," he continued, hooking the rabbit onto his dagger and standing. "Gather as much brush as ye can hold. We will need it to get the fire going since the wood is wet."

After they had gathered enough wood and made their way back to the cave, she plopped down to the ground in weariness. Her head was pounding, and she felt as if it were filled with mist. She pressed her fingertips to her temples to try to ease the pain, but a chill took her. She drew her knees up to her chest, wrapped her arms around her knees, and laced her fingers together as she watched Callum build the fire.

He worked silently with a furrowed brow as he struggled to get the wet wood to light. He muttered to himself, and Marsaili could not help but smile at how concentrated and determined he was. Finally, a spark appeared. And then another, and another. She let out a relieved sigh as delicious heat caressed her cold body and warmed her face and hands.

Callum looked up, and his gaze stopped on her. "I'm sorry that took me so long."

"And I'm sorry I did nae help ye," she said, her teeth

chattering as she spoke.

Callum circled the fire in a breath and kneeled down beside her. He touched his hand to her arm. "God's blood! Ye're freezing."

"Aye," she agreed.

He sat beside her, wrapped an arm around her back, and drew her into his side. "What are ye doing?" she asked wearily, but she was too tired to move away.

"I dunnae have any dry clothes to give ye or a blanket to wrap ye in, so I'm giving ye my body heat."

He was amazingly warm, so despite the fact that it was dangerous to be so close to him, she did not protest or make an effort to shove him back. "I'll take it, but only because I'm so cold."

He chuckled at that, and they sat in silence for a long while, the fire crackling and flickering on the cave walls and the heat increasing until Marsaili finally quit shaking. Her head still ached and felt full of wool, but at least she was not fearful a chill would take her. "I'm warmer now," she said.

Callum glanced at her, and his rugged handsomeness made her breath catch in her throat. "Ye're certain?" he asked, the concern from earlier still there.

"Aye," she replied.

When he removed his arm and shoved over so they were no longer touching, she felt his absence acutely. She thought he might get up and start to cook the rabbit, but instead, he turned toward her once more.

"Tell me how was it that ye came to find out ye had half brothers?"

It was an innocent enough question, so she didn't mind answering. "Well, ye recall Helena?" she teased.

"Who?" he teased in return.

Marsaili laughed at the lighthearted moment among all

the heavy ones they had shared. "Oh, I'm certain ye recall my beautiful sister."

"If ye recall, I told ye back then that she did nae have yer inner, as well as outer, beauty."

"I remember," Marsaili said. "She was enraged that she failed to seduce ye."

"She should nae have been. I could nae see her because of ye. Ye bewitched me," he admitted. His voice had dropped low, his gaze as hot as the fire that blazed before them.

She swallowed hard and licked her lips, trying to decide what to say. She thought he might be recalling the day they had joined. She knew she was.

"I can still see ye lying in the bright-green grass with yer dark hair spread all around ye," he said in a velvet murmur. Her stomach tightened with his words. "Purple heather surrounded ye."

She was acutely aware that if he were to lean over and kiss her now, she would not stop him. "I'm famished," she said, desperate for anything to think upon other than her yearning for him.

He gave her a long, searching look, then stood without a word to retrieve the rabbit and a stick. Soon, he had the rabbit over the fire and was cooking it. His focus was singular on the task, and she realized that when he was engrossed with something, he would catch his lower lip with his teeth. Did their son have that same habit?

"Tell me," she said, determined to learn all about his life for their son's sake. There would come a day, she was certain, when she would reveal to their son who his father was. There would come a time when her son would need him, and she would let him go, as she must. But not now. God help her for her selfishness, but not now. An ache sprang up in her throat, and she swallowed it. "Why was yer clan so weakened that ye were compelled to marry Edina? Did it have to do with the MacDonald Clan attacking yer clan?"

He flicked his gaze to her as he slowly turned the rabbit. "I'm surprised ye dunnae ken the history from yer family."

"Are ye?" She could not keep the sarcasm from her voice. "I was set apart from my family most the time I lived at Innis Chonnell. I ate in my chamber as ordered. I was not allowed to attend the great hall when guests arrived, so I did nae ken the happenings of other clans. The servants feared speaking to me, for they feared my father's anger. Maria was my only friend, but she had a family of her own and our time together was always in brief slivers. When I learned that Jean was nae my mother, that I was born of my father ravaging the MacLeod laird's wife—"

"God's teeth," Callum swore.

"Aye," Marsaili agreed. "He is nae a good man, which ye ken. I realized once I learned all of this that Jean had likely always hated me. I represented my father's indiscretion, and he hated me, as well, I think." She shrugged. "I kinnae say for certain."

"I'm sorry," he said. "It was a foolish thing for me to be surprised that ye did nae ken the history."

"Nay. It was nae foolish. Ye could nae have kenned my life there."

"I suppose nae," he said, looking angry. "I wish—Well, I wish I had kenned. I would have—"

"Dunnae," she interrupted, fearing to know such wishes. "Tell me the history that has weakened yer clan."

A resigned look settled on his face, and he nodded. "We've been under attack from the MacDonalds for years, as I told ye long ago at the Gathering, since King David's advisors granted Urquhart Castle to my father in the king's name for services rendered. At least that was the reason they gave."

She frowned. "Do ye mean to say yer father did nae aid the king?"

"What? Och, nay." He waved his free hand. "My father fought truly for the king, but the king, with his advisors telling him what to do, likely gave my father our particular castle because the MacDonald laird had wanted it and had demanded it. I imagine the king's advisors wished to send a message to the laird that he was nae in a position to demand things from the king, even one who was but a child as David had been then."

"Wise advisors," she murmured.

"Aye," Callum said. "Since Urquhart became our home, we have suffered frequent raids from the MacDonalds, which weakened us considerably. It did nae help matters that we were not near as large as the MacDonald clan in the first place, so my father sought out an alliance, and Edina's father answered the call. He gave my father warriors, and in exchange, I was offered as Edina's husband when we both grew older. I was but ten summers at the time the promise was given."

"And when ye broke yer promise to wed Edina...?"

"We came under attack from the Gordon clan, as well," he supplied. "When my father was killed, my mother begged me on her knees to mend the breach, but I could nae because of what I felt for ye."

He had that same tortured look he'd had earlier on his face. She stilled, her body screaming to touch him. She trembled with the effort to hold herself back.

"*Christ*," he muttered, slammed the pointed edge of the stick the rabbit was on into the ground, stood, and turned away from her. "Telling ye this does neither of us any good, yet I find I kinnae stop myself."

Her heart lurched at his words.

He swung toward her, his gaze swirling with emotion. "Even when I thought ye dead, my grief, my love for ye, obliterated my desire to do what I should as laird."

She inhaled a long breath, each word hitting her like a pebble hitting water and sinking into her brain. Her chest felt as if it would burst, and a trembling took hold of her. "Why did ye think me dead?" she asked, fully believing him now.

"Shortly after I returned home from the Gathering, we received a letter from yer father announcing that ye had drowned."

Her father's betrayal roiled through her, making her feel ill with the knowledge. She had this space in time to say out loud how she had felt, how she still felt, or she was certain the words would never be uttered to him. Soon they would part, and he would marry another. She clenched her hands with indecision, nails biting into her palms.

He caught his lower lip between his teeth in the same unconscious gesture that had made her wonder earlier if their son did the same thing, and the tension that had been building in her since the first moment she had seen him again in the tent at his tournament, drove the truth up. "I loved ye," she blurted, her palms instantly damp. "Not that ye dunnae already ken it, but I loved ye. Completely. I wanted—" A sob tore through her for what she had lost with him and with their son.

Before she realized he had even moved, he was a hairsbreadth from her. Pain twisted his features and shone in his eyes. He raised a hand toward her but stopped partway there. "I want to touch ye, lass, but I—"

She grabbed his hand and pressed his open palm to her cheek. "I ken. I love ye still," she said on a choked cry. "I love ye."

"By God, Marsaili, I love ye, too." Misery was etched in every word, and raw pain glittered in his gaze.

And then his mouth was on hers, crushing her to him. His lips moved possessively, devouring her, worshipping her, but he abruptly pulled back. He cupped her face, his touch so tender and the look in his eyes so reverent that she gasped. "Ye have my heart," he vowed. "All of it. Ye have me in ways I did nae even ken were possible for a woman to take a man. I am yers, body and soul."

His confession released something within her. With a groan, she pushed his hands aside, kissing his neck and his chest, the passion and need pouring from her. She wanted him to take her in this moment, to pretend with her that they had not lost each other, that they had a future together.

His hands came to her midriff, and he hoisted her off her feet as he brushed his lips to her flushed chest, then blazed a trail of kisses across her collarbone and up her neck. He growled, tangling his hands into her hair before pressing his mouth close to her ear. "I cannot resist ye," he said, the desperate words hot against her ear. "I have struggled in vain to conquer my desire for ye." His lips captured hers, more demanding than before. She tasted his searing desire, the kiss turning slow, causing each of her senses to spark to tingling life. He pulled back, his brown eyes glistening with need. "I kinnae find the strength to turn from ye any longer."

His words cut her to the quick and filled her with a hot joy that was drowned by sorrow so awful that tears could never express it. He pulled her face close to kiss her, and in that instant, she knew that as much as she wanted to, she could not allow him to endanger his clan for her again. She shoved against his chest with a strength she had not known she possessed. The moment their contact was broken, she began to tremble as her emotions spun wildly out of control. She hated him, yet she loved him. She wanted to tell him of their son, but she feared that would be the very thing that would stop him from putting his clan first.

She turned from him, fearing he'd see the secret in her eyes. "I kinnae," she said, sucking in a jagged breath. She could hardly breathe. She pressed her palms to her wet cheeks, only then realizing she was crying. "I... We kinnae. Ye are to be wed."

"I'll nae wed her," he said in voice that was as unbending as the ancient bronze used to forge her father's sword.

"Ye must," she said, trying to make her own tone as hard as his.

"Nay, Marsaili." His hand grabbed her wrists, but she jerked her arm away and swung toward him. His gaze burned into her. "How can I? I kinnae. I fooled myself into thinking I could. I will find another way."

"What way?" she demanded, praying he truly had an answer.

"I dunnae ken," he roared, "but I will find it."

Foolish hopes. That's all they had.

"Dunnae touch me!" she sobbed. If he did, she knew she would simply let him do as he pleased. If they shared another kiss, she would tell him of his son, and then he would feel obligated to wed her, even if their union would weaken his clan and bring another enemy to his doorstep. She had tasted his love for her in his kiss, seen it in his blazing eyes, felt it in the way he touched her, and heard it as truth from his lips. She would protect him from himself now.

He gave her a beseeching look that tightened her belly painfully. "Lass—" He stopped abruptly and drew his sword. "Nay!" he roared, and behind her, she felt the sudden heat of a body. Then a hand was on her mouth, an arm around her waist, and she was jerked backward off her feet as six men charged past her. The last thing she saw as she was being taken was Callum's sword plunging into the first warrior who reached him.

Twelve

Callum managed to kill the first two Gordons who attacked him, but when four more entered the cave just as he was yanking his sword from the last one he had felled, they advanced quickly under the shouted directives of Robert Gordon, Edina's elder brother who despised Callum. Callum sliced one warrior across the chest, but before he could turn to ward off Robert, someone knocked him on the back of the head so hard that bright specs danced in his vision and the cave seemed to tilt.

He stayed on his feet for another breath, but then a second hit to his head came, causing pain so intense that he clenched his teeth and fell to his knees. His vision blurred, and he blinked his eyes to clear it as his left arm was grasped. He blindly swung his sword upward, felt it knocked from his numb hand, and then his right arm was restrained. Whoever stood behind him yanked his head back. He squeezed his eyes shut again, his vision starting to clear, and with a roar, he strained against the men holding him to no avail.

"I'd save yer strength," Robert Gordon said, standing in front of him.

Callum gnashed his teeth as he tried to bring his head forward to glare at Robert, but the grip one of the Gordon's men had on his hair prevented any movement.

"Leave go, Sully," Robert ordered. Instantly, Callum's head was released, and he brought his gaze to Robert's.

"Where's the lass?" Callum growled. Since the moment Marsaili had told him that she had loved him, he'd known he could not marry Coira, yet he could not repeat his past mistakes. He had to find a way to save his clan without the union and somehow break his promise to Coira without hurting her or making an enemy of her father. The tasks seemed impossible, but not fighting for what he and Marsaili had was unthinkable. He needed her. She had taken his heart the day he had met her, and without her, he felt empty inside.

Robert smirked. "Ye're nae in a position to demand information from me. Does this lass mean something to ye?"

"Nay," he replied without hesitation. If Robert thought Marsaili was special to Callum, he would purposely harm her.

As if Marsaili sensed she was being discussed, her scream of rage rent the air. Callum lost control, roaring in response and surging upward against the three men who restrained him. He managed to throw off the man who had been holding his left arm. He then drove his fist into the nose of his captor on the right. Bone crunched satisfyingly, and blood spurted from the wound. The man released him to grip his nose, giving Callum the opportunity he needed to gain his feet. He sprung up, spun around, and delivered two quick jabs to the windpipe of the man behind him.

The man fell to his knees, gasping and wheezing for air. Behind Callum, the air swished, alerting him to danger. He swung toward the threat, but he was not fast enough. He saw the hilt of Robert's sword coming but could do nothing to prevent the blow. He was struck once in the nose, then on the side of the head, which sent his vision black once again. But this time, he felt as if he were suddenly floating in the darkest loch he had ever seen. The water was warm, and he could not fight the temptation to simply close his eyes and drift.

The grip on Marsaili's chin made sharp pain throb on both sides of her jaw, but the tears swimming in her gaze were for Callum. He lay unconscious before her, blood trickling from a cut on his head and streaming from his nose.

"I'll only ask ye one more time," the redheaded man before her said in a calm and eerily patient tone. She sensed he would relinquish a great amount of time to happily torture her if he thought it would get him the answers he sought. "Who are ye? And who are ye to the Grant?"

Her thoughts seemed to collide with one another inside her head as she tried to determine the best way to answer. So far, she had refused to say anything, but that had caused Robert, as she'd heard him called, to have his men drag Callum outside the cave, his limp head banging against the ground as the men brought him to Robert's feet. Who she truly was would both damn and save her. She knew the Gordons were her father's allies, thus they would not kill her, but they would alert her father to where she was, and then any hope of escaping a life as the earl's leman would be lost. Her father would triple the guards to take her there, and it would separate her from her son that much more.

"Have it yer way," Robert announced, his voice cutting through Marsaili's thoughts. He waved a hand at his guard. "Cut off one of his fingers."

She gasped. "What? Nay!"

"Aye," the man said in that same calm voice, but this time he offered her a distinctively cruel smile. "For every lie ye tell me, I'll take a finger off the Grant."

Her heart raced furiously in her chest. "Why?" she asked. "Why do ye do this?" She knew, of course, but she was desperate for time, any little bit she could get.

Robert drew her face a hairbreadth from his. "This man shamed my sister when he broke his promise to wed her. He took her innocence, got her with child, and then the child died shortly after he was born. It near killed my sister, and she has nae recovered from the loss. He deserves to suffer, and I see before me the perfect weapon to bring him more misery. What a happy chance, too!" Robert said with a guffaw. "So are ye or are ye nae Coira, daughter of the Earl of Ainsworth, whom the Grant intends to wed to secure an alliance with Ainsworth to fight against my clan?"

Marsaili had to clench her jaw against the desire to gape. Robert Gordon thought her to be Coira? He believed he had happened upon Callum with his soon-to-be wife? No wonder the man was gloating. He likely thought God had given him the perfect gift of revenge. It was both a nightmare and her only hope.

"Aye, I am Coira," she lied. "Please, I beg ye, spare Callum's life and take mine instead."

"Dunnae fash yerself, lass," Robert said, his voice baleful. "I'll take yer life just to spite yer da, and I'll spare the Grant so he may suffer the rest of his life without ye. He'll ken well ye died a painful death because he's going to watch ye die. It does nae matter how long it takes. And when ye're dead, he'll be a broken man, as my sister is a broken woman."

With those ominous words, Robert made quick work of binding her hands and her feet, and then he slung her belly-down across his destrier. The wind gushed out of her lungs, and before she could even catch a breath, they were riding. With each jarring strike of the horse's hooves against the ground, her head pounded, but she concentrated on one thought: she had to find a way to tell Callum he had a son in case she did not live to find the child herself.

Callum's thoughts floated just out of his reach, and he could not seem to remember where he was or what had happened. Something was not right, yet he could not recall what, and there was a dull ache that seemed a constant part of him. In the distance, something hung in the air, dangling, and he thought he saw a woman floating. But that was not right. It could not be.

Heat washed over him for hours, light pressing on his eyelids, and then coolness came with dark and blessed silence. Then heat once more, brightness and noise. Time drifted by like this, repeating itself until he awoke with a start, rage and worry immediately washing over him and the realization that he'd been drifting in and out of waking, but for how many days, he did not know.

Trying to ignore the thundering in his skull, he opened his eyes, the sun nearly blinding him. Flies buzzed around the cut on his head, the one Robert had given him. He struggled to swallow, his throat raw and burning. His eyes watered as they tried to adjust to the daylight. He tried to move his hands but couldn't, then tried his feet to the same effect. Looking down, he grunted.

A stake. He was tied to a stake! He brushed his fingertips against the unmistakable grain of wood that was often used for a binding stake. The familiar noises of a working castle surrounded him, like the sound of a smithy laboring with iron. He inhaled, and the scent of baking bread filled his nose. He was in the inner bailey of the Gordon castle. The questions now were what had Robert done with Marsaili and what did he intend to do next?

Callum's eyes finally stopped watering, and when he opened them, he glanced immediately to his left and right. Guard towers stood on both sides of him. He craned his head back to see the roof of the gatehouse above him. Squinting into the sun, he looked across the bailey, where guards, servants, and members of the Gordon clan milled about. There was a small group of people straight ahead of him at the far end of the bailey. They seemed to be gathered looking at something. He swept his gaze around, searching for what they were watching, and when he saw a woman standing with a basket on her hip and her head tilted back as if staring into the sky, he quickly looked up. His heart lurched, and his breath left him. There, suspended from an iron cage from the castle wall was Marsaili.

He had dreamed she was floating, and she was, in a way. The cage was rectangular and not tall enough for her to stand. She had her face pressed against the bars, and her hands clutched the black iron on each side of her. At first, he thought she must be glaring defiantly at the crowd gathered to gape at her, but from the tilt of her head, it seemed she looked beyond them. Black rage choked him, and with a guttural cry, he lunged forward, only to be jerked violently back by the momentum of his own body.

"Callum!" Marsaili screamed his name. A shudder of relief coursed through him that she could call out to him. He opened his mouth to call back when she screamed again. "Callum! Callum, it's me, *Coira!*"

The crowd that was gathered in front of her turned his

way, and at the front of the group of onlookers was Edina. She broke away from the crowd and strode across the bailey toward him. His thoughts spun, trying to take in everything and put meaning to it. Marsaili had called to him and told him she was Coira for a reason. Did she fear revealing her identity for fear that it would bring her father to her? Callum would keep her deceit for now unless revealing the truth would save her life.

Edina stopped in front of him and set her hands on her hips. She smiled, but it did not reach her steel-gray eyes. Instead, hatred blazed there. "It took ye long enough to wake up," she announced.

"Ye can thank yer brother for that," he croaked, his voice hoarse from lack of water.

She chuckled. "I was so stunned when Robert returned here with ye in tow—shocked and ecstatic. I have prayed for yer death for years. Ye shamed me when ye renounced me. I lost my child, and it was yer fault."

"I am sorry for the loss of yer child, but it was nae my fault."

"It was," she said, her eyes becoming daggers. "My father beat me because I carried a bairn in my belly but did nae have a husband. He beat me until I did nae carry a bairn any longer."

Callum's gut clenched at the horrific news. "Edina—"

"Save yer pity for yerself," she hissed. "Ye will need it. I dunnae ken why ye were so foolish to travel alone so close to our land, but I'm awfully glad ye're such a fool. Now, vengeance is mine. I thought to kill ye, but my brother showed me a better way to hurt ye."

When Edina paused and looked toward Marsaili, Callum's blood went cold. "She has nae hurt ye," he growled. "Leave her be."

Edina's lips twisted into a vicious smile. "Ye hurt me, and I will hurt ye by slowly killing the woman ye love. Ainsworth will consider ye an enemy when he learns ye failed to protect his daughter."

"Edina," he pleaded, not caring that he was begging. He would grovel on his hands and knees if he could somehow spare Marsaili. "The lass, Coira, has naught to do with what I did three years ago. Set her free and simply kill me."

"How touching," she snarled. "Ye love her so much ye will give yer life for hers. I fear I kinnae comply. She'll be forfeiting her life *for ye*. It will be entertaining to see how long it takes. It is already beginning, ye ken. She has weakened much in the three days ye have drifted in and out of sleep."

"Edina!" Callum called, even as she marched away. "Edina!"

She swung toward him. "Save yer breath. Yer precious Coira's blood will be on yer hands."

He flinched at Edina's words. He had to do something, but he didn't know how long Marsaili would hold on. How weak was she? He toiled against his ropes, his flesh burning and sweat dampening his brow and his neck for what seemed like ages. He struggled with his binds until his vision blurred. He paused, blinked, and looked toward Marsaili's cage, surprised to see the crowd no longer gathered there. He was equally as shocked to see the sun had faded, and hues of orange and purple now tinted the sky.

"Coira!" he called, not caring if he was heard. He had to know she was still alive. He could not breathe without confirmation. When she did not move, anguish threatened to overcome him. He yanked, tugged, and pulled fiercely on his tied wrists, and after a while, warm blood slicked his skin. But no matter what he did, the binds would not loosen.

Despair pounded at him. "Damn ye, Robert!" he roared. "Damn ye to Hell, and damn yer vengeful sister to Hell with ye!"

"Shut yer mouth," a guard called from the tower. "Or better yet, I'll shut it for ye!"

Footsteps pounded down the stairs and then two figures clad in hooded capes and Gordon plaids appeared.

"Untie me ye cowards," Callum seethed. "Untie me and fight me like men. Unless ye're afraid…"

"I'm nae fearful," said the taller and much bigger warrior.

"I'm nae fearful, either, ye clot-heid, but I kinnae fight ye like a man."

Shock reverberated through Callum to hear a woman's voice answering, and when the woman pulled her hood back ever so slightly to reveal her face, he was struck speechless at the sight of Maria.

"What the devil are ye doing here?" he asked, unsure whether it was an occasion of gladness or worry. "Has my castle been breached by enemies? Is my family well?" The most plausible way she would have slipped by his brother's watchful eye was if Brice had his hands full with an assault.

She snickered and dropped her hood back over her face. "Yer castle is fine. Breached by none."

"Then how—" Callum started, but Maria cut him off.

"Yer brother was much occupied with yer future bride, so he was easy to escape," she said in a rush. "Now, do ye wish to stand here chatting or shall we free ye and go save Marsaili?"

"Escape," he said, but as the larger warrior reached toward him, Callum stiffened. "Who are ye?"

The man pulled back his hood enough for Callum to see

his face. His expression was hard and grim. "Broch MacLeod," the warrior answered. "I was sent by my laird, Marsaili's brother, to find and rescue her. I have been searching for some time now."

"Only ye?" Callum asked suspiciously. If the MacLeod laird cared so much about Marsaili, why would he only send one warrior?

"Nay," Broch said as he worked discreetly to untie Callum's hands, though the courtyard was empty and night was rapidly descending. "There are others. We broke apart and went in different directions to find her with haste. I went to the Campbell hold," he said, freeing Callum's right hand.

Callum's instinct was to immediately bring his arm forward, but he refrained. "How do ye two intend we escape?"

"Broch and I will feign we are Gordon guards with orders to take ye to the cage to give ye a closer look at Marsaili to torment ye."

"What of the other tower guards?"

"Dead," Broch answered, releasing Callum's other hand.

Callum stood still as Broch kneeled to untie the binds around his ankles next. "How did ye find yer way here from Innis Chonnell?"

"I was leaving the castle for Inverurie, after some hard persuasion of the laird's wife presented me with word that Marsaili was searching for the Summer Walkers," Broch said, standing once Callum was released. "Och!" Broch grunted and looked to Maria. "Why the devil did ye push me with yer elbow?"

"Because, ye big, burly, handsome Scot," she said in an exasperated voice, "we dunnae have time to waste chatting.

Marsaili can tell him all he needs to ken. Aye?"

"Aye," Broch agreed. "Pleasing to look at, did ye say?"

"Aye," she replied, and Callum did not miss the flirtatious look she gave Broch.

They moved to either side of Callum and each took an arm. Broch drew his dagger and held it to Callum's throat. "I want ye to remember the feel of my dagger at yer throat," Broch growled, his light demeanor from a mere moment ago completely changed.

"And why is that?" Callum demanded as they started across the courtyard to Marsaili.

"Because," Broch answered, "if ye do anything that will cause Marsaili harm or sorrow, I'll kill ye."

"I want to protect her, nae harm her, and I dunnae intend to cause her sorrow."

"Just like ye did nae intend it the first time? What did ye think would happen when ye took her innocence and then—"

"Broch," Maria snapped. "Ye speak too freely, ye big clot-heid."

Broch chuckled. "For some reason, lass, I dunnae mind so much when ye offend me."

They both fell silent as a guard came out of the shadows that led to the stairs where Marsaili was being kept.

"What's this?" the man demanded.

Callum yanked his arm free and jabbed the man in the windpipe. He fell in a wheezing fit at their feet.

"That was nae the plan," Broch growled, turning the man over and giving him a hard thump on the head so that he went completely still. "Nor verra smart," the MacLeod warrior added. "Now we have to hide him. Control yer temper, aye?"

"Aye," Callum agreed, helping Broch tug the guard

under the stairs. "It was foolish, but that man dared to touch what is mine."

"Yer sword?" Broch asked as they climbed the stairs.

"Nay," Callum answered, sureness swelling inside his chest. "Marsaili. She belongs with me, and I'll nae abide another man touching her."

"Finally ye staked yer claim," Maria murmured, and as the words left her mouth, two figures came around the corner at the top of the stairs, one of whom happened to be Robert Gordon.

Thirteen

Marsaili lay curled in a ball, cold iron pressing into her cheek, along with pebbles of sharp rock and gritty sand. She was too tired and hungry to move or even care about the discomfort of those minor things. She trembled almost violently with chill and fatigue, and the pain in her stomach had turned piercing. Her every nerve throbbed as she struggled to press her palms over her ears to block out a loud clanking noise that now filled the air.

Despair weighed on her, stifling and immovable. She could not think of a way to let Callum know that he—*they*—had a son. She could not shout it across the courtyard and chance any of the Gordons hearing her secret. She had no doubt Robert Gordon would hunt down their son and kill him simply to hurt Callum. And she feared she would not be making it out of this alive.

God's above, she had to rise and find a way to tell Callum of his son. Maybe she could bribe one of her guards. But with what? She glanced down at her hand and the ring she wore that had been her mother's. It was the only thing of value she possessed, but she would gladly relinquish it to save her son. She took a deep breath and struggled to push herself off the floor. The clinking and shouting now seemed to be coming from everywhere, hitting her eardrums with painful, almost deafening beats. Pressing up to her hands

and knees took so much effort that she was panting, sweat
beading on her forehead, and the cage seemed to tilt
precariously. She had no notion if it was really moving or if
she was simply feeling unstable. Either way, the result was
the same. She had to gulp air to fight back the sick feeling
roiling through her.

With her cheek dragging against the cool bars of her
cage, she pulled herself slowly up, her sensitive skin sliding
over the chilled iron and her body screaming for her to
simply release her hold and drop back down into a heap.
Thoughts of her son kept her going until she gained her feet
and slowly opened her eyes.

Her cage dangled from an iron hook fashioned into the
castle wall. On one side of her, blackness swirled with white
fog, taunting her. And beyond the endless black was a
rocky, steep drop to the frothy waters of the loch below.
She shoved away from the bar as the salty wind sprayed the
first drops of rain across her face to sting her chaffed skin.
She turned slowly toward the castle. Torches lined the
walls, illuminating the stone structure, but what else she
saw shocked her speechless for a breath. "Callum!"

Robert Gordon and Callum both stood on the narrow
ledge of the passage at the top of the wall, and Robert
swung his sword perilously close to Callum's face. Callum
jumped backward and, to her astonishment, turned his back
on Robert to race toward her.

"Callum, watch out!" she called, fear making her voice
weaker than she wanted.

Robert charged toward Callum, sword raised once
again. As Robert sliced his sword down toward Callum's left
shoulder, a deep voice called out, "Left!" and Callum lunged
to the left, making Marsaili's breath catch with the fear that
he would plunge over the edge to his death. He teetered for

a moment before he righted himself, ducked another oncoming blow, and turned back toward her.

She blinked in shock at the sight of Broch, a big, burly MacLeod Highlander, who was visible for one brief moment when Robert ducked an oncoming blow from him. Though she knew Broch had been pursuing her to return her to Dunvegan, she was glad to see him. He'd fight for her life with Callum, and as close as the Gordon land was to Inverurie, she felt certain that if they did rescue her, Broch would help her find her son or, as fate may have it, aid Callum in the quest.

Callum came toward her with such force he almost barreled into the cage. As it was, he grabbed at the iron bars, which made the cage sway backward and knocked Marsaili, weak as she was, to her bottom. The fall jarred her entire body, and she let out a deep groan.

"I'm sorry, lass," he murmured, followed by a loud curse and then several hits of his sword to the lock that had been fashioned to keep her in. "God's blood!" he roared, kneeled, and reached his arm through the bar. "Give me yer hand," he demanded, his tone harsh, but the worry in his gaze was a gentle buffer.

She complied immediately, and his fingers gripped hers tightly. "Dunnae fear. I will get ye out of here."

A horn sounded loudly, and she knew enough about castle defenses to know that meant the Gordon men had been alerted to intruders. Though had she not known, Callum's string of curses would have told her the situation had just become even more dire. Shouts rose from the inner courtyard, and fear, along with a certainty that if he stayed he'd die with her, stabbed at her heart.

"Leave me!" she ordered him and tried to tug her hand away from his, but it was impossible. His grip was like a steel vise.

"I will nae ever leave ye from this day forward." His words vibrated with the intensity of his emotion and made tears come instantly to her eyes. "I will retrieve the key and return. Dunnae fear!"

When he released his grip and stood, she felt momentary panic. If he could not return, if she died—

"Callum!" she called, as he had already moved several steps away. He turned, and behind him, she saw a wave of advancing men. She scrambled clumsily to her feet and gripped the bar, the cage now rocking in the wind. "We've a son," she blurted. There was no time to ease into telling him the truth. He had to know. It had not been right to keep it from him, no matter her fears; she understood that now.

When he simply gaped at her, she repeated herself. "Ye have a son—our son. My father took him from me and told me he died at birth. That is who I'm looking for."

She flinched at the raw hatred and rage that swept his face. She had no notion if the black anger she saw in him was mostly directed at her. He turned with a guttural war cry and raised his sword above his head, then advanced straight down the line of enemies, swinging his weapon side to side, cutting men down. He appeared crazed and unstoppable, almost frightening in the destruction he was leaving in his wake. Near the end of the passage, Broch joined him, and a woman, who Marsaili recognized instantly by her hair. How Maria and Broch had both come to be here, she could not guess.

The nausea and fatigue hammered her relentlessly, and helpless to offer aid or to even escape, she slid to her knees, deciding the best thing she could do was conserve her strength in the unlikely event that Callum was able to free her from this cage. When nausea twisted her stomach and rose in her throat, she doubled over her knees and pressed her head to the cold iron floor as she inhaled long, slow breaths.

A rattle came from above her, and she shoved herself up with shaking limbs. Callum stood outside the cage, covered in blood with his sword at his feet, gripping an iron ring of keys. He did not speak, did not lift his eyes to hers; he simply kept methodically trying the keys. With each failed try, his curses grew louder and fouler, and her hopes dwindled. When he got to the last key, he finally looked up, and the stark fear glittering in his gaze made her throat ache with the need to cry.

As he brought the key to the lock, he said, "I'll die with ye before I leave ye. Dunnae mistake it."

Hot tears rolled down her cheeks as she nodded, knowing well that to fight him would be useless. He inserted the key, and with a click that reverberated through her entire body, the door swung open. But as she stood and he reached for her, Robert appeared behind him, and she could not get the scream out soon enough to warn him. Robert plunged his sword through Callum's left shoulder and then kicked out at Callum's stomach. Callum caught Robert's foot, and with a twist of his wrist, he sent the man over the ledge and likely to his death.

Something greater than nausea consumed her. Her stomach cramped, and she was instantly hot, then cold. Her vision blurred, the cage tilted, and then she felt herself falling as everything went black.

As Callum jerked the sword from his shoulder with a hiss,

he decided that he was glad Marsaili had fainted because there was no way to get out of the castle other than jumping from the ledge into the loch below. He'd studied it and judged it deep enough, but without going into the water to check, it was only a guess. Yet to stay on this ledge with the Gordon warriors advancing on them was certain death.

With Broch steadying the cage, Callum retrieved Marsaili, gripped her around the waist, and prayed for God's mercy on their souls in case this was the day he brought them to him. But as Callum locked eyes with Broch, who stood hand in hand with a very frightened-looking Maria, he also prayed that God would judge this day a bad one for taking them. Then, with his shoulder screaming in protest, he scooped Marsaili into his arms and jumped.

They hit the water within seconds, the impact taking his breath and jarring Marsaili into him as if he'd hit a wall with his chest. He lost his grip on her legs but grasped her wrist as the force of the water pulled her violently from him. As he recovered his grip, hands suddenly clawed at him. Her panic pierced him through the cold, dark water as her nails scraped him, and then she was pummeling and kicking him. With a jerk, he managed to turn her around and grab her around the chest, effectively pinning her arms so at least she could not hit him anymore.

She kicked out, though, as he swam toward what he hoped was the surface. When he broke it moments later, he sucked in one large breath of air before pressing his lips to Marsaili's. It was the quickest way he could think to reach her through her panic. She stilled after a second, and he pulled away, aware they had to flee and put distance between them and the Gordons who would be pursuing. He'd almost certainly killed Robert, and that would not be forgotten, nor forgiven.

Even in the cold water, the burning heat of her skin caressed him. Fear twisted around his heart at the fever that raged in her. "I love ye," he said, keenly aware there was not time to say much more. Later would be the time for anger, forgiveness, questions, joy—please, God, that there was time for joy. Callum had a son. *A son.* His heart swelled with an almost-choking sort of love.

"I have been a fool to try to turn away from ye. What we have kinnae be denied. We will find a way. Do ye hear me? I love ye," he said again and kissed her full on the mouth, tasting her salt, her heat, her tears.

"Ye can kiss the lass later, if we live," Broch called from the dark beside Callum.

"Maria?" Marsaili asked weakly.

"I'm here, dunnae fash. A bit bruised, but I'll live. And ye will, as well. I managed to keep my medicine bag."

"That's good," Marsaili said, her voice barely above a whisper.

A tight knot of fear formed in his throat. He'd be damned if he was going to let her die on him after everything they had been through and all that they had left to experience together. He surged toward the shore on his back, with her resting against his front. At first, she kicked with him, but after a few strokes, she went limp in his arms. The knot in his throat seemed to shoot out darts of pain and fear to his head, his heart, and his chest. He could not reach the shore fast enough, and when he did, he laid her down, straining to see her face in the little bit of moonlight. Rain drizzled down, he realized suddenly, as he pushed her hair back from her face and leaned in to see if she still breathed. Her chest rose in shallow breaths, but it was enough.

Maria and Broch came to kneel beside him. Maria

placed a hand on Marsaili's head and hissed. "She burns with fever." She dug in her bag. She produced a small bottle and motioned to him. "Lift her head."

He immediately did as commanded, dismayed at the way her head lolled and she did not stir. Maria pressed the bottle to Marsaili's lips as she opened them and slowly poured in a liquid. Some dribbled out of Marsaili's mouth, but she seemed to immediately swallow most of it.

"What did ye give her?" he asked.

"A potion of coriander for her fever. We need to bring it down. If it rises any higher, she could have a fit, which can affect the brain."

He clenched his teeth. "How can we ease the fever?"

Maria looked at him steadily. "There's nae much we can do. The potion is our best defense. Other than that, we need to keep her warm, though it may sound odd. Soon, the fever will make her cold and miserable," Maria explained while running her hands about Marsaili's head, raising Marsaili's limp arms to check them for broken bones or cuts, and then sliding her hands along Marsaili's body. "She dunnae appear injured. I believe perhaps exhaustion, and mayhap hunger, made her weak and more susceptible to fever."

He thought of the rabbit he had cooked, but they'd been captured before being able to eat it. "Aye. I dunnae believe she has eaten much since leaving my home."

"We have horses tethered just on the other side of the loch," Broch said. "We'll ride toward Inverurie, which is a two-days' journey from here if ridden hard—four if we need to stop often, which we might."

Callum nodded. "Once we're safe, I'll hunt for food and feed her."

"I'll hunt the food," Broch said. "I'm her clansman."

"And I'll be her husband," Callum shot back without thinking.

Both Broch's and Maria's eyes widened, and he could feel their gazes still on him as he scooped Marsaili into his arms, wincing at the shooting pain in his shoulder. He set a clipped pace to the other side of the loch. Above him, torches began to flicker on the cliff, and he ran, stopping only when he reached the horses.

Broch was directly behind him. "Take the one on the left," Broch said, indicating the white destrier. "The other is mine. Maria can ride with me."

Callum nodded again, and as he shifted Marsaili to swing them both into the saddle, Broch laid a hand on Callum's arm. "Have ye asked Marsaili to wed ye?"

"Nae yet, but we've a son," he said, the truth still hardly seeming real. "We will be wed, whether she wishes it or nae." Though he prayed to God that she did wish it. Now that he had come to realize how futile fighting his love for her was, he hoped he did not have to fight *her*.

Broch chuckled. "I've been privy to a fair amount of courting of stubborn lasses by the MacLeod brothers, and I can tell ye, if ye approach Marsaili with directives of what she will do, she will likely do the exact opposite."

"I'll take that into consideration," Callum replied as the sound of shouting grew louder, coming closer. Without another word, he swung onto the horse with Marsaili, situated her in front of him, and took off toward Inverurie, where he prayed they would find the Summer Walkers. He had no notion what they had to do with finding his son, but that is where Marsaili had been heading, so that was where he would go.

Fourteen

Hours later, still under cover of night, Marsaili began to whimper and tremble almost violently in her sleep. Callum decided it was safer to halt and seek shelter than to keep riding. They seemed to have lost the Gordon warriors in the mountains, and Marsaili could well die if he pushed on farther.

"We stop," he called to Broch. Callum looked around the thick woods, slowed his panting destrier, and led him toward a nearby stream. Once there, he dismounted, steadying Marsaili, then slid her off the beast.

Broch pulled his own panting charger up beside Callum's. "I dunnae care to be ordered about," he growled, dismounting his horse and then helping Maria down. Callum noted the lingering look that passed between the two of them, and he also noted the way Broch's fingers stayed in contact with Maria's hip, even after they were both standing and she clearly was not in need of his aid. Something was developing between those two.

"Tell me," Callum said to Broch, "how did ye come to be in Maria's company? I ken that she escaped my castle, but how did she come to meet up with ye?"

"I'll tell ye what ye wish," Broch said in a fairly amicable tone, "but I want ye to acknowledge what I said to ye. I dunnae take orders from any man but my laird, ye ken? So if ye wish for me to do something, propose it, ask it, but dunnae command it."

"Fair enough," Callum said, then strode to where Maria had made a pallet from a plaid Broch had given her and was now waving him over. He squatted and gently laid Marsaili on the plaid that Maria had spread out under some trees. "What should I do?" he asked, his chest tightening with worry that Marsaili had still not awoken.

Maria waved a hand. "Ye'll sit and let me wrap yer shoulder quickly, and then ye'll take yer leave. I need to examine her, and ye and Broch need to hunt. When I've a need of ye, I'll call ye to return."

He nodded and did as she bid. Maria made quick work of wrapping his shoulder, and then she gestured for him to depart. But he lingered a moment, so many questions in his mind that he longed to have answered. He knew Maria had been Marsaili's friend and at the Campbell hold with her. "Did ye ken I had a son?"

"Nae until verra recently," she replied, "but I saw the child when he was born. He was a braw bairn with a head of dark hair. I marked his foot with an X. I thought his mother was Marsaili's chambermaid, and that she might reconsider ridding herself of him. If he is still with the Summer Walkers, ye will be able to ken him from that marking."

Callum nodded, too choked up to talk. He was reluctant to leave Marsaili's side, but he knew she needed to eat; therefore, he needed to hunt. He withdrew his dagger and started toward the thick woods. He'd hunted many times at night with nothing more than a shaft of moonlight to guide him, so he was not overly worried that he would not be successful. Broch fell into step with him as Callum shoved through the thick shrubs to find the best spot to conceal himself and wait.

"So," Callum said, picking up his earlier question to Broch that had gone unanswered, "how is it that ye find yerself with Maria?"

"As I was leaving the Campbell hold, a band of four men tried to rob me. I fought them off, killing all but one. He had a MacLeod plaid stuffed in his bag, and with a little persuasion," Broch said, a deadly tone in his voice, "he admitted he'd taken a plaid from a lass named Marsaili who he'd helped their leader, a man named Lucan, take to yer home to wager away. So I went to yer castle, but on the road that led up to yer home, I found Maria racing away. She saw that I wore the MacLeod plaid and told me what had occurred, and of Marsaili being taken to Ulster."

"But the earl's home is in the opposite direction from here," Callum said, not ready to trust this man just yet, not totally.

"Aye, it is. We started toward the Earl of Ulster's and came across Lucan, who was almost dead."

Callum inhaled a long breath. "And?"

Broch held Callum's gaze a long moment. "And he told us Marsaili had spared his life. So Maria gave him a potion to aid him and we offered him food and water. I'll nae undo the good deed of another," Broch said defensively.

"Nay, nor would I. So ye started for Inverurie after aiding Lucan?"

Broch nodded. "We had just gotten to the edge of Gordon land when we came across two bards. We sat to take a short respite, and one of the bards started composing a song he called 'The Caged Woman of the Gordons.' I recognized Marsaili's description in the song"—he smiled—"as did Maria, and we kenned Marsaili had to be here, somehow having been captured, likely when the two of ye were trying to travel to Inverurie. Ye ken most of the rest already."

Callum nodded and paused, shoving a low-hanging branch out of his face. "Ye said when ye left the Campbell hold that ye were headed to Inverurie because of learning that the Summer Walkers may well have Marsaili's—*my*—son. How did ye ken they might be there?"

"Marsaili's half brother Graham MacLeod married Isobel Campbell, who ye surely ken is Marsaili's half sister on her father's side."

Callum shook his head, feeling the fool not knowing such important things about Marsaili's life. "I did nae. I still have much to learn about Marsaili."

Broch chuckled. "Dunnae fash yerself too much. Isobel, who told me of the Summer Walkers once and where they travel, did nae ever live with Marsaili, so she likely did nae think to mention Isobel to ye when the two of ye kenned each other." Broch's face suddenly took on a fierce, angry expression. "Regarding that—"

The MacLeod warrior shot out his fist so fast that Callum managed only to jerk to the left enough to avoid his nose getting punched again. His right cheekbone, though, felt the Scot's blow down deep in the bone, which seemed to vibrate with the punch. Seething, Callum grabbed Broch's hand as the man was pulling back from the freshly delivered hit, and he held him still. "What in God's name was that for?"

"That," Broch said, trying to jerk his fist from Callum's grasp, which Callum responded to by jerking back, "was for seducing Marsaili when ye were to marry another, getting her with child, and then nae ever returning for her and the child. I dunnae ken why she has nae killed ye yet."

"First," Callum said, releasing the man's fist, as he did not wish to make an enemy of Marsaili's clansman, "I did nae seduce Marsaili." If anything, the lass had beguiled him. "And at the time I met her, I already had broken my promise to wed Edina. I take it Maria is the one who has told ye what ye believe ye ken?"

"Aye," Broch confirmed, sounding and looking unconvinced that Callum was speaking the truth.

"Well, she did nae have good information because Marsaili did nae have good information." He would have gone through Hell itself to reunite with Marsaili had he known she was alive, but he was not going to speak of such things to anyone but Marsaili. "I was told the lass was dead," he said instead. "So 'tis plain to see that I did nae ken about my son, either, and she did nae tell me until we just rescued her from the cage." His pulse sped up just trying to imagine his son, and quickly following that thought was one about Marsaili. How had she felt when she had been told their son was dead? It enraged him to even think upon it. What had she endured and suffered, with child and alone? Had she been shunned? Treated poorly? He wanted to kill her father for all his treacheries. The man had lied to Marsaili, was intent on using her, and had lied to Callum and his parents when he had told them Marsaili was dead, among other things.

Anger pulsed within him. *Three years.* He had lost three years he could have been with her. Two years they could have been with their son. His chest squeezed so tightly, he had to suck in a sudden breath. "I will kill the Campbell," he ground out.

"Ye will make an enemy of the king if ye do so," Broch replied.

"I have to wonder if he dunnae still see me as such from my father's disloyalty. I have long wanted to pledge myself to his service, to align myself with him, but he would nae take the pledge."

Broch nodded. "King David is slow to forgive or forget, and unfortunately, he has put yer father's disloyalty upon yer shoulders."

"Ye speak the truth. I need an alliance," he said bluntly, allowing his pride to fall away. "I was to wed Coira Ainsworth to gain one, but I kinnae wed her."

Broch cocked his eyebrows. "Marsaili?"

"Aye. I will wed her. Yet my clan still needs an alliance. We have been weakened by constant sieges by the MacDonalds and the Gordons."

"I ken," Broch said.

"Tell me," Callum said, thinking on what Broch had said about making an enemy of the king if Callum killed the Campbell. "Why would the king wish to let the Campbell, who tries to thwart him at every turn, live?"

"Because the king sees many ways to use the Campbell, and as long as the king holds more power than the Campbell and the Steward, then he would rather the man live—for now."

"Is yer laird nae close with the king?"

"Aye," Broch answered. "Iain says King David is the best choice as king, though still a flawed man. But if ye repeat Iain's words, I'll deny them."

Callum nodded, and as he did, a darting flash of white caught his attention near the brook. "Rabbit!" he shouted. In a flash, his dagger and Broch's flew in unison toward the animal, hitting it at the exact same moment. "Ye throw a dagger true," Callum said, impressed with the man's skill.

"As do ye," Broch returned.

Callum retrieved the rabbit and the daggers, and after handing Broch his blade, he said, "Iain sounds like a wise laird." What he really needed to know was if Iain would be an enemy of Callum's because of whatever Marsaili had done or if perhaps an alliance could be found there. It would be much a needed reprieve if the MacLeod laird could be considered an ally, but if the man meant to punish Marsaili, to set her out of the clan for whatever deed she had done to him, then Iain MacLeod would be Callum's enemy, which meant the king may well be his enemy, too. What he would do then, he did not know. But he'd come up with a plan somehow. There was no choice. He would protect Marsaili always, and he would find their son, no matter what it took.

"Why did Iain send ye to find Marsaili?" Callum asked as they started back to Marsaili and Maria.

"She is his half sister," Broch said. "Therefore, she is his to protect. And when she was ordered taken by her father, who she forsook and broke ties with in favor of living with and accepting Iain's protection, it was his duty to find her and bring her back to the fold of the family."

Callum nodded. That all sounded good, but… "In spite of her treachery against Iain and the MacLeod clan?"

Broch glared at him. "What ken ye of what she has done?"

"Nae much," Callum said. "She simply told me she had done awful things—things she hoped would be forgiven."

Broch grunted. "She did nae make wise choices, 'tis true. Yet Iain kens she did nae do anything more than what any woman would have done when she discovered the bairn she thought dead was actually alive. Her da told Marsaili that he would only reveal where he had sent her child—"

"My child, as well," Callum interrupted, his anger at the Campbell roiling in him like a violent wave.

"Aye, yer child, as well. She was ordered to learn which nobles the king intended to take castles from next and get the information to her da. His goal was to make the Steward's position stronger so that his position under the Steward would grow stronger, too. He meant to use Marsaili to make this happen."

Callum curled his hands into fists. Marsaili had felt she had no choice but to betray the king, but the king would likely not care about that. "Does the king ken what she did?"

"Nay," Broch answered quickly. "As I said, Iain is a wise laird. What good would it do to tell the king that which did nae cause him harm?"

"What will Iain do with the information? What punishment must she face for her treachery?"

"He will banish her from Dunvegan—secretly to only her and the few of us that ken—for a period of one year, but he will bring her to him first to tell her he will forget and forgive."

Callum nodded. "'Tis a fair punishment, but if it were nae for me, where would she have gone?"

Broch smiled. "To the MacLean hold. Alex MacLean already offered."

Callum smiled, feeling relieved to discover Iain MacLeod was an honorable and good man. He very much hoped they would someday be allies. It could depend, he knew, on the whims of the king. Or perhaps not…

"Does Iain have sway with the king?" Callum asked.

A slow, knowing smile stretched Broch's lips. "Aye. More than anyone. If ye sway Iain to ye, the king will follow."

"That is good to hear. I will speak with him of my matters with the king when I speak with him about Marsaili. She will, of course, come with me now, instead of going to the MacLean hold."

"If Iain agrees," Broch replied. "He is the one to give his blessing on yer union, if ye can get her to consent."

"I'll get her to consent," Callum assured Broch, willing it to be so, willing Marsaili to recover fully. And hopefully, her brother would offer an alliance, but even if he did not, Callum would wed Marsaili *and* he would find a way to protect his clan.

After several attempts by Callum and Maria, they managed to rouse Marsaili enough to get her to take a few bites of the rabbit, but she was near delirious, mumbling about the bairn and moaning about how he was dead. Callum rocked her in his arms and whispered to her repeatedly that their son lived, though, he had no notion if he spoke the truth or not. He had to believe it. To consider that he—they—had a son they might possibly never know was unthinkable.

The chills hit Marsaili hard close to dawn, even with the fire they had built near to the blanket where Callum lay with Marsaili in his arms. Fear gnawed at him that the chills would make her worse, so he slipped under the plaid he had her swathed in and drew her against his bare chest. He wrapped his arms tightly around her and entangled his legs with hers. Slowly, she ceased trembling, and after a bit, her ice-cold hands, which had been pressed against his chest, slipped between his legs and she burrowed her forehead into his chest. Then she let out a long sigh, and her breathing became deep, even, and peaceful.

Shadows that he had not realized darkened his heart lifted, and he exhaled his own long sigh of contentment. She was meant for him. She always had been. He pressed his mouth to her forehead, giving silent thanks to God for bringing her back to him, for making him realize the futility of trying to forget her, and then he prayed for the right words to say to her brother to forge the alliance the Grants needed.

Callum's other concern was Coira. He had told her very plainly that he wished to wed for the sake of an alliance, and while he knew the lass did not love him, he had seen how vulnerable she was. He was more than willing to let Coira tell the world she wanted to break their promise to wed, but he had no notion if that would be enough to soothe whatever hurt feelings she might have. He was going to have to talk to her privately, and that caused him unease because he didn't want Marsaili to worry for a moment that he was moved to speak with Coira alone by anything other than guilt. It was with all these worries fighting for his attention, that he finally succumbed to sleep.

Fifteen

Marsaili awoke feeling as if she was lying in a cocoon of warmth. It was so very pleasant that it seemed near impossible to open her heavy eyelids. But she could sense the sunlight, and it beckoned her to wake completely. Her thoughts were muddled, but as they slowly started to clear, she remembered being put in a cage, the hunger, the sleeplessness, the pounding pain in her head that would not go away. Yet, the loudest memory, the one buzzing in her ears and burrowing into her heart to fill it with joy was that of Callum's words. He'd said he would never leave her again and would die with her before leaving her. He'd said that he loved her.

She opened her eyes slowly and found herself staring at Callum's bare chest, corded with muscle. He breathed evenly in her ear, still slumbering. She tried not to move. The task wasn't too hard, given weakness seemed to permeate every part of her body. Her stomach growled, and her throat felt coated with gritty dirt, but despite the discomforts, a sense of peace and bliss filled her. She was in Callum's arms! She swept her gaze up to his face. Even in sleep, he appeared as if concentrating on something. A frown line was prominent between his thick, dark brows. Was it her? Was it worry about his clan and what would happen with the Earl of Ainsworth should he break his promise to wed Coira? Was it worry over how the Gordons would retaliate since he had killed Robert? She shivered with the memory. She had no notion how Callum had managed to free them, but she knew he would tell her when he awoke, and she also knew she could not let go of him now.

God help her, she was too weak to release him from their love, from what they shared, but together, they would find a way. She would speak to Iain, beg his forgiveness, prove herself somehow to gain an alliance for Callum. Iain would soften.

And they would find their son! She could not think otherwise. The very tip of the idea made tears come to her eyes and slide down her cheeks. She wanted her son to have his father in his life, and she wanted Callum as hers, too. She had given herself to him completely, and no matter how inconvenient it was, their love could not be undone. Callum had not forsaken her. He'd thought her dead because her father had lied to his family.

"What's this?" Callum's finger brushed her cheek as the question rumbled from his chest. "Are ye in pain?"

She lifted her gaze to meet his brown one. "Nay. I feel fairly well, except weak, hungry, and well, worried. For ye, for me, for yer clan…for our child."

His gaze darkened, and he squeezed her tight. "Lass," he said, stroking her cheek and then cupping it in his large palm, "we will find a way. I love ye."

"I love ye, too," she replied, feeling better hearing him say that he too believed they would find a way. "Where are Broch and Maria?"

"They went to the stream earlier," he said. "I imagine they are still there. I drifted to sleep, and when I awoke, ye were awake, and they were still gone. I believe they like each other."

Marsaili's eyes widened. "Ye're certain?"

Callum nodded. "They've exchanged many a look. Mayhap they will stay at the stream for a spell," he said with a wink.

She chuckled. "Ye are terrible."

He grinned and brushed his thumb over her lips before pressing a gentle kiss to her mouth. "Nay. I just wish ye to myself for a moment. I-I'm nae one for flowery declarations, but—" He grabbed her hand and placed it over his heart, which thumped steady and hard under her fingertips. "From the first smile ye gave me, ye have had my devotion, and ye will have it until my last breath is taken. This I vow to ye."

Fresh tears sprang to her eyes, but these were tears of happiness, of dreams she had lost and now once again seemed found. She took his hand, and as he had done seconds before, she placed his palm on her heart. Heat pooled low in her belly at the pressure of his hand on her. "Ye took my heart the first day I met ye, and though we were divided by lies, my heart did nae ever forget ye. I vow to ye now that, ye will forever be the only man who holds my heart and who I hold in mine."

He parted her lips with a series of slow, feathery kisses that had a dreamlike quality to them and made her feel as if she were floating on a soft, wispy cloud. Under the blanket, his hand slid down her cheek, over her neck, then traced her collar bone and feathered to her breast where his fingers circled her bud in slow, languorous strokes. Her nipple firmed instantly under his touch, yanking a moan from her lips and a tormented groan from him. The sound of his need was a heady invitation to forget they were in the forest, that Broch and Maria were near, and almost that they were being hunted.

He must have had that same last thought because he broke their kiss as he brought his hands up to her face and cupped it. His dark gaze reflected the desire he kept under control as did the tic in his jaw. "I want ye, and if we were alone, I'd take ye, if ye wished it."

"I'd wish it," she replied, her voice a low, husky murmur. He released her face to pull her against the length of his body, and she felt his yearning for her, pressing low and hard against her belly. "What would ye wish to do to me?" she asked, teasing him as she had so long ago.

He grinned, and she knew then that he remembered her asking him that very same thing before she had consented to join with him at the time of the Gathering. "I would worship yer body until ye begged me to take ye, and then I would spread yer creamy thighs, plant myself in ye, and fill ye with my seed to make another bairn. But this bairn," he said, placing a hand between them on her belly, "I would watch grow in ye day after day. I will ken the happiness of seeing my next son or daughter swell yer belly with life, and I will be there to protect ye, to dote on ye as yer body nurtures our child, and when the time comes for our bairn to enter the world, I will kneel beside ye and hold yer hand until the squalls of our bairn fill the world."

A sob escaped her, and Callum swiped at the tears running down her face. "I thought," she said through more sobs, "that ye said ye were nae good with flowery words."

"I'm nae," he replied with a shrug. "These words were in my heart, put there the moment I found out ye had our child, and I began to think upon all I had missed. I had to tell ye."

She nodded and pressed her head to his chest. "I'm glad ye did. All the things ye said, I want, as well." She looked up, worry suddenly overwhelming her. "Callum, did ye say those things about another bairn because ye fear we will nae find our son?"

A startled look crossed his face, and then he kissed her fiercely. "God, nay." He kissed her forehead, her nose, her cheeks, and then her lips once more. "I will find him. I will rip apart Scotland to do so, if need be." She sighed in relief. "When ye feel strong enough," he said, "we will ride to Inverurie."

"I feel strong enough now," she replied, pushing away from him to sit up, but when a wave of nausea hit her, she clenched her teeth on a hiss.

He sat up beside her and slid his arm around her back, then tugged her against him. "Ye need to eat and quench yer thirst."

She nodded. "But then," she said, turning to meet his gaze, "we will ride."

He studied her for a long moment, looking as if he might argue, but then he nodded. "I dunnae wish to tarry, either." He squeezed her shoulder. "I saved rabbit for ye," he said with a smile as he rose and fetched it along with some water. When he sat again, he offered her the rabbit one piece at time, cautioning her to eat slowly. When she was finished, he handed her the skin of water, and she drank her fill before lowering it.

She felt his gaze upon her, studying her. "What do ye wish to ask me?"

"Why did ye nae tell me we had a son when ye first had the opportunity?" he asked. "Why did ye nae come to me for aid in finding him?"

She glanced away, her stomach tightening with anxiety at all the terrible choices she had made because of fear. "When I learned of him, I feared telling ye because I

believed ye dishonorable and that ye would take him from
me if ye kenned of him. And then I learned Coira was
barren, which increased my fear that ye would take our son
to raise as yer heir. And when I saw ye were honorable, I
still feared ye would take him as yer heir. I kenned ye
needed to marry Coira for the alliance, and I ken well how
men need heirs."

"God's teeth, lass, I am sorry for making ye doubt me."

She took his hand and squeezed it. "I am sorry I doubted ye. I am sorry it took fearing I'd die to tell ye the truth."

His tortured gaze impaled her. "I failed ye, and I failed
my clan, but I will nae fail again. If I could have simply put
ye out of my heart and my head and married Edina, my
father would be alive, but I could nae do it. Nae even when
my mother told me ye were dead. I felt dead, too, and could
nae imagine ever giving to another what I had given to ye."

She swallowed the lump in her throat at his admission.
"Was yer mother angry at ye when yer father died?"

"Aye. She dunnae let me forget that it was my fault. So I
must be careful how I break with Coira, but I *will* break the
promise."

Marsaili fidgeted. She did not like that Callum's mother
held her to blame for her husband's death, but Marsaili did
not see that anything could be done about it. "What of yer
brother? How does he feel about yer father's death? Does he
blame ye? Do ye think they will both hate me?"

Callum tugged her close once more. "Dunnae fash
yerself, aye? My mother will soften."

"That dunnae answer my question fully. What of yer
brother?"

"Oh, och. I forgot." Callum smiled at her. "Ye will find a
friend in him."

"That's comforting," she said. There was so much they

needed to say but simply not enough time. She thought of all she wanted to know, of all he might wish to know about her, but before she could ask any questions, he spoke.

"I will need to speak with Coira alone, ye ken."

He sounded so uncomfortable that her initial surge of jealousy ebbed a bit. "I ken. Ye wish to try to avoid making another enemy."

"Aye," he said, looking utterly relieved. She realized then that he had been worried about how she would react, and his worry actually comforted her. It was good to know she was not the only jealous one. She supposed not having been around each other in three years and not having had much time together when they had fallen in love, it would take time to learn who they were now.

"I want ye to tell me everything about yer life from the moment I left ye," he said, startling her out of her thoughts.

She gaped at him. It was as if he had known her thoughts! He squeezed her hand. "I ken that, though I fell in love with ye, there was much I did nae ken about ye, that I still dunnae ken. I did nae even ken ye had a half sister named Isobel."

"I'll tell ye all," she promised him, feeling as if her heart would burst. She had imagined this very conversation after he had first left her so long ago, and she had considered the many things they had never had the time to discuss.

He helped her up as she started to talk, and as they gathered their things to depart, Broch and Maria finally returned from the brook. By the mussed, bemused expressions they both wore, as well as Maria's swollen lips and flushed cheeks, it appeared her friend had found someone to help her forget her deceased husband and mayhap, with luck, someone to love.

Broch came straight to Marsaili and hugged her, but

when they separated, she could see that he looked uneasy as if he had unpleasant news to deliver to her, but he did not wish to. Callum moved to her side and took her hand, and it was not Broch who spoke, but Callum. "Once we have our son, we will need to travel to Dunvegan Castle."

Her stomach clenched at his words. She turned to him, ignoring Broch and Maria, who had approached Broch and taken his hand. "Callum, I must tell ye what I did," she started. "I...ye may nae wish to have me once ye—"

"I already ken," he cut in, squeezing her hand. "I would have done exactly the same thing had I been ye." He said it so reassuringly and lovingly that her eyes blurred with tears once again, but she blinked them away. She'd done enough crying for one day.

"Ye dunnae think me dishonorable?" she asked.

"Nay," he assured her. "I believe ye were desperate to save our son, and for that, I can nae ever feel ye are anything but meant for me."

"Mayhap Iain will forgive me and offer ye an alliance," she suggested hopefully.

"He will forgive ye," Callum said in a gentle tone. He looked to Broch, and Broch nodded.

"What has he decided?" she asked, tension tightening her stomach. She knew her half brother to be fair, but she also understood what a terrible thing she had done.

"He will banish ye from Dunvegan for one year," Broch said. The tension seemed to spread to her chest.

"But," Callum said, "he had planned to send ye to the MacLean hold to live with them."

"Had planned?" she asked with a frown.

He nodded. "Ye will, of course, live with me now." He looked as if he wanted to say something else, but when his gaze flicked from Maria to Broch and back to Marsaili, she understood that whatever he wanted to say would wait until they were alone.

Warmth and love filled her. "Will I now?" she teased, feeling much lighter than seconds before.

"Aye, ye will," he replied, his tone unbending, making her aware he would not have taken no for an answer, not that she would have refused. "It is my hope that yer brother might offer an alliance, but even if he does nae, ye and I will nae be parted again. Together, we will face whatever may come."

She smiled. "Aye. Together."

Sixteen

Fires blazed toward the heavens from the valley where the Summer Walkers were known to dwell, and fear lodged itself in Callum's heart. He and Broch exchanged a look, and then they both drew their swords.

"My God," Marsaili said from her perch in front of Callum on his destrier. "It appears as if the entire valley is burning!"

Though the sun was now high in the sky, Callum could no longer see it, for the smoke that rose from the valley was thick and gray. He slowed his horse to a stop. "Marsaili, I want ye to wait here."

She twisted around to look at him. "Nay! Ye said we would face our problems together."

"Aye, I did, but we dunnae ken what has occurred below. I dunnae think it can be peaceful, given the fires. I want to keep ye safe."

She placed a hand on his cheek. "And I love ye for that and so much more." Hearing her say she loved him made his chest squeeze warmly. "But I'll nae let ye ride into possible danger alone, and if ye try to leave me here"—she tilted her chin up defiantly—"I'll just follow."

He didn't doubt it. Her stubbornness was one of the reasons he had fallen in love with her. That combined with the bravery she displayed now made him feel so much love that he ached. He wanted to argue, but he knew it was pointless. He nodded. "Stay by my side, ye ken?"

She nodded and held out her hand. "Give me a weapon please."

He withdrew a dagger from the holder at his hip and handed it to her, then turned to Broch and Maria. He settled his gaze on Broch, who looked disgruntled. Callum assumed it was because he had relented to Marsaili's wish to ride down below with him, but when Broch glared at Maria and said, "This one refuses to stay, as well," Callum realized the Highlander was irritated that he'd not been able to convince Maria to do as he bid.

Maria smiled sweetly. "Ye need me there to aid ye."

Broch frowned. "Ye're a lass."

She snorted. "Therefore, I must be weak?"

"Aye," he agreed.

"Lean close, ye big clot-heid. I will kiss ye farewell, then." When Broch leaned forward to kiss Maria, she snatched his dagger out of the holder on his hip and held it to his throat. "I may be a lass," she said in a cool tone, "but I am nae weak."

Broch pushed the dagger away with the tip of his finger. "Ye may come, but dunnae ever hold my dagger against me again, lass."

"Dunnae offend me, then," she shot back.

"Fair enough," he replied. "Let us ride."

They set a slow pace down the hill. Callum scanned the surrounding woods for enemies as best he could, but with the smoke so thick he knew they were easy targets to ambush if someone was wishing to do so. The closer they came to the camp below—or what was left of it—dead bodies began to litter the ground.

Marsaili clutched at his leg. "Someone has laid waste to

the Summer Walkers," she said, her voice trembling.

"Aye," he whispered, pulling his horse to a halt. "We walk from here so we will nae be so easy to spot."

Marsaili nodded, and he quickly helped her dismount, as Broch did Maria. With Marsaili behind him, they climbed down the steep embankment, the smoke so heavy now that Callum's eyes burned and he had to swallow repeatedly to keep from coughing. He looked toward the river, where fires burned almost in a straight line.

"Someone has set the tents on fire," he said.

Marsaili moaned an almost animalistic sound, but Callum did not need to ask why. If their son had been here, he could be dead. If he had not been here, where was he? Black rage swept through Callum as he considered the possibility of never knowing his own son. He cursed himself for not riding to Marsaili's home so long ago to see her dead body with his own two eyes. He cursed himself for ever leaving her in the first place. He should have taken her with him the day he'd departed her home. He'd lived with guilt over choosing his heart over his clan, but he realized in this moment that by choosing his heart, he would strengthen his clan with Marsaili by his side. Their love was a mighty alliance all on its own.

The camp was eerily quiet, so when a child cried out, the screeching pierced the silence. It was a lone cry, high-pitched before it turned into a wail. The cry seemed to echo to the very chambers of Callum's heart, as if his soul recognized his son. He could not explain it, but he glanced back at Marsaili and saw her eyes wide, her face white as snow. She knew it, too.

"Callum," she sobbed.

The cry came again, louder, and then through the thick smoke, they became visible—a sea of warriors clad in the

Campbell plaid. In the front of the hundreds of men, one man sat on a great, black charger with a wailing boy sitting in front of him.

All logic fled. With a bellow, Callum raised his sword to charge the men, but a dagger pierced his sword arm from behind, and he dropped his sword. Shocked, he turned as Broch swooped upon him and slid the flat of his blade across Callum's neck. "If ye move," the Scot said, "I'll slit yer throat."

The anger and betrayal he felt was almost numbing. "I will kill ye," he replied, nearly choking on the words.

Broch had given her a look, hadn't he? Marsaili's heart beat wildly with doubt as two of her father's guards seized her. They started to drag her toward Callum.

"Marsaili!" he roared, straining against the four men who were now holding him.

She winced at the blood that dripped down his arm and the raw pain that twisted his features. He loved her. She would have that knowledge in her heart for the rest of her life, no matter what was to come.

"Marsaili!" he bellowed, his voice buffeting her back like a violent wind as she was led away.

She trembled as she walked toward her father and her son. It was her child; she was sure of it. His cherubic cheeks were red from crying, his big, dark eyes glistened with tears, his brown, curly hair was a tussled mess.

He was perfect. And he had Callum's eyes—they hadn't remained blue as they were at birth—and she was grateful for it. Her heart clenched with a strange mixture of love and pain. As she was stopped in front of her father, she tried to recall exactly what she'd seen in Broch's gaze right before he had thrown his other dagger at Callum. Broch's eyes had pleaded, she thought. His look had beseeched her not to fight what he was doing. Doubt battered her, but she trusted Broch. He was honorable to the core. He had, she was sure, known instantly what she had when Callum had charged toward her father: Callum was going to die. Fear had frozen her mind and her body, rendering her useless.

She prayed now as her father's cold eyes swept up over her that Broch had a plan that would save Callum's life and somehow enable Callum to rescue their son. As for her, as long as her son was safe with Callum, she could withstand anything. She would do her part.

Out of the corner of her eye, she caught a glimpse of Broch as he strode up and stopped to stand beside her.

"What business have ye here, Broch MacLeod?" her father growled. It did not surprise her that her father recalled Broch. They had met briefly at the Steward's home, not long ago, and her father had an excellent memory for people.

Broch stepped as if to move toward her father, and the guards who had pointed the swords at her before, swiveled them to Broch. He offered an indifferent look, and with a shrug, he said, "Ye may nae wish others to hear what I have to say, but if ye dunnae care…"

Her father waved his hand at his men. "Stand down. If the man so much as flinches as if he means ill, kill him."

The guards nodded and moved away. As Broch stepped forward, Marsaili took advantage of not having the guards trained on her and followed Broch. She would know what he was going to say and what his plan was.

"The MacLeod sent me to retrieve yer daughter to come before him in reckoning for her crimes of betraying his clan and the king."

Her father's face remained expressionless. "I dunnae have any notion what ye speak of."

"Ye do, and we both ken it. Yer daughter did yer bidding to retrieve her child, whom ye hold in this verra moment. Ye asked her to betray the king's mission, and she did. She must be punished for her crimes."

Broch gave her a hostile look that she prayed was all part of his plan. In that hope, she returned his look with a narrow-eyed scowl, then faced her father once more. Fear rose in her throat, but she swallowed it back, sensing the importance of the next few minutes.

"She will be punished," her father replied. "She is to marry an English earl and will be parted from her son."

"'Tis nae enough. She owes much for her sins. The MacLeod will wage war on ye if he dunnae receive compensation for her betrayal."

"Take the child," her father tossed out, as if he were offering a bag of coin. Marsaili clenched her hands into fists. "He can suffer the sins of his mother."

"That is a start," Broch agreed with a nod of his head. "I wish to take the Grant prisoner, as well."

Her father's eyes widened at the news. "What crime has he committed against the MacLeods?"

"He feigned to want an alliance and then killed some of my laird's favored guards," Broch lied. "He will be staked at the castle for all to see what happens to those who dare to cross us."

"Fine." Her father waved his hand negligently toward Callum. "Take him and kill him as ye will, but hear me now, if he somehow lives and comes to bring me trouble, ye can tell the MacLeod that I will nae hesitate to wage war with yer clan myself."

Broch bared his teeth in a semblance of a smile. "I'll be sure to relay yer message." Broch held his arms out toward her father. "The boy." His tone was commanding, and Marsaili feared her father would become angry and change his mind about giving her son to Broch.

"I would hold my son before ye take him," she blurted as much in desperation to do so, as in a bid to distract her father from becoming angry that Broch had dared to command him.

Her father settled an impassive gaze on her. "Ye're verra predictable, Marsaili. Though I will say I am impressed with how resourceful ye have proven to be escaping the castle and getting yer stepmother to confess to the whereabouts of my grandson."

She gloried for a heartbeat in the confirmation that the boy was hers. Not that she had needed it, but hearing her father verify it, made it that more real. "I want to hold my son," she demanded, stepping closer only to have the guards upon her in a flash. One drew his sword and pointed it at her. From the corner of her eye, she saw Broch tense, and behind her, Callum's bellow of rage echoed. She longed to turn to him, to assure him with a look that she was not scared, but she dared not. "I will go with ye peacefully, Father, if ye but allow me to hold my son before ye hand him over to Broch."

She did not bother to ask to take the child with her; she knew well her father would deny the request, and at least she knew he would be safe with Broch and pray God above, Callum, if all went according to plan. When he simply stared at her, but did not refute what she asked, she knew him well enough to understand he was contemplating her request.

"Just once," she said softly. "Let me hold him just once.

And then I will go with ye to the earl." If Callum could not come for her, or did not reach her in time, she'd become another man's wife. It was a thing that could not be undone. She inhaled a long breath to steady her nerves. She had to have faith that Callum would come for her and that he would reach her before she belonged to another in the eyes of God and of the king. She raised her arms toward her son. "Give him to me."

Her father's eyes widened a fraction, and a slow satisfied smile pulled at his lips. "Finally, ye are becoming a Campbell, Daughter."

She clenched her teeth on the desire to tell him that she was a MacLeod, instead saying, "I'm glad to finally please ye. My son, if ye will."

Her father scooped her son up and thrust him toward her. When her fingers touched his warm chubby arms, her heart felt as if it would explode. Tears filled her eyes, which she did not bother to try to dash away. She closed her grip around him, his skin like silk, and held him tightly. She brought the boy to her chest and wrapped her arms around him. He squirmed a bit, but his crying stopped, and when he nuzzled into her, pushing his head under her chin, a sob caught in her throat.

She lifted her trembling hand to his head and ran her fingers through his soft hair. "Ye're a fine lad," she whispered, deeply breathing in his sweet scent. His head popped out from under her chin suddenly, and he looked at her, his eyes so much like Callum's that she smiled with joy. He brought his tiny hand to her face and patted it. "I hungry."

"Oh, aye?" She cleared her throat of the clogged tears and brought her gaze to her father, who watched her with a dispassionate look. "Do ye have any food?"

"Norbert!" her father bellowed, bringing one of her

father's menservants scrambling.

The skinny young man rushed over to her father. "My lord?"

"Give my daughter a hunk of cheese."

The servant did as he was bid, and Marsaili broke off a piece and handed it to her son. His tiny fingers grasped it before he popped it in his mouth and chewed. As he did so, she touched the top of his foot, which dangled near her hip and turned it just enough so that she could see the bottom. She knew before looking that the X brand that Maria had told her about would be there, but when Marsaili saw it, her throat tightened with the final confirmation that the child in her arms was hers.

She glanced down at him and caught his gaze. "I'm yer mother," she said, not wishing to frighten or confuse him by telling him who she really was, but she feared she may never get another chance. The possibility that she may never see him again loomed in her mind.

He frowned, as if confused, and she quickly said, "Ye can call me Marsaili. *For now*," she added, under her breath, praying they would be granted a future where he would know her as his mother.

He grinned, making two dimples appear in his round cheeks and showing he had most of his teeth. The sight of the little white teeth made her feel warm with joy. He touched her hair, winding a strand of it around his finger. "I Brody."

"Brody," she whispered, trying the name out and deciding she liked it. She had not gotten to name him, but it was a fine name, and it was his. He knew it, and she would never dream to confuse him by changing it. She turned then, just enough so that she could see Callum's face and he could see her and his son. Mayhap it would be the only time he ever saw them thusly.

Their eyes locked over the distance, and through the mask of anger on his face, a smile, as intimate as a kiss, emerged. She felt her own lips trembling with happiness.

"Time to depart, Marsaili," her father said from behind her.

She turned toward him, hating him more in this moment than she had realized was possible. "The Summer Walkers?" she asked, not lessening her hold on her child. "Did ye kill them?"

"Only those who dared to resist me and did nae wish to hand over the child. The rest fled. Now give the boy to Broch."

Her chest ached, but she did as bid, and the moment Brody passed from her hands to Broch's, the child began to wail. Callum roared his anger in the distance. She knew Broch would not hurt her son. She understood in her gut what he had done and said was to try to save them all, yet she felt the loss of her child like a dagger to her heart. Her father flicked his fingers from his guards to her, and they scrambled toward her and seized her. The last thing she saw before she was thrown on a charger behind one of her father's warriors was Brody being handed to Maria and Callum being bound at the wrists by Broch.

Clinging to the knowledge that Callum would be with their son, she had to believe all would be well for them, and that somehow, she might be saved. To believe anything else was unthinkable.

Seventeen

Callum watched Marsaili being taken away from him on the back of a destrier, and the anger burning within him felt as if it would consume him. His son cried beside him, despite Maria cooing at the child. When Callum could see Marsaili no more, he dragged his gaze from her and the last of the Campbell warriors, and he locked gazes with Broch, who stood by Maria and Callum's son.

"I want to kill ye," he bit out, struggling to control his temper.

"Aye," Broch replied with a nod. "I'd want to kill me, too, if I were ye. But I saved yer life."

"Aye, ye did. Now untie me so I can save Marsaili."

"Nae just yet," Broch replied.

Callum's temper snapped. He lunged at the man, and Maria yelped. Callum barreled into Broch, sending them both flying to the ground. With his hands tied, he could not do much, but he managed to roll on top of the Scot, pin him with his thighs, and ram his head forward into Broch's nose.

Blood spurted out, which felt satisfying for a moment before the cries of his son penetrated the red haze of anger and the swelling tide of loss. He shook his head in disgust at himself, rolled off Broch, gained his feet, and glanced at Broch who was shoving off the ground to stand. As he swiped the back of his forearm across his nose, Callum said,

"I'm sorry."

"Dunnae fash yerself. I kenned ye'd be angry. I'd be the same. Ye just watched the woman ye care for—"

"The woman I *love*," Callum interrupted, shocked at his words in front of Broch and Maria.

Broch nodded. "Aye. 'Tis apparent. Turn around."

Callum did as he was commanded, and Broch quickly untied Callum's binds as he spoke. "I could nae think of another way to save ye, secure the lad, and give us time to rescue her."

Callum felt the binds fall away from his wrists. He immediately turned toward Broch, toward his son. His heart clenched as he looked at the crying boy. He motioned to Maria. "Give him to me, please."

"Ye mind yer temper then," she grumbled but passed the child to Callum.

As he held the small boy in his arms, he felt awkward and strange, but his heart felt so full that it hurt. He kissed the top of the child's head, his throat aching with emotion. "I'm yer da," he said, his voice catching.

The little boy quit crying and frowned. "Da? Nay." He shook his head. "Da dead. I Brody."

He squeezed the child tight, wanting to tuck this brief moment away in case there was never to be another. He'd send Brody on to safety with Maria, and he would go after Marsaili, and with God's grace, they'd return to retrieve the child and journey back to his home where they would wed and live out their days together.

The boy smelled of sunshine and spring water, and he was a squirmy, curious thing. He raised his fingers to Callum's growth of beard and giggled. Callum caught the child's small fingers and pressed his lips to them. Determination filled him. "I am yer da, and as God is my witness, I'll be back for ye. We will nae ever be parted again after that."

"Ye leave?"

Callum nodded, having to swallow the emotion before speaking. "I must retrieve yer mother, Marsaili—the woman from earlier." The last words were lost on the child as he had leaned back and started laughing and singing a tune. Callum brought him forward once more, gave him a hug, and then handed him to Maria. "Take him to Dunvegan with Broch."

"Ye kinnae go after her alone," Broch said as Maria took the boy in her arms. "Come with us to Dunvegan. We'll gather men there and then storm the Earl of Ulster's castle."

Callum shook his head. "Nay. I kinnae delay and take the chance that the earl will wed Marsaili." The thought of another man touching her, of claiming her body, made him feel crazed.

Broch set his hand on Callum's shoulder. "I'd do the same," he said softly, his gaze straying momentarily to Maria. "But dunnae attack the Campbell and his men. Ye will die."

"I ken," Callum replied. "I'll overtake them and track them. If I see an opening, I'll take her; if nae, I'll breach the castle somehow and take her from within."

"We'll make haste," Broch said. "And Lachlan, Alex, and Cameron are still searching for her, too. They are surely closing in on us, as they are all excellent trackers. If we come across them, we will send them to ye."

"God willing," Callum responded.

Broch nodded. "I will return to aid ye with Iain, and we will bring an army with us."

"The Campbell will wage war on the MacLeod if he aids me," Callum said, taking his sword from Broch, who was holding it out to him.

"Aye," Broch agreed, a grim smile twisting his lips. "We've many scores to settle with the Campbell. Iain will welcome the excuse to possibly kill the man. The king has stayed his hand, but I believe Iain has come to the end of his patience."

The news surprised Callum, as he knew that the MacLeod laird had always been one of the greatest supporters of King David, which was the main reason Callum believed he had no hope of gaining an alliance with them. "Will the MacLeod break with the king, then? Surely, he will nae support the Steward?"

"Do ye?" Broch asked, eyeing Callum expectantly.

Callum understood that Broch was making certain his loyalties lay with the king now. Callum sheathed his sword and then took the dagger Maria silently handed him, sheathed it, and then blinked in surprise when Maria handed him another. He raised an eyebrow in question.

"For Marsaili," Maria said. "It was knocked from her hand by her father's men. She'll be wanting it."

"Thank ye," he said, accepted the weapon, and sheathed it, as well. He looked to Broch once more. "I dunnae support the Steward as my father did," he said. "I vow it. I will pledge my fealty to the king if he will but have it."

Broch nodded. "Ye will have an ally in the MacLeods. On that ye can be certain. I ken ye have a promise to wed that ye need to break, but once ye do that, I feel confident in speaking for Iain and vowing that by wedding Marsaili, ye will have an alliance."

The news was most welcome. He could not tarry much longer, but it was important to settle these things so he knew exactly what he would be facing and whom he may consider an ally. "I thank ye for that. It is welcome information. I will break my promise to wed the earl's daughter, but I will keep the alliance with the Earl of Ainsworth if the earl is willing. I dunnae believe it will be good for the Lord of the Isles to gain more power by taking the earl's home and growing his territory into English soil. In my opinion, the MacDonald is greedy. What would Iain say to that?"

"Iain shares yer opinion, as does the king."

The news was surprising and good to hear. He glanced at his son for a long moment, memorizing his face and smile. "Ye will watch him as yer own, aye?"

Broch squeezed Callum's shoulder. "I would give my life for him. Dunnae fash yerself. I will send ye any allies I encounter on our journey to Dunvegan, so dunnae kill a stranger without inquiring who they are, aye?" Broch smiled.

"Agreed," Callum replied, allowing a chuckle and a moment of brevity in the darkness that seemed to surround him.

They walked together in silence to the tethered horses, and once they were all mounted, Callum took hold of his son's small hand. He wanted to leave the child with something to look forward to. "Do ye ken how to swim?"

Brody cocked his head, a contemplative look coming over his son's face that made him want to laugh. After a moment of quirking his mouth this way and that, he announced, "Nay."

"I will teach ye when we are together again. Would ye like that?" Brody nodded. Callum thought then of Marsaili. "We will teach yer mother, as well. She dunnae ken how, and a braw lass such as she is should be able to swim."

"Ma dead," the boy said.

"Nay," Callum said fiercely. "She is verra much alive, and we will be together, the three of us, verra soon. I vow it."

⌘

Marsaili's father set a casual pace to the Earl of Ulster's castle, which suited Marsaili just fine. Her father's certainty that neither Callum nor Broch would dare to pursue him would hopefully be his undoing, though when she thought about what would occur if they did pursue her, black fright nearly choked her. As they made camp that night, and she lay in her tent unable to sleep and guarded by three of her father's men, she prayed that Callum had sent Brody to safety. Then she prayed just as ardently that Callum did not simply charge in and attack her father. She did not think he would. He was cunning, and he had to realize that there was no way one man, or even two, could defeat her father's warriors.

Worry haunted her for the two long days of the journey as she tried to work out how and if she could be rescued before she was forced to wed the earl. The only hope was if Callum could breach the castle or if she could escape it. As they traveled another two days, her thoughts were divided between what the castle might look like and how Callum and their son were faring. She had a perfectly clear image of Brody in her head now, and for that, she was eternally grateful. The boy had been hearty and obviously had been well cared for by the Summer Walkers, though it pained her greatly that he did not know her and possibly never would. Yet, she found a measure of comfort in the fact that he would be with Callum if she ended up wed to the Earl of Ulster. It was that last thought that plagued her and knotted her stomach. She would almost rather be dead than wed to a man who was not Callum, but if she lived, there was always a chance she would get to see her son someday. But then she'd think of the pain that seeing him and Callum but not being able to be with them would cause, and she felt bottomless grief all over again. She was pinning her hopes, all her happiness, on the earl's castle not being greatly fortified.

As the first signs of night were beginning to fall in shades of purple and black across the gray sky, their party broke through the thick woods. In the distance, rising to the sky, was one of the most formidable-looking castles she had ever seen, and worst of all, it was surrounded by a moat. A wail of despair swelled in her throat, but she pressed her lips together and did not let it burst forth.

The castle was triangular, made of red stone, and had a tower at each of its points. The drawbridge was raised, and she was further dismayed that before they were even completely out of the woods, horns filled the night, surely announcing to the guards that someone was approaching. On the top of the wall, along the walkway known as the allure, men filed out one by one until it seemed thousands of guards stood there to kill any who are unwelcome. Fear and certainty that the castle was near impossible to breach made her shiver. She had to escape somehow. That was the only hope.

Her father's guardsman raised the Campbell flag, another horn was sounded, and after what seemed like an eternity, the bridge was lowered and two long lines of knights riding large destriers flooded out of the castle. They were dressed in full battle armor, swords drawn, and some had pikes. Her despair deepened. The Earl of Ulster was a careful man, as well he should be. Her father's favored warrior drew forward to meet with one of the earl's, and soon, they were being led across the bridge between two guard towers and into the inner courtyard.

She had not had a chance to even dismount before Ulster himself appeared, ruby robes billowing out to the sides as he strode down the stairs and straight up to her horse. He held his hand out to her. He was, she realized, much younger than she had remembered. He appeared to be perhaps thirty summers. It occurred to her then that he had likely been compelled to marry a woman not of his choosing. Perhaps he was the tender sort and she could appeal to that side of him?

He had kind green eyes and dark-brown hair with a thick beard. He smiled up at her. "I've been waiting for this moment since the day I first met you," he said, his heavy English accent making it difficult to understand him.

She cast her mind back to the day her father had ordered her to try to sway the earl to her.

The earl frowned. "You do recall when you met me, do you not, Marsaili? You tended to my wound after your foolish brother shot me with an arrow."

"I recall it," she said, locking gazes with her father. "My father ordered me to gain yer attention," she said, boldly speaking the truth.

Her father raised his hand as if to strike her, but the earl bellowed, "Stand down, Campbell," before focusing on her once more. "What wicked lies do ye speak, Marsaili? Why do ye try to injure me?"

Unease edged along her spine, the realization that she had likely made a grave error sinking in. The earl was a prideful man and was never going to welcome the truth.

"I—"

"Leave us," he barked at her father.

Her father's gaze narrowed dangerously, but he complied. The earl waved a hand to one of his men, and they came to her and helped her dismount. He took her hand and led her away from his men, up some sidesteps, and to the ramparts she had seen when they had first approached.

The guards there scrambled away to give them privacy. The earl stopped near the wall and faced outward toward his vast estates. "All I have ever wanted," he said slowly, "is to share this with someone I desired. And that certainly was not my last wife. I detested her, actually." He turned to Marsaili, the strong wind fluttering his hair. She grabbed at the edges of her own flapping hair and braided it to keep it from whipping her in the face. "You ripped your dress to tend my wound, and then later that night, you danced with me. You were flushed, your skin kissed by the sun, your eyes sparkling. You laughed when I twirled you about the room. Why would you say your father ordered you to do such things? You could not have feigned such emotion."

God's blood. Her father's plan had worked all too well. There was no way to tell him that would not injure and anger him, yet she had to try to find words to sway him. She licked her lips nervously. "Lionel," she said, remembering he had wished her to call him by his given name, "there has been a grave confusion between us."

"What do you mean?" he asked, surprising her when he jerked her hands to his lips and nipped her fingertips with his teeth.

Her unease increased tenfold. She cleared her throat. "Ye see, I—My father threatened my friend if I did not gain yer attention."

"I do not believe you," he thundered, his face turning red.

Marsaili flinched. This was not working. "It's true, but it's not only that... The day I met ye, I met another. And when I danced with ye, well, it was him in my thoughts."

A dark look swept across the earl's face. "You will not speak such lies anymore, or I will make you very sorry, do you understand?" He brought his hand to her face and squeezed her chin.

Her breath caught with fear. She recognized a cruelty in him that mirrored her father's, though the earl was better at hiding it when he wished to. "I ken," she whispered.

His grip on her chin became harder, pain radiating from the spot. "You will forget this other man, and if you cannot, I will kill him to help you do so. Perhaps I should dispense of him anyway. What name does he go by?"

She was not about to tell him Callum's name, but her father would gladly reveal it if the earl asked him. "He's dead," she blurted, trying to think of something that would prevent the earl from seeking Callum's name from her father.

"Excellent," he replied. He gave her chin a final hard squeeze before he moved his hands to cup her face. "Sweet Marsaili, I knew you were pure of heart, and this proves it. You will forget him once we are properly joined. Don't fear. Your heart will be filled with only thoughts of me." He yanked her to him then and kissed her. It was sloppy, unpleasant, and harsh. That one kiss told her much about Lionel. Most importantly, he was used to being obeyed and wanted, and he'd not tolerate anything less. So she did not fight the kiss. Instead, she pretended to enjoy it. She prayed he would be convinced he had lit her desire and then become careless about guarding her. Mayhap the door to her bedchamber would not be locked, even.

Her mind raced with hopeful possibilities. She wrapped her arms around his neck, offered a few encouraging sounds, and struggled inwardly not to gag. When he finally broke the kiss, it took all her will not to scrub at her mouth.

He smiled at her. "Do you see now that what I say is true? You will desire me."

"Aye," she said breathlessly. "I do. I kinnae wait to be married."

He pulled her to him once more and kissed her hard on the mouth, nicking her lip with his teeth. She tasted the metallic of blood as he pulled away. "I'm eager, as well," he told her as he dabbed a handkerchief at her lip. "We will be wed tomorrow night."

She clenched her teeth in an effort not to gasp her displeasure. "Wonderful," she choked out.

He nodded. "I refuse to wait longer than necessary to make you mine. And I don't mind telling you now that I don't care for your father overly much. I want him to depart, and I feel he would want to see you wed and joined with before he does so."

The thought of lying with any man other than Callum made her feel ill. She forced a smile. "I presume there is a feast tonight?"

"Yes," he said. "But you, my pet, will not be attending."

She frowned. "I will nae?"

"No." A dark look swept across his face. "You displeased me with your words. You—" he patted her roughly on the cheek "—will stay alone tonight and think upon how you will never say anything to displease me again. Your punishment is no food or drink, but next time it will be much harsher. Don't forget this."

"I will nae," she promised him, wishing she had a dagger. She would gladly use it at this moment.

A satisfied smile came to his lips. "I have chosen the most beautiful chamber for you. It overlooks the moat, and the window will provide a lovely breeze."

Her heart raced as an idea came to her. If the window

was large enough, she could possibly escape through it and drop to the water below. Of course, she could not swim, but she would address that when she came to it. "Am I to go to my chamber now?" she asked, hoping she did not sound too eager.

"No, my sweet," he replied and motioned to his guards. "You will spend tonight in my dungeon where you will do your penance," he informed her as the guards came to either side of her.

Her hope for escape tonight plummeted and tomorrow she was to be wed. "Lionel," she said, making her voice sound pleading, "will ye allow me to go to my bedchamber before our wedding so I may be refreshed for ye?"

"Convince me of your affections with a kiss, and I shall agree," he said.

She swallowed past the desire to gag. Instead, she stepped toward him, wrapped her arms around him, and kissed him, pretending that he was Callum. When the kiss broke off, she felt nauseated, but when he smiled at her and said, "Ye may go to yer bedchamber to cleanse before we are wed," she knew the small sacrifice had been worth it.

Eighteen

From his vantage point in the woods, Callum watched Marsaili on the rampart with Ulster. It had surprised him when she had appeared there so soon after arriving at the castle, and it surprised him even more when Ulster drew Marsaili to him and kissed her. Granted, he could not see the reaction on her face from a distance, but he could see that she circled her arms around the earl's neck. She had not pulled away, and the kiss went on far longer than Callum cared for. Jealousy gripped him in a merciless hold. His blood strummed in his ears as he reminded himself that Marsaili was most certainly doing what she needed in order to survive, but that did not mean he had to like it.

When the kiss was finally over, he exhaled a ragged breath, only to catch it again moments later when she stepped toward the earl and kissed him. Callum gripped his sword in hand and waited for the kiss to end. It felt like an eternity before it did. She had done what she had needed to, and he would, as well. He glanced toward the castle. Somehow, he had to breach it and rescue her, and he feared he did not have long.

Callum spent the night discovering as much as he could about the castle, and what he learned did not fill him with much hope. It was greatly fortified, and the only way he could find to breach it was to swim the moat and try to gain the bridge. He waited as patiently as he could for darkness to once again descend, and as he waited, he plotted how to distract the guards so he would have a chance. The only thing he could think to do was set a fire in the woods. Near nightfall, he gathered brush to put his plan to action, then went back to his position, where he could see the castle clearly and wait.

Before the darkness set in, Marsaili appeared on the rampart again. She was accompanied by two guards who led her to Ulster. After they stood speaking for a moment, she dropped to her knees at Ulster's feet, and Callum's stomach lurched. What had occurred the night before? What had the man done to her? Callum could barely see her past his red haze of anger, and when Ulster yanked her to her feet and covered her mouth with his once more, Callum swore. "God's blood!"

Behind him, wood cracked underfoot. He swiveled into a stand, sword drawn, legs parted, and anger coursing. Before him stood three men, one of whom he recognized as Alex MacLean, laird of the MacLean clan. The other two men he did not know.

"Ye should nae let yerself be so distracted by a harmless kiss that ye dunnae hear when someone approaches," the man standing directly in front of Callum said. They locked gazes, and the man assessed him with keen green eyes.

"And ye are?" Callum demanded.

"Lachlan MacLeod," the man replied. "Half brother to Marsaili.

Before Callum could respond, the fair-haired warrior

standing beside Lachlan said, "I'm Cameron—also half brother to Marsaili. Dunnae pay heed to this clot-heid." Cameron elbowed his brother in the side. "If Lachlan came upon his wife, Bridgette, kissing another man, his logic would flee, and he'd likely get himself killed storming an impregnable castle to retrieve the stubborn lass."

"I hate to admit it," Lachlan said, "but my brother speaks the truth. But the difference is that Bridgette is my wife. Marsaili is nae yers. If she cares to kiss another man, then—"

"She dunnae," Callum interrupted. "She simply does so as a deceit. I'm certain."

Alex waved a hand at Lachlan and Cameron. "Dunnae pay heed to these two. They ken how Marsaili feels about ye. Broch told us."

Callum had already concluded that Broch must have crossed paths with them and sent them here to aid him. "When did ye see him?" he asked Alex.

"Shortly after ye parted ways with him. We came upon him in the woods on the edge of Inverurie. We had received word of the Campbell traveling there and had followed in hopes of finding Marsaili. We tried to close the distance to ye after Broch told us what had occurred and where ye were going, but ye made impressive ground, and we trailed ye almost all the way here. How long have ye been here?"

Callum glanced to the darkening sky. "One day."

Lachlan motioned to the castle. "We will have to swim the moat to reach her."

"Aye," Callum agreed, studying the castle and its fortification again. "We'll move when it's dark."

"Dunnae ye think we should wait until the residents are slumbering?" Alex asked.

"Nay," Callum answered immediately. He had a bad

feeling in his gut.

"I agree," Lachlan said, an odd tension emanating from the man. "My wife was taken before we were married, and I reached her too late." He paused for a moment, and Callum could hear him audibly swallow. "I will nae ever forgive myself for that."

Callum had heard some news of what had occurred, and by the tone of Lachlan's voice and the tortured expression on his face, Callum knew what he had heard was true. Stony anger made Lachlan's green eyes look like green crystals. The man rolled his shoulders before focusing once more on Callum. "Ye need to ask yerself, if ye are too late, if she is married, if she has been defiled—"

"I will kill the earl with my bare hands," Callum spat.

Alex clamped a hand on Callum's shoulder. "He dunnae wish to ken what ye would do to the earl. It's given ye would kill him." All three men nodded at Callum. "What Lachlan wants to ken is, would ye still want her?"

"What?" Callum asked, astonished. The three warriors stared in silence at him. "Aye," he replied. "I would want her always. It does nae matter what happens."

"Then we will aid ye," Cameron said.

Lachlan bent over and picked up a stick then crouched near the dirt. "Let us plan how we will breach the castle."

Callum nodded, kneeled down beside Marsaili's brothers and spoke. "It's as ye said. We must swim the moat, but in order to gain entry into the castle, one of us must get the attention of the tower guards, compel them to lower the bridge, and while they are occupied with that person, the rest of us will loop a rope to the bridge, gain it, and enter through the main courtyard. I also considered starting a fire."

"Nay," Alex said. "I'll distract the guards while the three

of ye gain entry to the castle.

"Nay," Cameron replied. "Lena—" He glanced at Callum as if realizing he may not know who Lena was. "Lena is Alex's wife and our sister, and so she is Marsaili's half sister."

"Aye," Callum said. "I ken."

"Lena would kill us if anything happened to ye, MacLean. Ye kinnae take the most dangerous task. Ye will be a father soon, and ye need to be there for the birth of yer son."

Alex grinned, but the grin quickly faded. "Lachlan is a father, and Cameron will be a father soon, as well."

"Brother!" Lachlan exclaimed. "Why did ye nae tell me?"

Cameron scowled. "There's nae been time. I did nae tell Alex, either."

"Yer wife told my wife. Ye ken the lasses kinnae keep a secret." Alex shrugged. "We will draw a stick. The man with the shortest stick will distract the guards."

All four men grunted their agreement.

"How will the one distracting the guards get away?" Cameron asked.

"Whoever has that task need only distract them long enough for us to gain the bridge. Once that is done, we can signal, and the man can run. He needs to be fast. Are any of ye faster than the other two?" Callum asked.

"I'm the fastest," Lachlan said without any smugness.

"And I've the best bird call," Cameron said, showing them by example.

"I believe it's decided, then," Alex said, "without the need to pick sticks. Lachlan will distract the guards, Cameron will signal when we have gained the bridge, and it will be up to the three of us to find Marsaili once we are in the castle and then escape, likely by swimming the moat once again."

"Now we wait," Callum said grimly, rocking back on his heels and glancing to the sky, which was not yet completely dark.

"The hardest part," Lachlan said.

"Aye," Cameron and Alex agreed.

Callum fixed his gaze on the spot he'd last seen Marsaili and wondered what she might be thinking. Did she fear he would not return for her? Did she fear she would never see their son again? His mind turned with all the worst sort of possibilities. He squeezed his eyes closed, trying to shut out the roaring din of worry, but it was to no avail. Until they were together again,—Marsaili, himself, and their son—he would have no peace.

"My lady," the chambermaid assigned to bathe and dress Marsaili said, "shall I braid yer hair for the wedding?"

Marsaili shook her head. She feared she did not have long before one of her father's men, or her father himself, came to fetch her to take her to the chapel. "Nay," she said. "I prefer it down. Now, if ye'll leave me, I'd like a little time alone to pray to God for counsel."

Technically, it was not a lie. She would pray to God, just not for counsel. She would pray for the courage to jump into the moat, and that she would not drown. She had swam a few strokes long ago on the day she had almost drowned because of her Campbell half brothers, and she remembered the euphoria she had felt on her first time ever of gliding through the water. It was also her last.

She tried to recall what she had done. She had pulled the water with her hands and arms, it seemed, and she had kicked her legs. She prayed she remembered correctly and would be able to overcome her fear. If there were any other way, she would have taken it, but there was not. She and the maid were locked in this bedchamber by the earl's command. Marsaili had only one possible way to avoid being forced to marry the earl, and that was the window.

"As ye wish," the maid answered, went to the door, and knocked. "My lady and I are finished."

The lock on the door scraped and clicked as it was opened, and then the maid exited the room. The door shut immediately, and the lock once again snapped into place. She wasted no time rushing straight to the window. She tried to open it, but the thing would not budge. Muttering, she strode to the bed, yanked off the quilt, and hauled it over to the window where she dropped it in a pile on the floor. Then she tried to pick up the chest at the foot of the bed so she could stand on it to open the window and escape. The chest was too heavy, though, and she feared that when she moved it, it might draw the attention of the guards and they would open her door. But what choice did she have?

She first tried pressing her hands against the chest, but try as she might, the blasted thing would not budge. Her brow was damp from the effort, and her head and heart pounded. She crouched near the chest, lodged her back against it, and dug her heels into the ground while she pushed with all her might. The chest barely budged, and tears sprung to her eyes. But so did an image of her son. She had to keep trying.

Gritting her teeth, she once again positioned herself against the chest and shoved. This time it moved with a great loud scrape. Her breath caught with fright, but a burst of men laughing came from just beyond her door. She started to expel a relieved breath when she heard her father speak, and then the men laughed once more. She breathed in quick, shallow gasps as she grunted and shoved at the chest, finally moving it in front of the window.

She shook badly as she grasped the quilt, wrapped it around her hand, and then rearing her hand back, she threw her body weight into her fist and shoved her hand through the window. The quilt protected her skin and muffled the noise, and without hesitation, she knocked the last of the glass from the window, rid herself of the quilt, and placed her hands on the window ledge, hauled herself up, biting her lip to keep from screaming in pain. Shards of glass sliced into her palms, but behind her, the rattle of the door being unlocked made her entire body tingle with terror.

She dangled for a moment, her arm muscles burning as she struggled to find the strength to pull herself all the way up. Digging deep, she shoved, propelling her body up to wiggle through the space. She ignored the sharp pain of the glass cutting through her gown to slash her thighs, hip bones, and stomach. Her father's voice boomed from the other side of the door, and she thanked God that he had always loved to be the center of attention. It sounded as if he was telling another one of his hunting stories.

The cool wind hit her hard as she poked her head out of the window. Black had swallowed the night, but the full moon illuminated the area around her enough for her to realize she could not see the loch below. It was so steep. Fear lodged in her throat. The loch was there; she knew it to be so, for she had seen it earlier. But she would be falling blind, eyes open yet unseeing.

She absolutely did not want to plunge into the water headfirst, so she turned onto her bottom, scrunched herself as small as she could, and slid her legs under her. Then, gripping the ledge, she put her legs out the window and dangled there, heart pounding and blood roaring. She could not seem to release herself, though. Terror had frozen her ability to move, but her fingers were slipping, and soon, the inevitable would happen.

Nineteen

Callum crept along the ground, keeping his body as flat as he could manage, not daring to get up until he was at the moat. He rose only enough to slip over the edge of the moat wall, yet when he glanced toward the castle, his heart felt tripped within his chest. The moon shone on a window, and hanging there, seemingly by her fingertips, was a woman. He would wager his life that it was Marsaili.

"Alex," he hissed, pointing at her.

"God's blood," Alex swore under his breath.

Before Callum could reply, she dropped and the darkness consumed her, the only trace of what had occurred a single splash and then horrid silence.

"She kinnae swim," he growled, not waiting for a response. He dropped into the cold, black water and was swallowed immediately in a slimy liquid with a foul stench. He broke the surface, gulped in a breath, then swam toward where he thought she'd dropped, fear making his strokes choppy. Above him, he heard shouting, and then one by one, torches began to flare to life on the castle allure. A horn blasted from above, and a volley of arrows rained down. He went under again, searching for her, as did Alex and Cameron, who had pulled up beside him.

Nothing! He felt nothing but slime, grass, and water. He rose, gulped in air, and dove back under again. Still nothing.

Dark despair entered him as he rose to and dove under the surface several more times, Alex and Cameron doing the same. Arrows dropped into the water around him when next he surfaced, and Alex and Cameron swam over to him.

"We have to flee," Alex said. "She's lost, Callum. And if we dunnae go, we will surely die here, as well."

"I'll nae leave until I have found her," he bit out, refusing to believe she was gone.

"Callum," Cameron said, his tone harsh. "Would ye make yer son lose both his parents? Marsaili would nae have wanted that!"

"Damn ye both!" Callum bit out and dove once, twice, three times more. And when he came up after his last desperate attempt, chaos filled the night, and grief filled his heart. He had failed her. She had drowned, and he had failed to save her. "I kinnae leave her," he choked out to Alex and Cameron, who were treading water before him.

"For yer son, ye can," Cameron said.

Yes, for his son. He had to. He nodded, a thousand regrets, a thousand memories, assaulting him. He shoved them down and swam through the darkness toward the shore.

Another volley of arrows flew toward them, and they all ducked under the water to swim the rest of the distance under the surface. When Callum came up for air, he was at the rocky wall of the moat. He gained his purchase at the same time as the other men did. They began to climb upward, toward the sound of shouting. Armed men raced across the bridge on horses, and when they reached the top, Callum paused as confusion swept over him. He had expected knights to be standing there waiting on them, but what he found was mass chaos and fighting.

To the left of him, Cameron muttered, "'Tis the Summer Walkers." Cameron pointed at the flag that fluttered in the moonlight which bore no emblem. It was white and devoid of anything. As Callum glanced around, he counted, as best he could, twenty Summer Walkers. They were vastly outnumbered, but they had provided a much-needed distraction.

All three of them retrieved their swords from where they had left them, and when Callum stood, he raised his sword as Ulster's men charged them. He fought through one knight only to be surrounded by three more. He lost sight of Alex and Cameron while he battled the man to his left and then the man to his right. When a sword whistled through the air behind him, he whirled around to meet his foe, his heart lurching. The blade of the knight's sword came swooping toward him, but then the man grunted, swayed, and stumbled forward. As he did, Callum noticed the dagger protruding from his back, and when he searched the fighting throngs to see who had come to his aid, he could not believe his eyes.

Marsaili stood not four feet away beside Lucan. He had a sword in one hand and a dagger in the other. She closed the distance between herself and Callum and jumped into his arms, hugging him fiercely.

"How?" he managed to ask, emotion closing his throat.

"I dropped from my bedchamber window." She pulled back and bent down to yank the dagger from the fallen knight.

"Aye. I saw ye. I searched in the moat for ye. I thought ye drowned. I—" He shook as he spoke. "I thought ye dead."

In the moonlight, her eyes widened. "I did nae see ye! I swam!" He could hear the happy shock in her voice. "I swam under the water, but then a hand grabbed me and I thought myself discovered."

As a knight came toward them, Callum shoved her behind him and fought the man, felling him just as Lucan reached his side. Instinctually, he raised his sword to the man he considered an enemy, but Marsaili shook her head. "Nay, Callum. Lucan followed us. He went into the water to save me and guided me to the wall."

Callum's eyes flew to the man who looked battered and ill. By all accounts he should be dead. "Why?"

"She spared me," Lucan said as a cough racked his body. "I owe her a debt, and I pay my debts."

Callum nodded. "Take her from here," he pleaded to Lucan.

"Nay," she replied. "I will fight with ye. This night we will live or die, and we will do it together."

He wanted to argue, but he knew she would never agree to leave him. "Together," he said.

In that instant, she screamed for him to duck.

He fought with Lucan through four of Ulster's knights, striking down his opponents with ruthlessness to make his way to the woods, but as the three of them reached the tree line, three more knights appeared. As he battled one, he could hear Marsaili's grunts as she fought the other. He cut his opponent down by slicing across his legs, but when Callum turned, all he saw was a knight thrusting his sword toward Marsaili's heart. She threw her dagger as she jumped sideways, and though it lodged in the man's shoulder, it did not stop him. Callum raised his own sword as he closed the distance to her and took the knight's head off in one quick blow.

Callum grabbed her hand as Lucan turned to them both. His gaze rested on Marsaili. "We are even now, aye?"

"Aye," she croaked.

"Then let us flee before we all die," Lucan said.

Callum shook his head. "I kinnae leave her brothers, the MacLean, and the Summer Walkers to this battle."

Marsaili gasped. "My brothers are here!"

"Aye," a voice said from behind them. "It's good to ken ye would nae leave us, Callum." Callum turned to see Alex, Lachlan, and Cameron standing there. Lachlan winked at him. "The Summer Walkers are fleeing, what's left of them. We should, as well."

With a nod, he turned, taking Marsaili with him as a volley of arrows came through the woods after them, one striking Lucan in the throat.

Marsaili screamed as the man dropped dead to his knees, eyes wide. And then Marsaili's father and the earl came toward them from out of the mist. Without thought, Callum threw his dagger, and it lodged in the earl's thigh. The last thing Callum heard as he took Marsaili's hand and they continued to flee was the earl bellowing her name.

The ride to escape her father and the earl's men was relentless and exhausting. On the second day of being awake, Marsaili succumbed to sleep, slouching against Callum in the saddle. She awoke to darkness and a much slower pace than the frenzied one that all the men had insisted was necessary to reach allied territory. Her first reaction was fear, but when Callum squeezed her from behind and pressed a kiss to her head, her fears dissipated.

"Sleep, *mo ghraidh*."

The sound of being called *my love* by Callum made her smile, even as her eyes drifted closed once more. "We have entered yer brother Graham's territory, and his men have joined us. Neither yer father nor the earl's men can follow without threat to their lives." Relief made her sigh as she nodded. Callum pressed his lips to her ear. "Soon, we will be with our son."

"Aye," she replied drowsily and drifted to sleep once more, where she was met with a dream of Brody and Callum.

They were all floating in the water, the sun shining down on them. The day seemed perfect. But then a shadow appeared of a figure holding a dagger. She could not see its face, and she jolted awake with fear and dread in her heart. They traveled through the day and into the night without stopping. There was no time for talk with the pounding hooves and jolting road. She fell asleep once more near the break of a new day, and when she awoke sometime later, the sun was high and Dunvegan Castle loomed before her. Her breath caught in her chest as joy flowed through her.

The courtyard was filled to capacity with MacLeods, but at the front of the gathered men and women stood Iain, who held his son Royce's hand. Beside Iain stood Marion, his wife. In her arms, she held the most beautiful thing that Marsaili had ever seen—Brody. He was giggling as Marion tickled him, and then she pointed toward Callum and Marsaili and whispered something in the child's ear.

Behind her, she felt tension ripple through Callum's body, and she understood why because she felt the same thing, had the same worries. What if Brody feared them? What if they were terrible parents? What if—

"Together," Callum whispered to her.

She nodded. Callum dismounted and helped her to do so, too. They interlaced their fingers and walked to their son as one. When they stood before him, Brody reached for Marsaili, holding out his chubby arms, and said, "Mama."

She promptly burst into tears.

After greeting her brothers, her sisters-in-law who were present, and Maria, Marsaili made her way to her bedchamber to wash and spend some private time with Brody. Callum followed. She could sense he was reluctant to part with her, and she was with him, as well, but Iain had asked Callum to attend him in the laird's solar before supper, which did not give them much time.

When Marsaili opened her door, she was shocked and grateful to see a beautiful crib within, nestled under the window. Callum rested his hand on her shoulder as she bounced Brody on her hip. From behind them, someone cleared their throat, and Callum and Marsaili turned as one.

Marion stood there and gave a radiant smile. "Iain commissioned the crib to be carved for you," she said, her English accent not as heavy as it once had been. Marion brushed a hand over Brody's head. "When Lena wrote to him and told him of the bairn and what had occurred—"

Marsaili tensed knowing that Marion was referring to Marsaili's treachery. Iain had been kind enough when he had greeted her in the courtyard, but she had not expected him to denounce her on the spot. She assumed he would discreetly call her to him for her reckoning.

"He was angry," Marion said, ever truthful, "but Marsaili, he does understand. I told him I would have done exactly as you did."

"Truly?" Marsaili asked. Marion was one of the most honorable, bravest women Marsaili knew, and if she would have done as Marsaili had when put in such a terrible position, it somehow lessened the guilt she felt.

Marion nodded, then hugged Marsaili as she held Brody. "Truly."

"Down!" he pronounced, wiggling out of Marsaili's arms. She set him down, though reluctantly. He marched over the bed on still-wobbly legs and picked up some toys that had been left there for him before settling on the floor to play. Tears of joy came to Marsaili's eyes.

Marion patted her as Callum drew her near and squeezed Marsaili's arm reassuringly. "We will have a thousand of these moments," he said quietly.

She nodded, knowing it was true.

Marion cleared her throat. Marsaili looked over at her, but Marion's green gaze was focused on Callum. "I took the liberty of putting you in the bedchamber next to Marsaili. I presumed you would want to be near her and your son."

"Thank ye," he replied, his voice catching with obvious emotion that made Marsaili's heart squeeze.

Marion looked at Marsaili now. "I had the gowns you left here washed and the wrinkles shaken out. I'll have them bring up a tub and water. I gave Brody a bath this morning. Royce helped me," she said with a chuckle. "Those two boys will be the best of friends."

"Thank ye for taking care of him."

Marion waved a hand. "He's a joy to have around, and I am his aunt, at any rate. We will have to visit you a great deal after you are married—" she gave Callum a pointed look that made Marsaili chuckle "—so the children will all grow older together and be close."

"I could nae agree more," Callum said, taking Marsaili's hand. "And I'm certain that Marsaili will wish ye all to travel to our home to attend our wedding."

"When will that be?" Marion asked, giving Callum another pointed look that left no doubt in Marsaili's mind that Marion had heard Callum was promised to wed the Earl of Ainsworth's daughter.

"In the next fortnight," Callum replied, glancing at

Marsaili. "If ye agree, that is?"

Marsaili barely got out the "aye" that cracked on her lips. The swirl of emotion inside her stealing her ability to speak.

"I'll leave you now, but I will see you both shortly at supper." Marion started to walk away, then turned back around. "Oh, Brody usually takes a nap right about—" She laughed suddenly and pointed at something behind Marsaili. She turned to find her son curled up on the bed with his thumb in his mouth, his tiny chest rising and falling with sleep. "I'll send a supper tray up for you, Marsaili, if you prefer to stay with him."

Marsaili nodded. "I'll stay with him until he wakes. Does he sleep long?" She hated that she did not know.

Marion shook her head. "Actually, no. So you should likely be able to attend supper if he wakes and is not fussy. He has only woken fussy once, though, so all should be well."

Once Marion departed, Marsaili and Callum made their way to the bed. Callum very carefully scooped Brody up, set him in the middle of the bed, and then the two of them lay on either side of their sleeping son, facing each other. Below Brody's curled-up feet, they interlaced their fingers and each of them set a palm on their child. Marsaili could see in Callum's eyes that he had just as much need as she did to touch their son and ensure he was here, that it was all real.

For a long time, they lay in silence, alternately staring at each other and at Brody. Then Callum spoke. "When we return to Urquhart, I will need to speak with Coira alone to break the pledge of marriage given to her."

Marsaili nodded. "I ken. I am nae vexed about it. But I am fashed that yer mother will be angry with ye. Will ye ask Iain for an alliance to help continue to defend against the MacDonalds, the Gordons, and now possibly the Earl of

Ainsworth?"

Callum rubbed a gentle hand down their son's back. His tender touch to their child made Marsaili's chest ache with happiness. She could see he was contemplating things, so she did not speak. She simply enjoyed watching him with their son.

After a moment he said, "Aye, if ye are fine with my doing so?"

She smiled, pleased he asked her thoughts. "Aye."

He smiled. "I dunnae wish to be like my father, but I see and ken that he did what he needed to in order to keep the clan safe. He made an alliance and used me to do it. We will need alliances, but I dunnae wish to use our children, unless it is something they wish for."

"We are of a like mind," she said, relieved. Her father had always used his children, and she had thought for a long time that all families did the same until she had met her half siblings and their partners. They had all married for love, and only one of those alliances had been dictated, and that had been Iain and Marion's. Yet, even then, Marion had chosen Iain. Albeit, her only other choice had been an evil English knight, but she had picked Iain. Marsaili would give her children the opportunity to marry for love. Trying to deny the love between herself and Callum had almost destroyed them both, and she did not want that for her family.

"We will find a way," she said, squeezing his hand, "but I believe Iain will be agreeable."

"I believe so, as well. Iain has a heart for ye, lass. He is yer family."

"I felt alone all my life, and now I dunnae. I feel so blessed. It scares me a little."

"Why?" he asked, giving her a perplexed look.

She felt foolish telling him, but she did not want to hold

anything back from him. "I have nae ever had such good fortune. I feel as if something bad must surely be brewing."

"I will nae let anything bad happen to ye again, Marsaili," he vowed.

"Nor I to ye. We will have to guard each other well, aye. We will have many enemies to contend with."

Brody started to stir. Callum and Marsaili both went to pat him at the same time and in the same spot. They laughed, and Callum moved his hand down to pat their son's bottom as Marsaili patted his back.

Once he stilled, Callum said, "I hope the MacDonalds will pull back if I secure an alliance with yer brother. That reprieve would allow me needed time to strengthen fortifications and train new warriors so that the need for an alliance is nae so great. The Gordons will want my blood always, but I dunnae fear them. As for Ainsworth, I am hoping that he will see reason when I offer to keep the alliance with him and help defend his land against sieges from the MacDonalds."

"Ye have given this much thought," she said, impressed.

"Aye. The moment I kenned I could nae deny my feelings for ye and honorably marry Coira, I started to think on how I could protect my clan and also have ye. I love ye, lass. I would rather wage a thousand wars than live another breath without ye."

"I love ye, too." She wiped away a happy tear as their son's eyelids fluttered open.

Large, brown eyes stared first at her and then at Callum, and then Brody promptly announced, "I hungry."

"That's my, laddie," Callum crowed, scooping the child into his arms. "He already kens his mind, and I will teach him to stay true to it."

"*We* will teach him," Marsaili corrected with a chuckle.

Twenty

The meeting with Callum and Iain went better than Callum had hoped. Iain proved to be a generous man, offering an alliance before Callum could even broach the subject. Having the weight of that worry off his shoulders allowed him to concentrate fully on Brody, Marsaili, and her family at supper. As he watched Marsaili's half brothers with their wives and children, anticipation for his future built for the first time in a long time. Soon he and Marsaili would be wed, and he would sit at the dais in his own great hall with her by his side, along with Brody, until he likely wiggled away to wander around the great hall as children were prone to do. Royce, Iain and Marion's son, had sat at the dais for a time between his parents, as had Lachlan and Bridgette's son, Magnus, but both children were already squirming and trying to get down.

Marsaili was bouncing Brody on her knee when Iain asked her to attend him in the solar. She rose and started to hand Brody to Marion, but Callum stopped her. "I'll take the lad," he said, holding out his hands. Marion smiled at him, but Marsaili gave him a questioning look.

"Are ye certain?" she asked. "What if he cries?"

Her new motherly worry pleased him. His own mother had been rather cold all his life and had shown more concern for how much coin was in the chests than for her two sons. He'd thought most women were like that, but in his short time at Dunvegan, he'd seen that his mother was not like most other mothers. "If he cries, I will soothe him."

"What if he wets himself?"

"Then I'll clean him," Callum assured her. "And if he's hungry, I'll feed him. If he falls, I'll pick him up. Dunnae fash yerself, lass. I am his father, and I will care for him always."

"Ye are proving to be a good father," she said, her voice hitching.

He grinned as she left the dais with Iain. Lachlan leaned around Cameron and said, "Dunnae make the rest of us look bad, ye ken?"

Everyone on the dais laughed, and not long later, Callum found himself on the dance floor, swinging Brody around while Royce clapped and shouted, "Me too!" Then Lachlan's son tugged at Callum's arm for a turn. He was having such a good time that he did not notice Marsaili had returned until she tapped him on the shoulder and then held her arms out for Brody.

"'Tis his bedtime." She gave Callum a smile and look that heated him. "And mine and yers, if ye are intelligent."

Desire thickened in his blood. "Do ye mean to say ye wish me to come to yer bedchamber?"

"Ye are intelligent," she teased, turned, and sashayed out of the great hall, provocatively swaying her hips.

He immediately started to follow her, but when he exited the great hall, he found himself face-to-face with her four brothers and Alex MacLean. The men all had their arms crossed and Iain spoke. "Ye will marry immediately upon breaking the other vow, aye?"

Their concern amused rather than irritated him. "Aye. The verra next day."

"Why nae that day?" Lachlan demanded.

"I thought to give the earl and his daughter time to depart."

"Likely wise," Alex agreed.

"We will all come to witness the wedding," Graham said.

Cameron nodded. "And our wives."

"And bairns," Iain added. "So ready chambers."

"Gladly," Callum assured them. "Now if ye dunnae mind, I wish to see my son to bed. I've nae ever gotten to do that."

"By all means," Iain replied, sweeping his hand toward the stairs that led to the bedchambers.

"But after that," Lachlan said, "find yer own chamber, aye? Marsaili is our sister, and we give ye liberties for we ken a wedding is to come and—"

"And well, ye already made a wee bairn," Graham said, which elicited chuckles.

"But it kinnae seem we condone ye being in her chamber before the marriage," Iain finished.

"Certainly nae!" Lachlan exclaimed with a wink. "We did nae ever do such things."

"At least," Alex added, "nae that anyone kenned. So be quiet."

All the men nodded, grins on their faces.

With a shake of his head, Callum made his way to Marsaili's bedchamber, and when he pushed open the door, he found her curled around their son, both mother and child fast asleep. Such strong emotion filled him that he rubbed his chest as he made his way into the room, crept carefully onto the bed, and fit himself behind Marsaili, one hand resting on Brody. Soon, he too fell asleep.

Callum awoke to a touch as light as a feather trailing down his chest. He opened his eyes to find the room in complete darkness, except for the moonlight that streamed in through the window. Marsaili sat atop his hips, her thighs on either side of his.

"Will we nae wake Brody?" he asked.

Marsaili chuckled. "He awoke crying nae long ago. I took him out so as nae to wake ye, and Marion was in the passage doing the same with Royce. She said the two of them like to sleep side by side, and I wished to have a bit of time alone with ye, so…"

"So Brody is sleeping with his cousin?"

Marsaili grinned. "I hope so. Callum, I had a dream," Marsaili whispered, running her fingertips down to his braies, hooking her nails under them, and then touching the tip of his staff, which had become painfully hard.

He hissed in an effort to hold in a groan of pleasure at her touch. "What did ye dream?" he asked.

"Of the time we joined our bodies. I have dreamed of that night many times. I dunnae wish to wait until we wed to feel ye within me again. And tomorrow we will be traveling and nae be alone, so…"

"So we have but this night," he finished for her, sliding his hands up the silken skin of her thighs, under her thin léine, and to her perfectly rounded bottom, which he squeezed. Need rushed through him hot and fierce. It was the need of three long years without her. His pulse spiked as he rolled her over to her back and climbed atop of her. "I dunnae think I can be slow, lass. I have longed for this too much. But the next time—"

"The next time?" she asked with a giggle as she slid her

palms up his bare stomach to his chest.

Lust strummed through him, making him tremble. "Aye, the next. Tonight, after the frenzy, there will be calm, slow, pleasurable torment."

"I look forward to it," she promised, wrapping her arms about his neck and tugging him toward her.

He did not need to be asked in any other way. He crushed his mouth to hers, as he pulled her léine up to her hips and slid the undergarment off. She parted his lips with her tongue, and the reckless abandon he tasted in her mouth, the feverish need he felt from her hands, and her thudding heart that matched his own took the little control he had.

He trailed his hands to her breasts as he kissed her and ran his fingers over her hardened buds. When she moaned her pleasure, he teased her there with pinches, but he needed more, and he sensed that she did, too. Breaking their kiss, he took her nipple into his mouth and sucked and pulled, spiking his desire with each luscious stroke. Her gyrating hips and the way she tossed her head back and forth told him her need was as great as his.

She clutched his arms and whispered fiercely, "I'll take tenderness later, aye. Come in me now, I beg ye."

He quickly kicked off his braies, braced her thighs, and slid into her with a groan. She fit him perfectly, just as he remembered, and the moment he started to move, so did she. They found a rhythm that made everything fade away but the two of them, and all the moments that they had lost, they reclaimed with each kiss, each touch, each whispered word of love. They found their climax together, covering each other's mouths to silence their screams of release, and when their wild joining was over, they lay panting side by side.

Once their breathing had calmed, Callum felt his need for her rising once again, but he hesitated. They had been through much, and he did not want to tire her, or if she was sore, he did not want her to feel she must acquiesce, but she turned into him suddenly and placed her hand on his hard staff.

"And now the slow," she whispered, nipping his ear, kissing his neck, and trailing her lips down his abdomen to between his thighs. And then she gave to him, and in return, he gave all of himself to her well into the night, then longer still until dawn, when they both fell into a weary sleep.

Hours later, they were awoken by Marion knocking on the door. Marsaili answered it, and a moment later, Brody waddled into the room to announce that he was hungry. They dressed and made their way to the great hall to break their fast before traveling on to his home. The great hall was mostly empty, as they had risen late, but as they finished eating, Broch and Maria entered. They approached the table, hand in hand.

Callum was pleased, and he could see that Marsaili was, too, by the way she grinned. He cocked his eyebrows at Broch, who shrugged as if to say he was not quite sure where things would lead with Maria but that he was pleased. "We wish to travel with ye to yer home so Maria can see her sister."

"Yer sister?" Callum asked, startled.

"Aye," Maria said. "She is married to a Grant, and when Marsaili and I escaped Innis Chonnell, I was traveling to Urquhart to ask to become part of yer clan."

Callum smiled. "We would welcome ye as an addition, if—" he glanced at Broch "—that is what ye wish."

"We shall see," Maria said, her gaze sliding toward

Broch, a blush tingeing her cheeks.

Later that day, they departed for Callum's home with full bags of food and a contingency of MacLeod warriors. The journey was peaceful, and it gave Callum time to truly contemplate what he had known for years. He had wanted a marriage born of affection, and now he would have one. He had given his love to Marsaili three years prior, as she had given him his, and once that had occurred, their love would not be denied for anything—not alliances, nor treachery, nor promises offered to another. He would do his best to fix the situation with Coira, but in the end, his most important task in life was to love Marsaili and Brody, and protect them with his life.

They rode into the inner courtyard of his castle at nightfall. His brother was there, along with at least a hundred of Callum's warriors. Cheers went up when he dismounted his horse. He glanced around the courtyard, noting his mother's absence, as well as those of Coira and her father. He wanted to draw Marsaili to his side, but he did not want to shame Coira and make things worse. He turned to Marsaili, and when he saw her looking so unsure, so anxious while she clutched their son, he thought he would lose his mind.

He reached out for Brody, eager to tell his brother about him, but at that moment, his mother came into the courtyard with Coira trailing behind her. Shock swept over his mother's face when she saw Marsaili, and Marsaili stepped away from him, holding Brody to her chest. Behind her, the MacLeod guards, led by Broch, closed in toward her. Callum clenched his teeth in frustration that Broch thought he needed to protect Marsaili in Callum's home. This had to be settled at once.

"Mother, take Marsaili and—"

"My son," she interrupted. "This is my son, Brody." She gave Callum a beseeching look. Knowing Marsaili and her kind heart as he did, he suspected she was considering Coira and how learning everything here and now in public would embarrass the lass. He nodded his acquiescence, though he despised not telling everyone of Marsaili and Brody directly.

His mother puckered her lips. "I dunnae ken why she is here, but I'll nae—"

"If ye dunnae do as I tell ye," Callum said, pitching his voice low so his clansmen would not overhear, "I will set ye out of my home and forget ye exist."

"Callum!"

"Now, Mother," he said. "Show Marsaili to a bedchamber and see that she has anything she requires."

After a long tense pause, his mother jerked her head in agreement, and with a huff, she motioned for Marsaili to follow her. Callum watched as Marsaili disappeared into his castle with their son in her arms, and then he turned to face his brother and Coira.

"How fares the castle?" he asked Brice.

"Well, Brother," Brice answered. "We have been attacked twice, but the men fought well and we were nae breached."

Callum nodded, having much to talk with Brice about but needing to settle matters with Coira first. "See me in the great hall before supper," he said to Brice. He expected his brother to depart, but when Brice stood there looking uneasy, Callum frowned. "Was there something else?" He noted that Brice exchanged a quick look with Coira before he answered.

"Aye," his brother said. "I—" Coira nudged Brice, surprising Callum. "That is, we"—he motioned between himself and Coira—"wish to speak with ye alone."

"Verra well," Callum said. He could only imagine what sort of things his brother might have done in an attempt to aid Callum. He prayed to God it was nothing that would further complicate matters.

They went directly to the solar, and once the door was shut and Callum turned to Brice and Coira, Brice blurted, "We are in love."

Callum could only gape at them.

Coira twisted her hands in front of her. "I'm sorry, Callum. I could not resist. You don't love me," she said softly, "and I don't love you. I have spoken with my father. He had to return home, for my mother took ill, but he has agreed to my wedding Brice, if you will allow it. And he wishes to remain allies, if you will have us. I beg you—"

Callum waved a hand, recovering from being shocked by the news, but then suspicion set in. "Brice, what is this?"

"It is nae as ye think. I admit I tried to seduce her to disembroil ye from yer promise to wed her, but I fell in love with her. Ye dunnae love her, Brother, but I do. And ye brought Marsaili back with ye, so surely…"

"I know about the lass," Coira said. "Brice—" she gave him an adoring look "—told me everything. I wish you all the happiness."

"As do I," Brice added. "Did ye ken she had a bairn, though? Whose boy is it?"

"Mine," Callum announced with so much pride he thought his chest would burst. "The boy, Brody, is mine. She thought he had died at birth. 'Tis a long story."

Brice grabbed Callum by the arm and hugged him. "Sit and tell us. There is time. Give Mother and Marsaili a chance to come to ken each other."

A thought struck him. "Does Mother ken about ye and Coira?"

"Nay!" Brice answered.

"We have kept it secret to all but my father," Coira said in an assuring tone that amused him given his own situation.

"I thank ye, lass," he replied.

"Do we have yer blessing?" Brice asked, clearly anxious.

"Aye, aye," he assured them both. The look they gave each other eased the last of Callum's concern. It seemed all had somehow resolved itself.

"Tell us of the boy," Brice encouraged.

"I will," Callum said, "but let me tell Marsaili about this first. It will ease her greatly."

Brice and Coira smiled. "We'll await yer return here," Brice said.

Callum nodded, departed the solar, and went to find Marsaili. He found her in one of the guest bedchambers with Brody. The door was open, and for a moment, he stood there watching her with his son. His heart was full. When she finally glanced up, he walked wordlessly to her, dropped to his knees in front of her, and told her of Brice and Coira. She was so relieved that tears filled her eyes. He cupped her face in his hands, and with their son between them, he kissed her tenderly.

When he pulled back, he started to sit beside her, but she shook her head. "Nay. Leave me time with yer mother so we can learn each other."

"Ye're certain?"

Marsaili nodded. "Ye can speak with her later and tell her everything, but nae here with me looking on."

"As ye wish, *mo chridhe*. Brice and Coira did want to hear about Brody…"

Marsaili laughed, "Away with ye, then I will see ye soon."

Twenty-One

When Callum's mother returned to the bedchamber after retrieving a refreshment for Brody, she greeted Marsaili with such a warm smile that Marsaili was immediately suspicious. She berated herself for feeling that way, though, as she had to learn that not everyone was out to harm her or use her, even if her own family had been.

Callum's mother carried a tray with a goblet of wine and a repast of cheese and bread. She strolled into the room, shutting the door behind her with her foot. She skirted around Brody without so much as a glance, and then she set the tray on a table and brought Marsaili the goblet. Lorna thrust it toward her. "Drink. Ye must be parched."

"Thank ye," Marsaili said, taking the goblet. She was thirsty, but as she brought the goblet to her mouth to drink, an odd scent wafted toward her. Frowning, she inhaled deeply, her gut clenching at the faint rank smell. She sniffed again, noticing that Callum's mother was watching her carefully. Marsaili had a vague memory of Maria once showing her the deadly berries of the poisonous nightshade, and she would swear it smelled like this. She lowered the goblet, her heart pounding, and moved to put herself between Brody and Callum's mother. But as she did so, Callum's mother withdrew a long dagger with a sigh.

"I was hoping," she said, pointing the dagger at Marsaili,

"that this would nae be difficult nor messy."

Marsaili's blood roared as she set the goblet down, not taking her eyes off Lorna. "Were ye intending to poison me with nightshade?" she asked, feeling almost numb with shock.

"Aye," the woman said, nicking Marsaili's chest with the tip of the dagger. "I tried to let ye live, and that was my mistake. I paid good coin to have that Black Mercenary take ye away."

Marsaili gasped. "Ye hired Lucan?"

Callum's mother nodded. "Aye. Did ye escape him, or did he simply take my coin?"

"Neither. Callum rescued me."

"Callum is a fool," his mother hissed. "He would throw away another good alliance for ye, and ye did nae ever even want him! Ye chose the Earl of Ulster!"

Marsaili frowned. "I did nae do such a thing. Ye were misled by my father, I'm certain," she said, her palms sweating as she glanced toward the door, praying Callum would return, even though she had told him to give her time. She darted her gaze to Brody, who thankfully was playing by the window and seemed oblivious to what was occurring. She feared what would happen if she did not keep Callum's mother talking, though. Her mind raced through what Callum had told her. His mother had told him that Marsaili had died, and Marsaili had assumed that her father had lied and told Lorna that was the case, but maybe Marsaili had it wrong.

"Did my father tell ye that I chose the Earl of Ulster over Callum?"

"Aye. So dunnae try to deny it. Ye bewitched my son!" she hissed. "Callum went to visit Edina and then to yer father's castle for the Gathering, and when he returned, he had broken his vow to wed Edina and refused to mend the breach because of ye!"

"Callum broke his vow to wed Edina before he ever met me," Marsaili said as calmly as she could.

"Lies! He tried to tell us the same ones, but I kenned better. He was obedient until he met ye! Ye were going to ruin everything, and ye did nae even want him!"

"Nay!" Marsaili shook her head. "I loved him! I love him still!"

"Dunnae lie to me. I wrote to yer father when Callum refused to wed Edina. I offered him an alliance and told him that Callum wished to wed ye. He wrote back and refused the alliance. He said ye would never wed the likes of Callum, and that ye chose the Earl of Ulster over my son."

Marsaili gasped. "That is nae true! He lied to ye!"

"Even when he thought ye dead, he would nae forget ye," Lorna continued, as if she had not heard Marsaili or simply did not care what she had said. His mother's face was mottled red, and her eyes bulged. "Ye must leave! He is to marry Coira, and I will get the coin her father had vowed to give me. The Grant clan will be strong again. Everything I do is for my son and our clan, and yer presence threatens to destroy it all."

"Oh, dunnae fash yerself," Marsaili said and reached down to pick up Brody. "We will leave immediately!"

When she rose, Callum's mother had the dagger in one hand and the wine goblet in the other. "Ye must die. 'Tis the only way. Drink the wine, or I'll kill yer son."

Marsaili found her voice with difficulty. "Then ye will murder yer grandson."

Callum's mother gasped and glanced at Brody. "Nay!"

"Aye," Marsaili said. "Brody is yer grandson. He is Callum's son."

When the door to the solar slung open with such force the hinges rattled, both Callum and Brice gained their feet and withdrew their swords. Broch strode into the room, fairly dragging a blond-headed man behind him. "This Black Mercenary was caught on the stairs slipping up to the bedchambers." Broch's gaze fell to Callum as Broch shoved the Black Mercenary forward and then to his knees. He jerked the man's head back, and only then did Callum see Broch had given him a beating in the face.

"He did nae wish to tell me why he was at the castle, so I had to be persuasive," Broch said simply.

Callum glared down at the man, anger beating in his breast. "And what say he?"

"That yer mother hired him to come seize a woman."

"Marsaili!" Callum cried out, something clicking in his mind. He shoved the Black Mercenary away and raced for the stairs with Brice close behind. Taking the stairs three at a time, he thought on how Lucan could have possibly entered the castle when he had come here. There had been no explanation, but now there was. His mother wanted Marsaili out of his life, and apparently, she would do anything to achieve her goal.

Callum reached the top of the stairs, and as he turned the corner toward the bedchambers, he heard a scream. He thundered down the hall, praying he was not too late. He kicked open the door to the bedchamber and came to a shuddering halt. His mother held his son, and she was crying. Marsaili stood in front of her, white as snow except for her knuckles, which had pinked around the edges from her grip on the dagger that she had pointed at his mother.

He closed the distance between himself and his mother,

and took his son from her. She did not try to stop him but wept openly, as he had only seen her do when his father had died.

"I'm sorry," she said, turning her tearstained face to Callum. "Everything I did, I did for ye and for our clan. I would nae kill yer son, though. Nae ever that. I would nae ever harm my own flesh and blood."

He placed a protective hand over one of Brody's ears and pressed the other side of his son's head into his chest. "What have ye done, Mother? God's blood, what have ye done?"

She crumpled to the ground as the words poured out of her, and he stood with his brother and Marsaili by his side and listened to her tale. Rage filled him, then disbelief, and then great, overwhelming sorrow. It was his own mother who had lied to him and told him Marsaili was dead, not the Campbell. The Campbell had shamed her with his response, and he had said Marsaili had wanted to wed Ulster but his mother had concocted the lie that Marsaili had died. She wanted him to forget Marsaili and marry Edina.

After a long while, his mother fell silent, and Callum and Brice looked at each other, as Marsaili leaned against Callum. The betrayal was deep and painful, and he could only imagine what Marsaili was feeling.

"Will ye put me to death, then?" his mother sobbed.

As he and Brice stared at each other, Marsaili answered. "Nay, of course nae. Ye are his mother."

Marsaili's capacity to forgive amazed him. He did not have the same ability. "Ye kinnae stay here, Mother."

"Aye," Brice agreed. "We will send ye to Aunt Claret's."

"To the heathens?" their mother gasped, referring to the MacKenzies, the clan to which their aunt's husband belonged. He was a poor man, and their mother would have no status, just as she deserved.

"Aye," Callum replied. "Yer greed is why ye did what ye did, nae love, nae a desire to simply make us strong. Ye kinnae stay here after such a betrayal to me, nor after trying to kill my future wife."

He saw Marsaili visibly relax, even as his mother's jaw gaped open, and he realized Marsaili had been worried. It was going to take some time for her to understand that she came first to him, but he would make certain that she knew it eventually. "Take her to the dungeon," Callum told Brice.

"The dungeon!" his mother screamed. "Brice, nay! Surely ye dunnae agree."

"Actually, I do," Brice assured her. "Completely."

Callum turned to Marsaili as Brice half dragged their mother out of the room screaming. He lowered his hand from Brody's ear and set his wiggling son down. He sighed. "I dunnae ken what to say. I wish I could say I will ken if ye wish to leave me, but I will nae. And I'd come after ye. I love ye. I'm selfish. I dunnae have an excuse for what my mother has done—"

Marsaili pressed a finger to his mouth. "I dunnae have excuses for all that my father has done, nor for what my Campbell brothers and sister did. We are nae our parents or our siblings." She cupped his face. "There is ye, and me, and Brody. What we have is true and pure, and we will build a good life."

"Together," he agreed, kissing her full on the mouth as Brody stood with his arms wrapped around his father's leg and squealed at them in glee.

A sennight later, Marsaili stood by Callum's side in the

courtyard of Urquhart Castle as his wife. They were surrounded by her brothers and their wives, including her half sisters Isobel and Lena, and Lena's husband, Alex. One by one, Iain's men knelt before Callum, pledging their allegiance to him as Iain had. Then, to her great surprise, a contingency of Alex's men and her brother Graham's men did the same. As the last man was about to give his pledge, the horn announcing an approaching enemy sounded.

They had been expecting her father and men from the Earl of Ulster, as the earl himself was recovering from the wound Callum had inflicted upon him in battle. They'd had men standing watch, and word had come early this morning that her father's birlinn approached by sea. She watched as the birlinn neared the shore, and her breath caught as a sea of warriors, men faithful to her and Callum, advanced from the castle to meet her father's men.

Grants, MacLeods, and MacLeans stood side by side with their swords raised, blades shining in the sun. When her father's warriors started off the ship, a cry of warning went out. She held her breath for one second, worrying her father might be so foolish as to try to battle his way through, but he was greatly outnumbered.

As she and Callum made their way to the shore, her heart began to pound. Callum squeezed her hand. "I can speak with him alone, if ye prefer."

"Nay. I will say my piece," she said.

Moments later, she stood in front of her father, who had been the lone man allowed to set foot on the shores of Callum's land. "I'm glad ye came," she said by way of greeting.

Her father's eyebrows rose in skepticism.

"I am," she repeated. "I wanted to tell ye that I will nae ever fear ye again."

"Ye should," her father bit out. "I will gather more of my forces and the earl's, and I will return."

"I'd nae do that if I were ye," Callum said. "I have made an alliance with the MacLeod, the MacLean, *and* the Earl of Ainsworth."

Iain came to stand by Marsaili's side. "And I have the king's word that if ye rise against the Grant, he condones us going to war with ye. So I will gladly kill ye if ye return."

"As will I," Callum added. Her brothers and Alex nodded their agreement.

Her father's face turned red. "It seems I must depart for now," he spat, "but one day, Marsaili, ye will wish ye had nae turned against me."

"My only wish," she said, "was that ye were nae my father."

The Campbell huffed and turned to leave. Callum slid his arm around Marsaili as they stood on the shore and waited until her father sailed away.

Callum leaned close to her. "Are ye sad?"

"Nay," she assured him as Marion came forward and handed Brody to her. Her son curled his fingers into her hair. "I've nae ever been happier."

Epilogue

$\mathcal{M}$arsaili normally detested Christmas, as it had never been pleasant in her father's home, but this year, Callum had cut down a rowan tree, and they snuggled together in bed under mounds of quilts, listening to the crackle and pop of the wood as it burned. The rowan was meant to clear away any lingering bad feelings about family members, and they both had thought it would be a good thing to do. Though the things their parents had done to them were unforgiveable, they both wanted to put it behind them and look to the future with Brody—and with the child that swelled in Marsaili's belly.

She smiled as Callum patted Brody's back with one hand and rubbed her stomach with the other. She could not recall ever feeling as content as she did in this moment by her husband's side. Soon, her half brothers and their wives, as well as her sisters, would arrive to celebrate Hogmanay with them, too.

She sighed happily and started to close her eyes when she felt the first movement from their unborn child. Tears sprang to her eyes, and she glanced to Callum, finding him staring agape at his hand, which still rested upon her stomach.

He slowly looked at her, love brimming in his gaze. "Did ye feel that?"

She chuckled. "Oh, aye. I do believe we will have another hearty lad, if that kick is any indication."

"I dunnae care if it's a lad or a lassie, as long as ye and the child are healthy."

A moment of fright grabbed hold of her as she thought on how hard Brody's birth had been. "Ye will be there with me when our bairn is born, aye? Ye vowed it."

Callum leaned close and kissed her soundly on the mouth, then trailed a hot path down to her breasts, but she stopped him with a tsk. "Put Brody to bed first."

He chuckled, scooped up their sleeping son, took him to his room, and then returned to their bed. He promptly picked up where he had left off. Between periods of dizzying attention to her breasts, he stopped long enough to meet her gaze. "I will be by yer side always," he said. "Dunnae fret. I will be there for every birth, every moment of joy, and every moment of sadness. I love ye, *mo chridhe*."

"Prove it," she teased, running her hands up his muscled bare chest.

He captured her hands, and with a wicked grin, he said, "Oh, I will, lass. I will."

And he made true his vow—over and over again.

Dear Readers,

I hope you enjoyed the book. I invite you to leave a review for it, and to try the first chapter of My Fair Duchess, A Once Upon a Rogue novel, Book 1.

Prologue

The Year of Our Lord 1795
St. Ives, Cambridgeshire, England

The day Colin Sinclair, the Marquess of Nortingham and the future Duke of Aversley, entered the world, he brought nothing but havoc with him.

The Duchess of Aversley's birthing screams filled Waverly House, accompanied by the relentless pattering of rain that beat against the large glass window of Alexander Sinclair's study. The current Duke of Aversley gripped the edge of his desk, the wood digging into his palms. He did not know how much more he could take or how much longer he could acquiesce to his wife's refusal of his request to be present in the birthing room. He knew his wish was unusual and that she feared what he saw would dampen his desire for her, but nothing would ever do that.

Camilla's hoarse voice sliced through the silence again and fed the festering fear that filled him. She might die from this.

The possibility made him tremble. Why hadn't he controlled his lust? After six failed attempts to give him a child, Camilla's body was weak. He'd known the truth but had chosen to ignore it. Moisture dampened his silk shirt, and Camilla screeched once more. He shook his head, trying to ward off the sound.

He reached across his desk, and with a pounding heart and trembling hand, he slid the crystal decanter toward him. If he did not do something to calm his nerves, he would bolt straight out of this room and barge into their bedchamber. The last thing he wanted to do was cause Camilla undue anxiety. The Scotch lapped over the edge of the tumbler as he poured it, dripping small droplets of liquor on the contracts he had been blindly staring at for the last four hours.

He did not make a move to rescue the papers as the ink blurred. He did not give a goddamn about the papers. All he cared about was Camilla. The physician's previous words of warning that the duchess should not try for an heir again played repeatedly through Alexander's mind. The words grew in volume as the storm raged outside and his wife's shrieks tore through the mansion.

Alexander could have lived a thousand lifetimes without an heir, but he was a weak fool. He craved Camilla, body and soul. His desire, along with his pompous certainty that everything would eventually turn out all right for them because he was the duke, had caused him to ignore the physician and eagerly yield to his wife's fervent wish to have a child.

As Camilla's high, keening wails vibrated the air around him, he gripped his glass a fraction harder. The crystal cracked, cutting his hand with razor-like precision. He yanked off his cravat and wrapped it around his bleeding hand. Lightning split the shadows in the room with bright, blinding light, followed by his study door crashing open and Camilla's sister, Jane, flying through the entrance. Her red hair streamed out behind her, tears running down her face.

"The physician says come now. Camilla's—" Jane's voice cracked. She dashed a hand across her wet cheeks and moved across the room and around the desk to stand behind his chair. She placed a hand on his shoulder. "Camilla is dying. The doctor needs you to tell him whether to try to save her or the baby."

Pain, the likes of which the duke had never experienced, sliced through his chest and curled in his belly. A fierce cramp immediately seized him. "What sort of choice is that?" he cried as he stood.

Jane nodded sympathetically, then simply turned and motioned him to follow her. With effort, he forced his numb legs to move up the stairs toward his wife's moans. With every step, his heartbeat increased until he was certain it would pound out of his chest. He could not live without her, yet he knew she would not want to live without the babe. If he told the doctor to save her over their child, she would hate him, and misery would continue to plague her and chafe as it had done every time she had lost a babe these past six years.

He could not cause her such pain, but he could not pick the child over her. Outside the bedchamber door, Jane paused and turned to him, her face splotchy. "What are you going to do? I must know to prepare myself."

Alexander had never been a praying man, despite the fact that his mother had been a devout believer and had tried to get him to be one, as well. His father and grandfather had always said Aversley dukes made their own fates and only weak men looked to a higher power to grant them favors and exceptions. Alexander stiffened. He was a stupid fool who had thought himself more powerful than God. The day his mother had died, she had told him that one day, he would have to pay for this sin.

Was today the day? Alexander drew in a long, shuddering breath, mind racing. What could he do? He would renounce every conviction he held dear to keep his wife and child.

Squeezing his eyes shut, he made a vow to God. If He would save Camilla and the babe, he would pray every day and seek God's wisdom in all things. Surely, this penance would suffice.

A blood-curdling scream split the silence. Alexander's heart exploded as he shoved past Jane and threw the door open. The cream-colored sheets of their bed, now soaked crimson, lay scattered on the dark hardwood floor. Camilla, appearing incredibly small, twisted and whimpered in the center of the gigantic four-poster. Her once-white lacy gown was bunched at her waist to expose her slender legs, and Alexander winced at the blood smeared across her normally olive skin.

Moving toward her, his world tilted. His wife, his Camilla, stared at him with glazed eyes and cracked lips. A deathly pallor had replaced the healthy flush her face usually held. Blue veins pulsed along the base of her neck, giving her skin a thin, papery appearance. The sour stench of death filled the heavy air.

Only seconds had passed, yet it seemed like much longer. The physician swung toward Alexander. He appeared aged since coming through the door hours before; deep lines marked his forehead, the sides of his eyes, and around his mouth. Normally an impeccably kept man, his hair dangled over his right eye, and his shirt, stained dark red, hung out from his trousers. Shoving his hair out of his eye, the physician asked, "Who do you want me to try to save, Your Grace?"

Alexander curled his hands into fists by his sides, hissing at the throbbing pain the movement caused his cut palm. His mother's last words echoed in his head: *Great sins require great penance.*

The duke glanced at his wife's face, then slowly slid his gaze to her swollen belly. "Both of them," he responded. Fresh sweat broke out across his forehead as the doctor shook his head.

"The babe is twisted the wrong way. Even if I can get it out, Her Grace will be ripped beyond repair. She'll likely bleed out."

Anger coursed through Alexander's veins. "Both of them," he repeated, his voice shaking.

"If she lives, I'm certain she'll be barren. You are sure?"

"Positive," he snapped, seized by a wave of nausea and a certainty that he had failed to give up enough to save them both. Rushing to Camilla's side, he kneeled and gripped her hand as her back formed a perfect arch and another cry broke past her lips—the loudest scream yet.

Alexander closed his eyes and fervently vowed to God never to touch his wife again if only she and his babe would be allowed to live. He would do this and would keep his sacrifice between God and himself for as long as he drew breath and never tell a living soul of his penance. This time he would heed his mother's warnings. Her threadbare voice filled his head as he murmured her words. "True atonement is between the sinner and God or else it is not true, and the day of reckoning will come more terrible and shattering than imaginable."

Alexander repeated the oath, coldness gripping him and

burrowing into his bones.

Moments later, his throat burned, and he could not stop the tears of happiness and relief that rolled down his face as he cradled his healthy son in his arms.

Then in a faint but happy voice Camilla called out to him. "Alex, come to me," Camilla murmured, gazing at him with shining eyes and raising a willowy arm to beckon him. He froze where he stood and curled his fingers tighter around his swaddled son, desperate to hold on to the joy of seconds ago, and yet the elation slipped away when realizing the promise he had made to God.

That vow had saved his wife and child. As much as he wanted to tell Camilla of it now, as her forehead wrinkled and uncertainty filled her eyes, fear stilled his tongue. What if he told her, and then she died? Or the babe died?

"You've done well, Camilla," he said in a cool tone. The words felt ripped from his gut. Inside, he throbbed, raw and broken.

He handed the babe to Jane and then turned on his heel and quit the room. At the stairs, he gripped the banister for support as he summoned the butler and gave the orders to remove his belongings from the bedchamber he had shared with Camilla since the day they had married.

As he feared, as soon as Camilla was able to, she came to him, desperate and pleading for explanations. Her words seared his heart and branded him with misery. He trembled every time he sent her away from him, and her broken-hearted sobs rang through the halls. The pain that stole her smile and the gleam that had once filled her eyes made him fear for her and for them, but the dreams that dogged him of her death or their son's death should the vow be broken frightened him more. Sleeplessness plagued him, and he took to creeping into his son's nursery, where he would send the nanny away and rock his boy until the wee hours of the morning, pouring all his love into his child.

Days slid into months that turned to the first year and then the second. As his bond with Camilla weakened, his tie to his heir strengthened. Laughter filled Waverly House, but it was only the child's laughter and Alexander's. It seemed to him, the closer he became to his child and the more attention he lavished on him, the larger the wall became between him and Camilla until she reminded him of an angry queen reigning in her mountainous tower of ice. Yet, it was his fault she was there with no hope of rescue.

The night she quit coming to his bedchamber, Alexander thanked God and prayed she would now turn the love he knew was in her to their son, whom she seemed to blame for Alexander's abandonment. He awoke in the morning, and when the nanny brought Colin to Alexander, he decided to carry his son with him to break his fast, in hopes that Camilla would want to hold him. As he entered the room with Colin, she did not smile. Her lips thinned with obvious anger as she excused herself, and he was caught between the wish to cry and the urge to rage at her.

Still, his fingers burned to hold her hand and itched to caress the gentle slope of her cheekbone. Eventually, his skin became cold. His fingers curiously numb. Then one day, sitting across from him at dinner in the silent dining room, Camilla looked at him and he recoiled at the sharp thorns of revenge shining in her eyes.

The following week the Season began, and he dutifully escorted her to the first ball. Knots of tension made his shoulders ache as they walked down the staircase, side by side, so close yet a thousand ballrooms apart. After they were announced, she turned to him and he prepared himself to decline her request to dance.

She raised one eyebrow, her lips curling into a thinly veiled smile of contempt. "Quit cringing, Alexander. You may go to the card room. My dances are all taken, I assure you."

Within moments, she twirled onto the dance floor, first with one gentleman and then another and another until the night faded near to morning. Alexander stood in the shadows, leaning against a column and never moving, aware of the curious looks people cast his way. He was helplessly sure his wife was trying to hurt him, and he silently started to pray she would finally turn all her wrath at how he had changed to him and begin to love the child she had longed for...and for whom she had almost died.

Series by Julie Johnstone

Scottish Medieval Romance Books:

Highlanders Through Time Series
Sinful Scot, Book 1
Sexy Scot, Book 2
Seductive Scot, Book 3
Scandalous Scot, Book 4

Highlander Vows: Entangled Hearts Series
When a Laird Loves a Lady, Book 1
Wicked Highland Wishes, Book 2
Christmas in the Scot's Arms, Book 3
When a Highlander Loses His Heart, Book 4
How a Scot Surrenders to a Lady, Book 5
When a Warrior Woos a Lass, Book 6
When a Scot Gives His Heart, Book 7
When a Highlander Weds a Hellion, Book 8
How to Heal a Highland Heart, Book 9
The Heart of a Highlander, Book 10

Renegade Scots Series
Outlaw King, Book 1
Highland Defender, Book 2
Highland Avenger, Book 3

Regency Romance Books:

A Whisper of Scandal Series
Bargaining with a Rake, Book 1
Conspiring with a Rogue, Book 2

Dancing with a Devil, Book 3
After Forever, Book 4
The Dangerous Duke of Dinnisfree, Book 5

A Once Upon A Rogue Series
My Fair Duchess, Book 1
My Seductive Innocent, Book 2
My Enchanting Hoyden, Book 3
My Daring Duchess, Book 4

Lords of Deception Series
What a Rogue Wants, Book 1

Danby Regency Christmas Novellas
The Redemption of a Dissolute Earl, Book 1
Season For Surrender, Book 2
It's in the Duke's Kiss, Book 3

Regency Anthologies
A Summons from the Duke of Danby (Regency Christmas Summons, Book 2)
Thwarting the Duke (When the Duke Comes to Town, Book 2)

Regency Romance Box Sets
A Very Regency Christmas
Three Wicked Rogues

Paranormal Books:

The Siren Saga
Echoes in the Silence, Book 1

Keep In Touch

Get Julie Johnstone's Newsletter
juliejohnstoneauthor.com

Join her Reading Group
facebook.com/groups/1500294650186536

Like her Facebook Page
facebook.com/authorjuliejohnstone

Stalk her Instagram
instagram.com/authorjuliejohnstone

Hang out with her on Goodreads
goodreads.com/author/show/2354638.Julie_Johnstone

Hear about her sales via Bookbub
bookbub.com/authors/julie-johnstone

Follow her Amazon Page
amazon.com/Julie-Johnstone/e/B0062AW98S

About the Author

Julie Johnstone is a *USA Today* and #1 Amazon bestselling author. Scottish historical romance, Regency historical romance, and historical time travel romance featuring highlanders, aristocrats, and modern-day bad billionaire bad boys are her love, and she enjoys creating both with a hefty dose of twists, plenty of heartstring tugs, and a guaranteed happily ever after.

Her books have been dubbed "fabulously entertaining and engaging," making readers cry, laugh, and swoon. Johnstone lives in Alabama with her very own lowlander husband, her two children – the heir and the spare, her snobby cat, and her perpetually happy dog.

In her spare time she enjoys way too much coffee balanced by hot yoga, reading, and traveling.